*To my mom and Michael, both of whom read
or listened to me read every draft and still
came back for more.*

I wouldn't be here without their love and support.

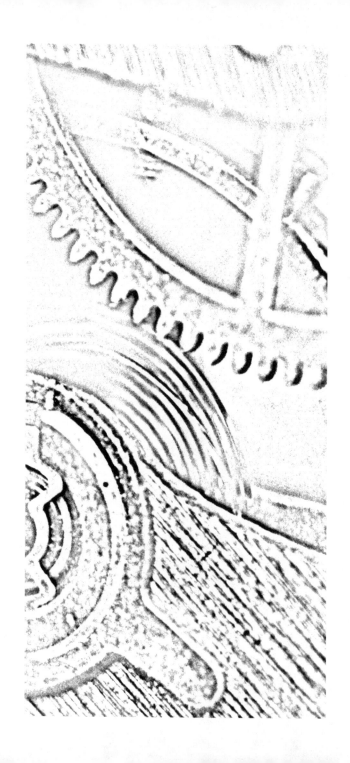

The windowsill ground into Maeko's ribs. Grabbing hold with both hands, she pushed her toes against Chaff's palms and lifted high enough to place the frame in that squishy area between her ribs and pelvis. Awkward. Painful. Discomfort, fear of discovery, and the potential payoff of success kept her moving. She rolled onto her right side. A soft whimper escaped as the narrow sill pressed deep into her flesh. The sound was lost amidst the ticking of so many clocks within the shop.

Bracing her hands against the top and bottom edges, she began to draw her knees up so she could squeeze her legs through and land on her feet inside the shop. Even with her slender build, it was going to be a tight fit.

One of many holes in her pants caught on some-thing. She tugged a few times, moved the leg out and back in a little. No luck. The pain of her position was creating a fog around her thoughts.

"Chaff," she hissed.

"Trouble, Pigeon?"

She could hear laughter in his voice. "It's not funny."

"It is a bit." There was tugging on her pants that shifted her weight and brought a fresh spike of pain to her side. "Blood and ashes," he cursed under his breath. "I can't get it from here."

She gritted her teeth. Pain translated to a burst of

anger and she jerked the leg. The sound of tearing fabric followed by freedom. She curled up in the window, maneuvering her legs and feet through, then twisted her body around to catch herself with a death grip on the sill. Her toes bumped the door.

She braced for the scream of the alarm. Nothing.

"You all right?"

A quick glance down to determine her proximity to the device. Close, but it appeared undisturbed.

"Splendid," she said. Which, in this context, was code for proceeding as planned.

"Brilliant. You're a cracking burglar for a bird."

"Better than any of your boys," she boasted and let go, dropping to the floor.

The landing was hard enough to draw a few bright sassy notes from a music box on the display table nearest the side entry. It was a fanciful and somewhat scandalous piece with a clock in the base and a woman on top wearing only a corset and underskirts, a tool belt hanging askew at her waist and a parasol in one hand. Disdained pirate regalia made palatable for the gentry in art.

The locked cabinet next to that held an elaborate brass bracer with an embedded clock. Several mechanized articulated arms folded in against it ending in various items including a pen, a pair of tweezers, and a magnifying glass. A black and gold plaque beneath it declared it THE PROPER PROFESSOR'S COMPANION FROM CLOCKWORK ENTERPRISES.

There were many such innovative items in locked cabinets around the shop. Items that were worth enough to pay off her mother's debt, but no fence would touch those pieces. They were much too easy to trace, therefore risky and hard to sell. Still, a satchel full of pocket watches and other trinkets would let her stash a good sum toward her goal.

Further in, on the opposite side of the shop, was the long flat case that held the less exclusive selection of items they were targeting.

First, secure the goods. That way, if she set off the unfamiliar alarm system, they could make a run for it before Literati officers arrived and still have a good payout. She padded over and made quick work of the lock on the case with the pick set she kept stored in one tattered shoe. She swept the entire cabinet, moving everything into the satchel one item at a time to avoid damaging the goods. Minutes clicked by on the numerous clocks, ticking their way into her nerves. By the time she had the satchel loaded, her fingers twitched in time with every agonizing tick tock.

No more clock shops…ever.

She started back toward the door, pausing for another longing glance at the Professor's Companion. Such a device had to be worth a tidy sum. She eyed the cabinet lock.

Maybe…

A rap on the side door caught her attention. She could see Chaff's hand through the long narrow window beside the door. He was pointing at the handle. She abandoned the cabinet and went over to crouch by the door, examining the connection wire between the piece on the inside of the door and the alarm itself, not surprised to see a Clockwork Enterprises logo on the device. A small switch appeared to release the tension on the wire that connected the two pieces. Easy.

Except the switch was already flipped. The wire was slack. There had been no blaring of alarms. Perhaps the shop owner had failed to finish arming it when he locked up. She disconnected it. No alarms went off. She grinned and unlocked the door.

"There! Get him!"

Her heart seized.

There shouldn't have been a patrol here this early. They'd watched for weeks to get the schedule down.

Run, Chaff!

He met her eyes through the glass, distress gleaming in his. He mouthed "hide," then spun and bolted, rapid footfalls retreating down the side street.

Hide? Not likely. Not so long as he was in danger.

"The street's clear! Shoot him in the leg, you bloody oaf!"

An officer stopped in front of the door and raised his gun.

Bloody Literati officers and their guns. The Bobbies had carried clubs, so you only needed to worry about outrunning them. What if the Lits nicked Chaff or, worse yet, if they shot him? She hated putting him in danger; without him, she wouldn't ever pull together enough to get her mum out of servitude. She needed his help.

She needed him.

Maeko threw the door open, hitting the officer in the shoulder and sending his shot wild. Two more officers were behind the first. She darted between them, catching a glimpse of Chaff disappearing around the corner. She ran the opposite direction. An officer caught hold of the satchel slung over her shoulder, jerking her back. There was a sinking in her gut. She twisted free, letting the satchel and their plunder go, and ran.

"After her, Wells! Jameson, guard the shop!"

"What about the other one?"

"He's good as gone, but this little rat's ours."

No, she isn't.

Maeko sprinted past three Literati steamcycles parked in the street, good reason to head for tight back alleys with lots of obstacles. She picked a route and ran, counting on the time it would take them to get the steamcycles going to give her enough of a lead to find a hiding spot.

The alleys in the outskirts of Cheapside were home turf for her. There were a million places to hide.

A million places and somehow most of them involved crawling in muck.

Maeko wriggled back into the narrow space behind a big metal ashbin, shoving between the wall and the rusted metal with hands and feet. Her fingers dug runnels in generations of slick grime that coated the surfaces, fighting for purchase while she gagged on the sickly stench of rotting waste.

Steamcycles rumbled past the alley entrance only to stop and turn back seconds later. Sharp exhales from the steamcycles warned that the Literati officers had pulled into the alley. She froze, her heart pounding in time with the rhythm thrumming through the back wall of the pub. The dark mixed beats of a band of pirate musicians.

Crushed like an ant between the Lits and the pirates. I'll be nothing but a smear in the dirt.

No one would care. No one would mourn another unwanted street rat lost in the dark dirty streets of London.

Rhythmic new music pulsed through her and a shaky smile danced across her lips.

Not crushed, protected. The heavy beats were her sanctuary, drowning out the sound of her labored breathing.

The music also masked the officer's approach so that she startled when he lifted the ashbin lid. When it crashed back down, she jumped again, her heart slamming into her throat and pounding in her ears so loud that she barely heard the music now. Myriad cockroaches, dislodged from their rusty abode, ran over one hand and up her arm. Her muscles tensed as she resisted the desperate urge to sweep them away, staying motionless while they explored her shoulders, neck, and face at their leisure. The tiniest whimper squeezed free when one bloated bug poked about in her left ear, but the sound drowned beneath driving drumbeats.

"Find anything?" A clear, young male voice edged with a rasp of exhaustion, but lacking the sharp hatred she often heard. He must be new to the job.

"Cockroaches about the size of a small dog." This came from a veteran of the streets, a man whose gruff voice held no warmth, like the chilly dark depths of the Thames in winter. "If the rat's back here, he can stay."

She shuddered and moved one hand behind her back to support herself, sinking it down into something slick and warm. Her stomach turned. She clenched her teeth and waited.

"Afraid of bugs," the younger man teased.

"I don't see you back here digging around the bloody ashbin in the dark!"

"I'm not daft."

"Bloody rats!" The veteran kicked the ashbin, sending another batch of cockroaches scurrying down by her feet and she closed her eyes.

Be calm. Be quiet. Basic rules every thief learned to follow.

A cockroach scuttled up her trouser leg and she ground her teeth, the urge to scream becoming a desperate tickle in the back of her throat.

"They're kids, Tagmet, not rats. Rats are large rodents with hairless tails. They're often found in alleys, reveling in the waste of mankind with the cockroaches. You're like to find one if you keep poking around back there."

Something in the younger man's voice tugged at Maeko, a whisper of lighthearted humor and warmth behind his sarcasm. But they were officers of the Literati. No circumstances would ever make them her friends.

"Don't try to be cute. Most of these kids are old enough to be making an honest living." The veteran,

Tagmet, growled a few crude insults at his partner under his breath before adding, "Besides, it's hard to tell the difference between the kids and the rodents half the time. They smell the same."

The song stopped and she held her breath. Someone moved near the corner of the ashbin, a shifting in the shadows so close to her hiding place. She heard the whispering whir and click of clockwork gears in the dark behind her where nothing but rodents and cockroaches should be. Her muscles trembled with fear, exhaustion, and hunger. Another heavy drum rhythm rolled out into the night. A cockroach crawled across her lips. Something coarse and moist brushed one of her fingers where they remained pushed into the warm muck behind her. She sucked back to hold in the scream lodged in her throat.

The steamcycles rumbled to life and she heard them pulling out of the alley. With fierce will, she managed to remain motionless until the sound of the engines faded in the distance. Then she scrambled like a startled rabbit, throwing disgruntled cockroaches in all directions in her desperate charge for the open air beyond the edge of the ashbin. One bony elbow smacked into the brick wall and she bit down on her lip to stifle a cry.

Sound is the killer. Silence carries one through the night alive.

Ripping free of the tight space, she spun and peered back into the darkness. Searching out a bit of fabric between holes in the tattered boy's trousers she wore, she wiped the worst of the grime from her hands. Something moved in the dark reaches of the narrow space.

Ashbins such as this one existed throughout the city. Despite regular visits from the big steam-powered collectors, the metal degraded quickly in London's soggy weather. On the up side, Literati officers rarely wanted to soil themselves by getting too intimate with the decaying bins, especially one as poorly maintained and richly pungent as this one. Therefore, they made for prime hiding places if one was small enough to fit behind or beneath them and a steam-powered ash collector didn't happen by at the time.

She couldn't loiter there. No telling when another patrol might happen by. They had been doing an aggressive sweep all through the last few weeks to gather in strays. It was a bad time to be wandering the night-time streets. She didn't dare go back to one of the usual lurks tonight, though, not without knowing if Chaff had gone back there. Most of the boys accepted her for her skills. Those who didn't left her alone because they respected Chaff, but they were far less pleasant when he was away. It stung to admit how much she still relied on Chaff. He was the closest thing she had to family on the streets, but what good was family if sooner or later everyone disappeared?

Glancing nervously at the alley exit, she took a few steps in that direction, but curiosity held her back.

With a grimace, she braced her feet against the wall and shoved the ashbin, hoping to shift it a few inches. It perched on little rusted wheels that refused to roll. A second push sent it collapsing forward as the corroded metal around the front wheels crumpled. The resulting crash, spilling a rank sludge into the alley, sent fear burning through her in a dizzying rush. She froze, a storm of panic welling inside. Still, her gaze went to the now open space behind the bin.

Dim moonlight pierced through the haze of soot into the alley, revealing layers of decomposed refuse she'd been sitting in and the freshly disemboweled corpse of a rat lying on a rusty grate, which explained the slick warmth she had sunk her hand into. Her stomach turned again. The one benefit of going hungry; she had nothing to heave up.

Panic continued to prick at her with needle-sharp fingers, warning her to move on before someone investigated the ruckus.

The grate under the dead rat had once covered a large venting in the back wall of the pub. From that shadowed space, she could see a pair of bright yellow eyes peering out at her. She moved in slowly and crouched near the opening, poised to run if the eyes belonged to something less than friendly. The music lulled. In the brief quiet, she heard another sound, a soft, insistent purring. The faint forlorn lament of a violin lifted into the night, resonating with her loneliness.

Reaching into the shadows, she found the cat's head and scratched behind its ears. The animal crept forward in pursuit of precious affection, its head emerging into the poor light. Too much dirt caked its fur for her to discern a color, a condition with which she could sympathize, but yellow eyes scrutinized her, full of vibrant curiosity. She crouch-walked back a few inches. The cat looked past her, scoping out the surroundings and checking for signs of danger.

Smart. "C'mon. You can't stay back there eating rat guts."

The cat glanced down at the grisly remains of its meal, then cautiously stepped one paw forward.

"That's right. C'mon." She held her hand out, wiggling fingers to entice the cat forward, and scuffed her feet back a little more.

After looking around again, the cat met her eyes and meowed, a soft querying sound. When she held her ground, refusing to give, it finally came to her hand, and she sucked in a sharp breath, staring in astonishment at the animal. An engraved, articulated metal armor fully encased its left back leg and hip, complete with little brass claws at the end of each toe. The cat rubbed its head on her hand and she absently scratched it, contemplating the mysterious appendage.

The leg, so perfectly made she wouldn't have been surprised to see the claws retract, gleamed through smears of grime. The sound of gears spinning smoothly when the cat moved further attested to the craftsmanship of the piece. She might not have a proper education, but any thief worth their salt would recognize the value of such an intricate device.

Worth enough to pay Mum's debt?

The cat walked over to sniff at the rat corpse, its tail high with pleasure at having friendly company, showing off its male parts to the world.

She averted her eyes and giggled. "Boy, huh?"

When she spoke, he turned and trotted back to her, rubbing into her offered hand, placing his trust in her. Desperate for companionship.

A lot like me.

What would happen to the cat if she sold him for his leg?

There was a sinking in her chest.

Nothing good. Nothing good at all. It was one thing to nick from people with more than they needed, but this cat wouldn't survive long without its leg.

He licked her fingers, then walked past her toward the alley entrance.

"Where're you off to? You'll be nicked in a heartbeat out there."

The cat stopped a few strides away, looked at her, at the alley entrance, then at her again and meowed.

She grinned. "Oh? Brilliant plan. A half-Japanese street rat and a cat with a mechanical leg traveling together. That won't draw unwanted attention."

A metal door halfway down the alley shrieked open. Maeko grabbed the cat, tucking him against her chest and wrapping her arms around him to hide the anomalous leg. The cat made a small squeak of surprise but didn't struggle when she cradled his warm body against hers. She pressed back into the shadowed corner and waited to see who would come out.

A tall, heavyset man stepped through the door and scowled at the fallen ashbin. The ends of his long moustache drooped below his chin, adding a comical exaggeration to the severity of his frown. Then his eyes tracked to her corner and the scowl deepened. His brow furrowed under the rim of the brown bowler balanced crookedly on his head.

He strode over to her, the anger in his eyes fading the closer he got until he looked more distressed than angry. A good sign. The expression on a person's face in the first few moments of contact often told volumes about how they were likely to treat her. This man seemed to suffer from a kind heart and good intentions. His type often caused more harm than good simply by misunderstanding her situation, but they tended toward generosity and were usually easy to slip away from.

He stopped, looming over her, and grabbed her upper arm, his big hand wrapping easily around it. Clinging to the failing dregs of his anger, he pulled her out into the reaching light of a gas-lamp and turned her to face the ashbin.

"Here now, what's the meaning of this mess?" His growl lacked conviction, and she began to sense an opportunity.

She sagged, letting his strong grip keep her from falling. He grunted and reached out to grab her other arm, supporting her until she was firmly on her feet again. His eyes focused on the cat, his big nose crinkling up with puzzlement. The cat stared back at him.

"Running from the Lits are you?"

She nodded.

"Cat got your tongue?" He had a hearty laugh. When she didn't join in his merriment, he nodded to the quiet animal in her arms. "You know..." She gave him a blank stare. "Forget I said it. Come along, you won't be running far in the shape you're in, and you smell bad enough to clear the city."

He turned her, guiding her through the open door with his hand still tightly clasped around one arm. She scuffed along, making a point of leaning on his hand so he wouldn't forget about her significantly weakened state.

"You should eat the damned cat," he muttered, pushing her ahead of him.

She frowned, clutching the cat a little tighter. Enough people she knew might do just that, but a person could starve for company just as they could starve for food.

Music thrummed down the hallway ahead of them, much louder now. They were in the pub. What a triumph! A bowl of food waited at the end of this hallway, she could smell it.

The man pushed her through an open doorway into a small, dingy room with a basin of murky water sitting in the middle.

"Clean yourself up a bit. Heldie's going to tan my hide for bringing you in here, but if you smell a little less offensive, she might not take my head completely off."

She walked around the basin, setting the cat discretely beside it to keep his unusual appendage hidden.

He sat politely and began to groom one paw, apparently aware of the washroom's purpose.

Smart indeed. She held back a grin. It wouldn't do to look less than miserable for her audience.

With the man looking on, she rinsed her hands and face, her motions slow and weary.

"There's a mass of dirty skin showing through them sorry trousers. You might as well rinse that too."

With a small huff, she scrubbed through the many holes in her trousers then scowled up at him.

The man chuckled. "You'd think I was beatin' you for the look on your face."

He snatched a stained towel off a narrow counter and tossed it to her. When she was dry, he beckoned her over. Carefully picking up the cat again, she walked up to him and he took hold of her arm, once more guiding her down the hallway and through a swinging door into a hot room brimming with the dizzying aromas of cooking food. This time she didn't have to fake it, swaying as the twisting ache of hunger made her lightheaded. The man supported her again, guiding her to a seat on a rough-hewn bench before a table facing into the kitchen.

She stared into the room, unable to think past the empty ache in her middle. A woman turned from a large pot and stared back at her, red curls in wild disarray around her face. The top laces of her red corset had popped loose under the weight of her heavy bosom and the sides of her skirt were tied up, revealing banded stockings and knee-high boots. Her face, already flushed with the heat from the cooker, burned a brighter red the longer she stared.

Finally, she pointed accusingly at Maeko with the wooden spoon she held. "What is that?"

The big man flinched and Maeko couldn't blame him. The woman had a shriek that would make a banshee cringe and the way she rested one fist on her hip brought Maeko's mum to mind with a flood of guilt and anger. Like this woman, her mum could throw out some alarming volume when riled. Maeko could see her clearly in her mind, her black hair pulled partly down from an ornate bone clip and one fist pressed into her hip.

"Don't you ever mouth off to the gentlemen who come here!"

"He hit you!"

"That's none of your affair, Mae!"

She remembered tears sparkling like small gems in her mother's dark, angled eyes, a spot of blood shining like a ruby on her lip. It was nothing compared to the injuries that had driven her mother out of the brothel.

Had that really been ten years ago? Oh, the things her mother would say to her if she knew what Maeko was doing now. Would her reasons for doing them even matter to her mother? She'd given Maeko up. Abandoned her.

Maeko stroked the cat's neck. "Don't worry," she whispered. "I'll take care of—"

"The poor thing weighs a feather," the man in the bowler hat said. "She ain't going to eat enough for us to notice the loss."

"We don't feed rats, Barman! Any minute now them players is going to be stormin' in 'ere to eat us out of 'alf our food. We ain't got enough for one more." The hand with the spoon pointed to the door now. "Get it out of 'ere!"

The man, Barman, puffed up his chest, ready to defend his decision. Maeko cheered him on silently. "Heldie, I..."

He trailed off when a group of people barged into the room. Maeko hadn't noticed that the music had stopped until then. Three men and one woman entered in a shroud of tired but enthusiastic chatter. They wore an odd mix of clothing that combined society panache with accents suggesting science, adventure, and a flair of danger. Typical pirate or anti-Literati fashion given a kiss of personal drama. They came and sat at the table around her as if they found nothing unusual in the arrangement. None of them appeared to notice her less than pleasant aroma under the strong stench of sweat, smoke, and liquor that entered with them.

An imposing, broad-chested man sat on her left, his short dark hair spiked rebelliously behind the aviator goggles perched above his forehead. He wore an elaborate brass and leather wrist brace with a watch face and several other instruments of uncertain purpose embedded in it. A lot less fancy than the one in the clock shop, but similar enough to be a bitter reminder of the failed heist.

His virtual opposite, an older, thin man with an elaborate headdress of woven material strips cascading down from the back of his crooked top hat, sat on her right. The blond woman, slender and seductive, decked out in a silky corset dress and feather hairpiece that swayed with every move of her head, sat across the table beside the third man who was rather average in this group, both for his more sedate attire and for his groomed look. Neither of the last two gave her more than a cursory glance.

The door opened once more and a younger man trailed in behind them, his dress more sedate in the manner of the man across from her. He had messy, overlong dark brown hair that edged toward black. He looked a little younger than Chaff, about her age. Where the rangy thief was tall and lean, he was shorter, with thick musculature and strong features that resembled those of the man sitting on her left.

When his gaze lit on her, she glanced away. Not out of shyness or embarrassment. Well, mostly not. He had the loveliest pale green eyes she had ever seen, framed by thick dark lashes that would make most women envious. Those beautiful judging eyes brought a flush to her cheeks and made her all too aware of her own appalling state.

The spike-haired man mussed Maeko's hair. "Joining us for supper, Rat?"

"I'm not a rat," she snapped, her cheeks burning with irritation. She was small for her age, and with her breasts bound down under shapeless boys clothing, people assumed she was much younger. The deception was handy for living on the streets, but always being treated like a child got bothersome, more so with those pretty green eyes looking on.

"It does speak." Barman grinned at her while he laid bowls out.

She glowered back at him, but he had already turned his attention to his task.

"Does that have to eat with us? It smells awful."

Maeko glanced up to find the young man still staring at her from where he'd sat beside the blond woman. He waved a hand in front of his nose to emphasize his point.

"Ash! Mind your tongue," the man next to her snapped at the same time the woman smacked him on the back of the head.

Ash stared down at the table with a defiant glower.

Barman cleared his throat. "Lively crowd tonight, Captain Garrett?"

"Very lively. We—"

Maeko glanced up at him. "Are you a real captain?"

Garrett looked at her, his spiked hair and the odd high collar on his stylishly worn jacket making him appear much bigger than he was. His charmed smile brought a shy blush to her cheeks. She looked down at the cat in her lap and began to stroke his head with determined intensity.

Barman set an empty bowl in front of her and the thrill of anticipation made her swoon. She rocked back on the bench and Garrett caught her shoulder, keeping her upright.

"I think you had best feed the rat first."

"And my cat," she croaked, now finding it hard to project her voice above a whisper.

Garrett chuckled. "It seems that the cat needs a bowl too."

"Bloody foreigners ought 'a take care of their own rubbish," Heldie snarled with a targeted look at Maeko.

The comment stung. She'd been born in London, even if she did look like her Japanese mother. She had every right to be here. Still, this was the best luck she'd had all week. She could tolerate a few abuses from a bar wench and a handsome over-privileged boy if it meant a hot meal.

"Be easy on the poor thing, Held," Garrett called to the woman.

Held?

"Yer always too nice to folks. It'll get ye taken advantage of," Heldie answered, but the smile she cast over her shoulder at him was a fond one.

Barman carried over a hot pot of stew, redolent with the faint otherworldly aroma of imported spices, and two warm loaves of bread. She started to lift one shaky arm toward the pot. Garrett pushed her arm back down and ladled some of the steaming stew into her bowl. He tore off a chunk of bread for her then accepted a smaller bowl Barman passed over to him, filled it, and set it on the floor behind her.

The rest of the group watched with interest now, their attention drawn by the captain's kindness toward her. The three across from her looked torn between disgust and pity. Maeko ignored them, turning around to hide the cat's unusual leg as she set him on the floor.

Then, her body trembling in anticipation, she attacked the stew and bread with gusto. The others soon started eating, chatting over their meal and forgetting their momentary interest in her until Garrett tapped her shoulder.

"Slow down, Rat, you'll make yourself sick."

She heard him and recognized the truth in his words, but she couldn't slow down. Chunks of real meat and potato and other delightful foodstuffs she hadn't tasted in some time urged her on. She continued shoveling until the bowl vanished out from under her spoon. She grabbed after it, but Garrett snatched it from her grasp. He pushed her back on the bench.

"Eat some bread. I'll give it back when you start showing sense."

She snatched the bread off the table and bent over it, forcing herself to take small bites. He just smiled, setting her bowl down on the far side of his, impervious to the longsuffering sigh of the woman sitting across from him and Ash's deepening scowl. When Maeko had nibbled her way through most of the bread, he moved the bowl back, even ladling in more stew in spite of the scathing glare Heldie gave him.

Though Maeko long ago made a vow not to trust strangers, she found Garrett's ministrations comforting. He was intelligent, but most likely not Literati. Outside of law enforcement officers and discrete visits to the brothels by some of the gentry, the Lits didn't come to this part of town. His music and his clothing screamed pirate, in open opposition of the Lits, which inclined her to trust him more than some. She thought of asking if he was really a captain again, but a soft meow drew her attention. It also caught the attention of the men sitting on either side of her.

"What the…"

The older man trailed off when Garrett reached down to pick up the cat. Pushing his bowl aside, he set the animal in front of him and started to examine the armored leg.

Maeko's stomach clenched and she stopped eating.

"He's mine," she muttered. Even to her ears, her voice lacked conviction.

They ignored her. All eyes were riveted on the cat. Garrett found a small latch on the front of the leg and released it. The cat stood patient, as though accustomed to such handling. A metal panel swung open to reveal a delicate arrangement of clockwork gears and pulleys where the real leg should have been. The open portion of the leg was separated off from the shoulder with a metal plate through which several tiny belts passed. The captain's brown eyes lit with feverish intensity as he felt around the shoulder, perhaps looking for another way in.

"How does it work?" he asked of no one in particular.

Only she was close enough to catch his quick intake of breath. Something caught him by surprise.

"He's mine," she repeated, putting more strength into the declaration.

"I don't think so." Garrett turned the cat so she could see the words etched into the inside of the open panel. Beneath an address, it read: MACAK, PROPERTY OF LUCIAN P. FOLESWORTH

Was it the name that caught his attention? It did almost sound familiar.

"Little thief," Ash accused, his pale eyes narrowing.

The woman caught him in the rib with a quick jab of her elbow. "Have some manners, Ash."

"She's a rat." Ash rubbed at his ribs. "You know she nicked it."

Garrett ignored him, turning a sober gaze on her. "Where did you get this cat?"

She lowered her eyes. The cat was as good as gone now. It shouldn't matter, she'd only had him for a short time. Who was she to look after him anyway? Even if she had a safe home to offer, the leg would require maintenance she wasn't qualified to give. But there was something liberating about having another living creature to look after.

Loneliness opened up in her like a fresh wound.

"I found him in the alley," she murmured.

"Curious."

"How does something like that end up in an alley frequented by street rats?" the older man asked.

"I'm not a street rat," she said. They ignored her again, the way most people ignored lesser things.

"Good question." Garrett examined the etching inside the leg again, running a finger over it before closing the panel.

"That kind of work's worth a fine stack of tin," the older man commented over her head.

"That it is," Garrett agreed. "I bet someone would pay a tidy sum to get this back."

Maeko glanced at Ash and caught a glimpse of something that might have been pity in his eyes, though his expression closed up too fast for her to be sure. Maybe he wasn't as cold as he acted, but she didn't want his pity. She spun around on the bench and stood.

Before she took more than two steps, Garrett leaned back and caught hold of her arm. "Where're you going?"

She stared at the floor. "I don't want to outstay my welcome."

"I'm sure Barman and Heldie will lend you a spot of floor tonight." The irritated snort from Heldie argued against this, but he didn't let go of her arm. "Sit down."

Against her better judgment, she sat back down. He placed the cat in her lap and it began to purr, settling there.

"Macak." She tested out the name.

The cat butted his head into her hand.

"He likes you," Garrett observed.

She relaxed a little, calmed by his pleasant tone, but when she met his brown eyes, the feverish gleam still lit them. She stared at the cat and stroked him, listening while they drank and talked of other things. When they finally broke up to go to sleep, Garrett insisted, to Heldie's obvious irritation and Ash's apparent displeasure, that "the rat" sleep in the kitchen with them. They shoved the table over against one wall and laid out sleeping rolls. Heldie found an extra blanket and tossed it down for Maeko. She stretched out under it with much misgiving.

It wasn't that she didn't relish the lingering warmth from the ovens and the chance to sleep under a relatively clean blanket, but when things were going this well, chances were they were going too well. Macak, less concerned, licked her on the nose once, then pushed in next to her and purred himself to sleep. Outside the door, she heard Barman and Heldie speaking in hushed voices.

"We should contact the Lits," Heldie insisted.

"Why, so they can take the girl and turn her into another brainwashed minion? Let her stay the night. We'll send her off first thing tomorrow with a full stomach."

Even stuffed as she was, her mouth watered at the suggestion of another meal. One night here wouldn't hurt anything so long as she stayed awake.

Garrett lay on the nearest bedroll. She didn't think he had time to fall asleep yet.

"Captain Garrett," she whispered, hoping Ash, laying on his opposite side, wouldn't hear.

Confirming her suspicions, he rolled over to face her. "Yes?"

"Do you have a daughter?"

"Two boys." He smiled then. "You're not implying that there's a young lady under all that grime, are you?" His eyes drifted to Macak and the smile faded. "Go to sleep, Rat." He turned over again, putting his back to her.

With a full meal weighing her down and the cat's warmth pressed against her, unwanted sleep overwhelmed her.

Rough hands grabbed her sometime in the night, jarring her awake. The last thing she saw before a black bag came down over her head was that the musicians, their sleeping rolls, and the cat were gone.

ool night air nipped at her skin through the holes in her trousers when her captors dragged her outside. The pungent stench of rotting waste from the dumped ashbin told her they were in the back alley. She struggled with the ferocity of a rabid dog, but superior strength and size worked in their favor. They twisted her arms around behind her and banded them with metal cuffs.

A worse fight went on inside her, a fierce battle against the welling despair that made her want to give up and let them take her. She'd been betrayed. How could she have been such a duffer? She let Captain Garrett lull her with his musician's charm and false caring. Probably the moment she drifted off, he and his group had taken the cat and left, reporting her to the first Literati officers they saw. She'd seen others wrestled into submission by the Lits, and this was how they always did it. They threw a black bag over your head, then secured you with tight cuffs that cut into the skin and dragged you away.

She struggled, but she didn't scream. No one would help, and years spent learning the value of silence weren't abandoned so easily.

A back kick connected and a hoarse cry rang out behind her. One set of hands vanished. Before she could take advantage of the moment, something struck the side of her head and she staggered, reeling with the im-

24

pact. Her knees hit down on the hard-packed dirt and her stomach turned, her recent meal making an abrupt evacuation into the bag.

"Get the bloody bag off!" The voice was familiar, tight with fresh pain and thick with loathing.

If that was Tagmet, then the other, who still gripped her arm with one hand while fussing with the tie on the bag, must be his younger partner.

She hung her head, trying to keep vomit away from her face while the young man loosened the bag and pulled it off, tossing it to one side. Her head continued spinning in the sudden rush of fresh air and she retched again, the last vestiges of a delicious meal discarded in the dirt. Something warm trickled down in front of her left ear.

"Hellfire! Did you have to hit her?"

The younger man took her chin and turned her face. He dabbed at her head with the corner of a dirty rag. It took a moment to recognize the tattered fabric as one sleeve of her shirt that had ripped the rest of the way off in the struggle. No great loss, it had only been hanging on by a few threads.

"Bloody rats!" Tagmet took hold of one of her arms in a viselike grip, hauling her to her feet. "Why are the quiet ones always so much blasted trouble?"

The younger man, a clean-cut brunette who looked dapper in his sleek black Literati uniform, gave Tagmet a sour look and resumed dabbing away the blood.

Maeko twisted her wrists, trying to get blood flowing through the pinching cuffs. Her hands felt like they were in danger of exploding. The image of them puffing up like red balloons forced a hysterical giggle through her lips.

"Stop squirming!"

Tagmet shook her and the other man grabbed her shoulder to keep her from falling before the onslaught.

She looked up at him, pleading with her eyes, the humor gone, leaving only looming despair in its wake.

The man turned her, moving her out of Tagmet's hands, and began fiddling with the over-tight cuffs. "They shouldn't allow you to handle kids. You've no compassion."

The cuffs loosened a little. Was this the right time to try fighting again? She didn't feel very steady on her feet.

"They're just rats, Wells. They don't respond to kindness."

Tagmet grabbed her shoulders and turned her, shoving her toward the waiting Literati steamcoach. She dug in her heels. Unimpressed by her effort, he shoved her again with enough force to send her sprawling. She turned her face, her ear and cheek smacking down on the hard-packed dirt. Garrett's smile flashed through her mind with the burst of pain and her throat tightened, tears stinging her eyes.

How could she have been so gullible? He had taken Macak. He had taken her freedom.

If I ever see him again...

Two sets of hands grabbed her arms, lifting her from the ground. They shoved her into the back of the coach. Wells avoided her eyes when he locked the door, perhaps feeling guilt for the rough handling. She considered spitting on him for his cowardice, but thought better of it. No reason to invite additional abuse. She'd had more than enough of that for now.

The coach wheezed and rumbled to life. Street signs and familiar landmarks passed by beyond the barred windows and she turned her mind to the task of using them to determine their destination. It was too late to drop her off at an orphanage or reformatory tonight. It would be a holding cell for the night, probably at London Juvenile and Adult Holding Facility, otherwise known as JAHF.

Doing her best to get comfortable with her hands bound behind her, she curled up and closed her eyes, listening to the sounds of the steam engine at work. The heat of the boiler warmed her back and the coach rocked when it moved onto newer, better-maintained streets. Her lips moved, repeating the address etched inside the cat's leg while she waited for the opportunity to escape. Sooner or later they would make a mistake. They always made mistakes.

The coach jerked to a stop and Tagmet came around to drag her out of the back. Her shin smacked the edge of the door as she struggled to keep up, a fresh blast of pain. With his crushing grip and her throbbing shin keeping her alert, she marched into the building. Wells followed close behind, muttering complaints about unnecessary force without once attempting to intervene. They took her to a white room with a table in the center and pushed her down into the chair behind it. Bright electric light made her head hurt more, so she squinted her eyes to filter it out. How did the Lits afford that kind of newfangled technology when they complained rather publicly of a shortage of officers and insufficient funds for recruiting?

Shifty blighters.

Tagmet walked to a desk tucked to one side and grabbed a clipboard and pen. Against the opposite wall, a floor-to-ceiling shelf unit held bundles of tagged items. Personal belongings and perhaps some evidence waiting for transfer with the appropriate prisoner.

Wells sat down across from her. "What's your name?"

His gentle pitying tone made her want to smack him. With her hands bound, she settled for glaring at him, clinging to the security of her silence.

"How old are you?"

She shifted her glare to Tagmet, giving him his share of her hatred.

Tagmet wrinkled his crooked nose and scratched something out on the tablet. He cleared his throat and read what he had written aloud. "Cell C1. Female street rat of Asian or part Asian descent. About 15 or 16." He jotted a quick note. "Maybe 17."

She continued to glare, doing her best to hide surprise at the accuracy of his assessment.

Wells gave his partner an incredulous look. "She's not more than 13."

Tagmet responded with a rude snort. "She's older than she looks." He resumed reading. "Long black hair. Dark eyes. Pale skin. About," he gave her a long scrutinizing look, "5 foot. Needs processing and transfer." He threw the clipboard and pen back on the desk. The pen rolled across the top and off, bouncing from the chair to settle on the floor under the desk. Tagmet sneered at it and left it there. "Come on. Let's lock her up and get out of here."

Wells retrieved the pen and put it back on the desk then urged her to her feet with a light touch. Tagmet grabbed an odd shaped key from a hook on the wall. He led the way through another door into a corridor full of iron barred cells and the stench of sweat and urine. After removing her cuffs, Tagmet pushed her into the first cell, locked the door, and left.

Wells hesitated in the doorway until she glared at him. With a resigned shake of his head, the young officer in his fitted black uniform, a pistol and club hanging from his belt, turned and left. She doubted he had the nerve to draw either weapon.

After the door shut behind them, she stood inside the bars and looked around. The few occupied cells held adult prisoners. Anyone under the age of eighteen was transferred as soon as possible to an orphanage for assessment, which took about a week. From there, most kids five years and older went to one of the Literati workhouses or reform schools for re-education. That meant placement in training for a trade based upon your social status and skills, something that didn't bode well for the illegitimate child of a toffer skilled at picking locks and pockets.

She glanced at the lock mechanism on the door. A unique style of lock that required a special key, manufactured by none other than Clockwork Enterprises, specifically made to thwart prisoners with her skills.

The other prisoners slept or pretended to sleep, all except for the hatchet-faced man in the cell next to her. He lay on his back with his head turned to the side staring at her, pale eyes unmoving under a rough stubble of light blond hair. His hardship-worn face bore numerous scars, a theme that continued down his chest where his tattered shirt hung open. He lay still as death for several seconds, then a slow grin curved his thin lips. A gap showed in his upper teeth where several were missing.

She had seen a leering grin like that more than once in her time on the streets, a clear warning not to go anywhere alone with this bloke.

Feel fear. Don't show it. Another essential rule for surviving on the streets.

Doing her best to ignore his disquieting stare, she sat on the camp bed and proceeded to pick at a hole in her trousers. She had almost managed to put the man out of her mind when he got up and walked to the bars separating their cells. He stood there and continued to stare. She resisted the urge to slide over to the far corner of the camp bed to maximize the distance.

He grinned again. "Yer a right slip of a bird." He had a soft, gritty voice, perhaps because of the long scar running across his neck just under his jaw.

She narrowed her eyes at him.

He squatted down and beckoned her with one hand. If he thought making himself shorter made him any less terrifying, he must not have looked in a mirror lately, if ever. With the bars separating them, however, it might be safe to indulge him, just to find out what he had in mind. She stood and approached, stopping inches out of his reach.

"Turn to the side." He made a rotating motion with his crooked index finger.

With a wary eye on him, she turned and his smile spread showing another missing tooth farther back on the top left.

"Come here." He beckoned with the crooked finger this time, his rasping voice dropping to a whisper.

She shook her head.

"You wanna get out?"

She nodded.

He beckoned again and she took a few reluctant steps closer. One filth-stained hand reached through the bars, calloused fingers touching her arm. His pale eyes picked up an excited gleam. She fought the urge to jerk away, hoping compliance would encourage him to disclose his escape plan. It worked.

"The waifs they bring in here is always so terrified. They cower in the corner like kicked puppies." Staring into his face, she could believe he knew exactly what a kicked puppy looked like. "Not you, though, little bird," he crooned. "I can see you're brave. A fighter like me." His tone made her tremble, but she stood her ground. "I think you can squeeze between them bars and get the key from the next room."

She turned, moving her arm away from his hand, and considered the space between the front bars. He was probably right. It would be a tight fit, but not impossible. Then there would be the door. She looked beyond the bars at the next barrier and he chuckled.

"Good. Yer thinking it through. The big bludger down the way kicked that door open when they brought him in. The lock's busted. You get the key and let me out. I'll handle the rest."

Seeing the excitement in his eyes, she knew she couldn't trust him. She couldn't trust the Literati either. If he could get her out of the building, then all she had to do was get away from one man. That didn't seem so hard.

She walked to the front bars, then cocked her head toward the door and listened.

Trust your ears to find what your eyes might miss.

Who had told her that? A plethora of pickpockets and other wily survivors she'd met since taking to the streets skittered through her mind. The Literati had captured so many of them over the years, but their advice remained. They'd all taught her something useful about surviving in the streets. She was just better at it than they were.

Satisfied by what she hadn't heard, she turned sideways and slipped one leg and arm between the bars. Then she tucked her face through. The bars caught on her ears so she shoved hard, bracing her outside palm against a bar for extra force. The ear that had hit the dirt when Tagmet pushed her earlier felt tender, stinging as she pushed it through, but it worked. Now for the rest of her.

How awkward would it be to become stuck half through like this? She almost giggled at the image, but the reality of the situation sobered her.

Behind her, the hatchet-faced man began to breathe faster, excited. She did her best to ignore him, pushing air out of her lungs and pressing into the narrow space. It wasn't as hard as she expected. Some pressure on her ribs, not even enough to be painful, and then she was through. Turning to face the empty cell, she grinned at her achievement, until she noticed Hatchet-face again. Sweat beaded on his scarred brow, the eager gleam in his eyes and his gap-toothed grin giving him a maniacal look.

Turning away, she went to the door and tried it. It wasn't locked. She nudged it open just a crack. The room stood empty and the one odd key hung by the door on its hook. She reached up, grabbing the key. Ducking back into the cellblock, she stood and considered him. Did she need him?

She was out now. Couldn't she just run?

"The next door's locked from outside and there's a guard beyond that," he said, interpreting her look. "You won't get past that guard without me."

The door lock she could pick. The guard was a different problem.

"He'll kill you, when he's done toying with you."

She glanced at the shadowed figure lying back on the camp bed in the cell beyond Hatchet-face. The figure there didn't move and didn't speak again. Hatchet-face ignored him.

She hesitated. "Why are you in here?"

Hatchet-face lowered his voice, likely to keep someone else from calling his bluff. "Burglary. Same as you I bet."

He was right, though she couldn't believe that was all he'd done. "Breaking out will give you a longer sentence."

"I've a job to finish. We're wastin' time."

Swallowing dread, she walked to the cell that had been hers and unlocked it. Then she went to the next cell. Hatchet-face hovered by the door, hands reaching as if he wanted to grab the key from her and trembling with the effort of restraint. He didn't want to frighten her too much, not yet.

"Hurry, before someone notices," he whispered.

She put the key in and turned it. The lock clicked free. Hatchet-face surged out. He crouched and grabbed her arms, his face close enough that she gagged on his sour breath.

"In the next room, I'll hide by the door and knock. You stand in the middle so the guard sees you. Understand, little bird?"

She nodded. She would do anything if it would get his hands off her. He released her and led the way back into the room. She hung the key up, then let him position her on the opposite side of the desk in full view of the next door. He crouched alongside the door and gave it a light rap.

A man's voice came from the hallway beyond. "What the hell?"

Moments later, a view panel set high in the door slid open and the man looked into the room. His small blue eyes, framed within the little rectangle, settled on her.

"How did…" He shook his head and the panel closed. She heard the sound of a key turning in the lock and the door swung in. He strode into the room, not worried about handling one girl. "How the hell did you get out?"

Hatchet-face rose behind him, a lethal shadow. Before the guard could utter a sound, the gap-toothed prisoner wrapped an arm around his neck and squeezed. Backing up against the far wall, she watched in horror while the guard struggled. Hatchet-face held on and the guard's face slowly turned purple, his struggles weakening as the color deepened. She looked away and bit her lip to keep from crying out when his body slumped to the floor like a marionette with cut strings.

She'd seen death, usually from illness or exposure. You couldn't miss it living on the streets, but watching someone die like this was different. It had a horrifying intimacy about it that made her feel ill.

Hatchet-face held a hand out to her and she hesitated. This man was far more dangerous than she first realized. This, however, wasn't the place to try to fight her way free of him. Drawing the attention of more guards would only get her dumped back in the cell.

A snake of terror coiled in her throat, tightening so it was hard to breathe. She walked around the table, stepped gingerly over the guard's body, and placed her hand in his. Grinning, he closed his fingers, his large hand making hers look small and frail.

"Good bird." He mussed her hair with the other hand the way Captain Garrett, another bloke she'd misjudged, had. Then he grabbed the club from the guard's belt and pushed the door open.

London JAHF wasn't well staffed at this time of night. The hall beyond the door held only silence. She chewed at her lip, fighting the urge to run from him regardless of the consequences, and hoped it would stay quiet long enough for them to get out. Hatchet-face was dangerous, he killed like he'd done it a thousand times before, but if he got her out of here, she could cope beyond that.

The slack look of the guard when he'd fallen haunted her as Hatchet-face moved them forward, his stance low, his steps uncannily quiet. The dead man's image hovered in the back of her mind like a ghost. She glanced over her shoulder. No one followed them, at least not that she could see, but she didn't suppose she would see a ghost. Or would she? Would the officer haunt her if he became a ghost or would he know that her vile companion alone made the decision to kill him?

She tripped over Hatchet-face's foot, surprised to find he had stopped moving. His hand tightened on hers as he yanked it back and up to keeping her from falling into the crossing hallway. This time, when she bit her lip to keep from crying out with the pain, she tasted blood. He scowled at her and she noticed with a remote amusement that the set of scars on his forehead resembled the shape of a duck when he furrowed his brow. She bit her lip harder to counter the hysterical giggle that bubbled up into her throat and his eyes narrowed as if he could see it trying to escape.

This is serious.

Looking into those pale eyes, she remembered how serious it was. Not only did they have to get out of this place, but the cold and calculating look in his eyes brought to mind the next problem she faced. His was the confident, fierce look of a man who could easily kill another full-grown man his size with his bare hands. A girl her size wasn't much of a threat to him. She would never overpower him. That meant she had to be on her toes. The first opportunity for escape could be her last if she let it slip away.

Burglary indeed.

With a sober nod, she turned away his anger. The glimmer of cold cruelty that crept to the surface in its place sent a shudder of fear through her. She managed to hold his gaze and he faced forward again.

In front of them, a hallway crossed the one they had come down, which continued on the other side in a mirror image of the hall behind them. She could only hope her unsavory companion knew which way to go. They all looked the same to her.

Hatchet-face remained still and silent, barely breathing. She mimicked him, waiting and listening while he did. She didn't hear anything. He leaned forward, slow and cautious, peering out into the crossing hallway. She mirrored the movement, learning what little she could from him.

His hand squeezed hers, more of a reflexive twitch than something meant to convey meaning. He led her on, pulling her into the hallway and down it on the left.

Every closed door they moved past presented a possible threat. The hall itself, dimly lit with occasional wall sconces, provided them with a few shadows to lurk in. Not that it would truly hide them if anyone came, but she found the darkest places between lights comforting.

Stay quiet, lurk in shadows and don't draw attention.
That was how you survived the nighttime streets and
avoided the Literati. *And don't trust anyone.*

How could she have forgotten that lesson with
Garrett? Although she still remembered that key bit of
information that might work in her favor. She remembered the address engraved inside the cat's clockwork
armor. If she went there, she could tell Mr. Folesworth
who had taken his cat. Perhaps he would be grateful for
the news, grateful enough to reward her and maybe, just
maybe, he would let her visit the cat when he got him
back. Then Captain Garrett would learn not to mess
with her. But that was all irrelevant until she got out of
this.

A set of double doors closed off the hallway ahead of
them. Hatchet-face stopped, putting his ear to the crack
between the doors. He rested one palm on the door as
if he might feel the presence of someone beyond as he
would hear them. She watched with keen interest. For
all that he terrified her, he had notable skills in the art of
stealth that were worth studying for the brief time she
planned to be in his company.

He pulled her close and she forced herself to meet
his frigid eyes. With a jerk of his head, he gestured to
the doors and nodded, letting go of her hand. The separation was like a storm cloud lifting.

Did he want her to go through?

She lifted one finger and pointed at the doors, raising her eyebrows in question.

He nodded.

Her mouth tasted like chalk and the sound of someone moving beyond the doors made a cold sweat break
out on the back of her neck. What was she supposed to
do? She couldn't overpower a guard.

He nodded again and she gave a tiny nod in response.

When she pressed a hand to the door, he coiled back
into the shadows and nodded once more, smiling what
she suspected was supposed to be encouragement. On
his face, the expression mostly made her want to run
screaming.

Taking a deep breath, she bit the inside of her lip
hard enough to bring tears and the coppery taste of
more blood then pushed the door open. The heavyset
man in the room, sitting facing the outer door, turned
and stood, his dark eyes popping wide, the whites
showing like a startled horse. He reached for the club at
his belt and she stumbled forward, swaying while tears
ran down her cheeks.

The man hesitated a second before taking his hand
away from the club and stepping forward to catch her.

"Blast it! How did you get in here? What happened
to you? Are you supposed to be out here?"

She leaned into him, making him shift his weight and
turn away from the door in order to keep her upright.
The man's hands held on to her, soft and gentle, not
like most officers. They felt like comfort, like the touch
of a loving home with soft blankets and warm food.
Then a wet crunching sound broke the brief spell of his
touch and his hands tightened in spasm before releasing
her. Something warm and wet spattered her face and she
cringed away from it, glancing up at Hatchet-face, his
pale countenance and the club in his hand also painted
in spatters of red. The man slumped to the ground at
his feet, his mouth hanging open in a posthumous mask
of surprise.

For an instant, she couldn't breathe. The face staring up at her changed, becoming her face, her dead eyes,
staring into an eternity of emptiness.

Then the face became that of the heavy man with
the gentle hands again and she wanted to scream at
Hatchet-face for what he had done. Her eyes tracked to

the Literati badge on the man's coat front. No, this man wasn't trustworthy. This man wasn't safety or comfort. He was death, a slow death that would strip her of everything she was.

But did he deserve to die for that?

She swallowed hard and looked up at Hatchet-face. The deliberate, calculating smile he gave her before he turned away made her shudder again.

He moved to the next set of doors and she felt the cool of night air seeping under them. This was it, the way out! Excitement charged her, readying her to run. Then he held a hand back to her and she recoiled, retreating from it. When her hand didn't enter his, he looked back at her, the peculiar duck shape reforming on his forehead as he frowned. The hand jabbed out with more force, demanding her acceptance this time. He stood between her and her goal, a lethal threat she couldn't hope to escape in this place.

Don't make him angry.

She held out her hand, forcing it forward, though every fiber of her being warned her away. The leering smile returned when his sinewy hand closed around hers with the ominous finality of Literati shackles.

Maeko met his eyes. *I will escape you,* she promised, letting him draw her after him as he turned and pushed the door open.

The welcome smells of the night air—soot, coal dust, and manure—greeted them when they slipped out the front doors. They emerged at the top of a run of shallow steps rising up from the street that Maeko remembered from when the officers brought her in. At the foot of the steps, a Literati officer stood chatting with someone in a coach pulled by a set of white horses. The animals matched in everything from the set of their fine heads to the thin layer of soot on their coats that turned them a greasy pale gray.

No one noticed their exit in the darkness. The officer laughed at something.

Might this be the opportunity she needed? A quick shout to draw attention, then she could make a run for freedom and give the officer a chance to accost Hatchet-face. His recapture had to take priority over that of a common street rat. He hadn't accumulated all those scars through a life of petty mischief.

But after years of training to avoid the Lits, when she opened her mouth to shout at the officer the sound stuck in her throat. What would come from getting the help of a Lit? At best, her recapture. At worst, his death. Her hesitation gave Hatchet-face time to pull her far enough away that the officer wouldn't have much hope of catching up.

Was that my one chance? Did I miss it?

Like it or not, she was on her own.

Hatchet-face turned a corner and yanked her along through the shadows with the speed and stealth of an accomplished predator, running down streets she knew well enough from years spent hiding out, lurking in the darkest corners and surviving, learning about the value of silence and dirty clothes in dark shadows. She did her best to keep track of the turns, but by the time he finally slowed, she stumbled along behind having long lost track of the streets and the details of the buildings. Despite all her time spent fleeing capture, his stamina put her to the test and his firm grip on her hand never loosened.

He pulled her into a narrow alley and stopped. She ran into him and sprang back, jerking to get her hand free. He held fast.

"I got you out. Go do your job."

"We're creatures of the street, you and I." Hatchet-face grinned, his eyes gleaming with excitement. "We do what we got to do to survive and we need tin for that, right little bird?"

She stopped pulling. His idea of survival went to dark places she'd never considered. He was a cold murderer. She would never go there, no matter how desperate. She did need tin though. He was right about that.

His grin stretched wide. "I knew you were my kind." He moved closer, still holding her hand, and lowered his voice. "This job, there's a pile of tin in it. I owe you for helping me out of there. You watch my back on the job and I'll give you thirty percent of the cut, plus full price for any goods you nick."

The wild in his eyes spiked her adrenaline and his words made her wary. Wasn't nicking goods the point of a job? Still, there might be opportunity here to make up for the failed clock shop job and stash something toward paying her mother's debt. "What's the job?"

"We need to break into a suite on the tenth floor of the Airship Tower." He rattled off the address.

Time stopped. The address was the same as the one etched in Macak's leg down to the flat number. Macak lived in the Airship Tower.

Macak is a moneyed cat.

How could that be? She needed to know more. Could he be after the cat? "Sounds brilliant. What are we after?"

"You watch my back and grab any valuables you can carry. I'll take care of the family."

It was hard to keep alarm from her voice. "Take care of them?"

"A wealthy toff hired me to drop them. Splendid payout when the job's done."

Drop them? Did he mean… Was he going to kill them? She saw the two officers he'd killed in her head and her gut squirmed. What had she done by letting this monster out? "You can't keep killing people."

His eyes narrowed, the grin fading. "What's it matter? Ain't like they're family."

She had to get away, but without upsetting him. "I can't. I have to meet someone."

He pulled, drawing her in. The rotting sour smell of his sweat wafted to her, making her gag. His arms were masses of ropey, scarred muscle, too much for her to escape on strength alone.

"That so? Here I thought we had a good thing going. Well, my employer tips his fine hat to you for your assistance." He grinned, pleased with himself, and pulled her even closer. "I can't let you go now. You know too much."

She tried to dig her feet in, clawing at the fingers crushing her hand. "No. Let go." It was almost a sob. She hated feeling weak and the look in his eyes said he didn't intend to let her go anywhere alive.

No! This isn't going to happen!

All men had a common weakness. Several weaknesses, in fact, but Chaff had taught her that one was more certain than most.

The dingy world narrowed down to the two of them. Her heart raced, panic threatening at the edge of a vital calm. She pretended a stagger, moving herself toward him and his hold relaxed a little. He trembled now, his breathing harsher than it had been when they first stopped running, a hideous smile curving his colorless lips, hungry for the kill. She swallowed the burn of bile rushing up into the back of her throat and, with all the power in her small body, rammed one boney knee into his groin.

The duck-shape of the intersecting scars on his forehead came out in sharp relief and his eyes bulged wide. He doubled over. She twisted away, breaking free. A blast of panic flared like lightning across her vision when his other hand clamped onto her upper arm. His fingers dug into the flesh, yanking her back and down as he curled around his pain. Tears sprang into her eyes.

Maeko spun, raking down his cheek with ragged fingernails. A swell of crimson rose in their wake. She kicked out at his groin again and he caught her leg with his other hand, jerking up so she fell onto the gritty dirt of the narrow street. She hit the ground with a small grunt and kicked out with her free leg, catching him in the nose as he bent over her. This time he let go, reeling back into the wall with a hoarse cry.

She didn't dare waste the chance. If he caught her again, after what she had just done, he wasn't going to be in the mood for a chinwag. She sprang to her feet, sprinted around the nearest corner, and down that street. All too fast, she heard the sound of heavy shoes slapping the wet street behind her as he gave chase. With little care for her destination, she darted around another corner. He was too close and gaining. She couldn't escape him with speed alone. She needed to be clever.

Sprinting around another corner, her eyes homed in on an ashbin at the end of the alley. Memories of the stench and cockroaches from the last one twisted her face in a grimace as she pelted toward it. Various sized crates were stacked haphazardly near the ashbin and two doors opened into brick buildings on either side of a narrow street that intersected the alley on her right. This was it. This choice would decide her fate.

The pounding of her heart was so loud in her ears now that she could barely hear the slap of his feet on wet ground. She tried one door. Locked. The other offered no resistance to her cautious touch so she pushed it open a few inches then hurried back to the ashbin. Squeezing in behind the last one worked well enough, but it might be tempting fate to expect the same results again so soon. Instead, she lifted the lid, letting it slam closed. Then she crashed through the crates, scattering them before returning once more to the ashbin. She dropped to the ground next to it and pushed out her breath.

Forcing herself under was harder than squeezing between the bars at JAHF, but the buildup of grime beneath the bin provided some lubrication. Her feet still poked out the side when Hatchet-face charged into the alley. With a last desperate shove, digging worn toes of her shoes into the ground, she pushed herself the rest of the way under. She couldn't suck back in the breath she had pushed out to get into the tight space and her head lay twisted to the side, making it impossible to track the movement of his heavy boots, the leather as scarred as his flesh. Winded from running, her lungs started to burn with lack of air. She closed her eyes, terror rising while she strained to breathe without wheezing.

"I know you're here, gutter rat."

His voice sounded strange, as though he had a bad cold. The kick to the face had done some damage. She might have felt good about that if panic weren't welling up so strong around the edges of her thread-fine grip on rationality. The need to stay hidden started to fade before a rising fear that she would perish here, suffocated beneath an ashbin. Of the many ways she could imagine dying in this cruel city, this had to be one of the worst.

The lid opened and smashed closed, the jarring vibration piercing through her. She flinched. Something cold and moist touched her nose and her eyes snapped open. A large gray rat stared back at her, sniffing the tip of her nose. She stared into the small black beads of its eyes, focusing there.

"If you come out now, I won't hurt you." Hatchet-face kicked at the crates now, making enough racket in the alley that she dared to hope someone might come investigate. "I'll find you! You know I'll find you!"

The rat sniffed her forehead then turned and ambled out from under the ashbin. A heavy boot slammed down, crushing it, and she squeezed her eyes shut to block out the sight. Her chest hurt. Stars began to flash behind her eyelids. Above them, she could hear an airship passing over and tried to focus on guessing what it might be—a Literati patrol, a bold pirate vessel, or spoiled wealthy folk out for a joy ride. In that moment, she didn't really care who it was, she despised them for being in a better place than this.

"Bloody rat!"

She heard his footsteps receding followed by the violent slamming of a heavy door. Had he gone through the open door into the building in search of her? She opened her eyes again and counted to sixty once, twice, using her strained breathing to set the cadence of the count. For good measure, she counted to sixty a third time, fighting panic and the lightheadedness of too little air. Finally, she started to struggle toward the front of the ashbin. She couldn't get her heels up to push with her toes, so she reached forward, digging into the dirt with her fingertips and pulling.

One ragged nail bent back and another tore up into the quick. She bit her lip against the sharp pain. When her chest came free, she sucked in a huge breath. Her head spun, making the alley tip and sway like a ship at sea. She heard the sound of footsteps coming back her way and terror burst through her again. She thrashed free of the ashbin and dove into a broken crate, tucking herself into the shadows and pulling her knees in to her chest. She put one grimy hand over her mouth and nose to muffle her breathing. The bent over fingernail stung. She pushed it back down, watching blood well beneath it.

Hatchet-face kicked the ashbin and swore. Then he kicked some of the crates again. If he hit the one she was in, would he notice the resistance of her weight? She tucked her head down into her arms to bury a panicked sob. Tears ran down her dirty cheeks as she silently cursed Captain Garrett for getting her into this mess.

"I'll find you eventually rat. I promise."

A door slammed somewhere nearby.

Hatchet-face took off at a run. His footsteps receded and she stayed there, curled and trembling, almost screaming when a hand grabbed her arm.

"C'mon, Pigeon. We need to get out of here before that bludger comes back."

The familiar voice sparked giddy relief. She climbed out of the crate with Chaff's help as raindrops began pattering on the street, echoing hollow on the metal top of the ashbin. She hurried after him on shaky legs, keeping her thoughts to herself in case Hatchet-face was in earshot.

The rain picked up, coming down hard enough to wash away some of the worst grime from crawling under the ashbin and rinsing out gummed blood in her hair from where Tagmet had struck her. Now that the immediate danger was past, she noticed stinging pain from that strike and the accompanying headache. It was just one of many aches, not the least of which was the throb in her bum from Hatchet-face yanking her over by her leg. Her injured fingers stung as well and she took a moment to chew away the hanging part of the torn fingernail, scowling at the well of blood. She wiped it off on her trousers.

With it overcast and heavy with rain, the only real harbinger of morning's arrival was an increase in traffic. Coaches, steam-powered and horse-drawn, increased in numbers along with the occasional steamcycle. Pedestrians began to fill the pavements and a few bicycles joined growing traffic. A lanky gentleman in top hat and spectacles trundled by on a peculiar clockwork bicycle. The contraption didn't have the speed of the steamcycles, but it was smaller, quieter, and the motion of gleaming gears created a lovely dance as it traveled along. It also didn't alarm horses the way the labored chugging and sharp exhales of steam-powered engines did.

Too bad the Lits don't ride those. I could outrun them without breathing hard.

They wove between ladies in bustled skirts and men in frock coats, doing their best to avoid attention while discreetly pointing out good marks to each other out of habit. They finally stopped at a shop front sheltered by a red and gold striped awning. A boy several years younger than either of them was waiting there. He greeted Chaff, staring at him with the wide-eyed admiration of a novice criminal in training.

Maeko turned to Chaff. "You got away."

"I did." His tone said there hadn't been any doubt. "Checked myself into that fancy new Lit orphanage for a late dinner. What do you think of the haircut and the fancy togs?" He gestured with flair to the ensemble, a pair of black trousers and a clean white shirt under a dapper black waistcoat. It gave him an upstanding appearance that he appeared to enjoy a little too much. Despite the trim, dusty blond hair still hung in his blue eyes that sparkled with the promise of mischief. "I took the togs and the meal and beat feet."

"How'd you find me?"

"Could've been the pen and ink." He waved a hand under his nose for emphasis and winked at her.

Recalling Ash with his pretty green eyes saying a ruder version of the same thing, she sniffed her arm and recoiled. *I do stink.* "Really, how did you find me?"

"Diggs tracked me to the orphanage to tell me he heard you'd been nicked by the Lits. I was headed to JAHF to see if I could perform a rescue when they moved you. I saw you running from that bloke. When he didn't give up, I made a ruckus to draw him off. I guess rumors of your captivity were exaggerated."

"Thanks for the help. I was nicked last night, but I took my leave before they could move me out of JAHF. There were a few smelly ashbins involved."

"Bugger and blast!" Chaff straightened. The devoted attention of the younger boy next to him became all hers. "How'd you scarper out of there?"

Sometimes less information was best. "I slipped out between the bars."

He laughed. "I always said you were about as wide as a lamppost. Good thing you haven't filled out too much up top yet."

She felt her cheeks grow hot and beat down the urge to wrap her arms around her bound chest.

He punched her shoulder playfully. "Don't go getting all shy on me, May."

The strands of her temper frayed. She'd spent the night breaking out of jail and fighting for her life while he got a haircut, new clothes, and a meal. The least he could do was pronounce her nickname correctly. "It's Ma-eh."

"Whatever, Pigeon." Chaff turned to face the young boy who shrank before the direct gaze of his mentor. He rested a hand on her shoulder. "This is Benny."

She sidestepped out from under his hand. He didn't get to be chummy if he couldn't be bothered to say her name right, not today. "Teaching him the ropes?"

A brief tightening around his eyes was the only indication that he noticed her evasion. "Indeed. I was about to explain to him how you shouldn't offend the delicate faculties of your marks, such as their sense of smell, if you want to be successful on the streets."

She swiped out for a punch, but he danced to the side, dodging her strike. His wink and roguish grin were almost as irritating as they were comforting.

"I nicked him from the orphanage when I snuck out. Told him to wait here while I went for you."

Recalling Garrett's betrayal and the meal she'd lost brought another welling of bitterness up in her. "So you thought you'd abandon me at the clock shop? Go have some warm food and relax?"

He stepped back from her glare. "I did look for you first, but you weren't in any of the usual places. I couldn't do much without knowing where you'd gone. It's a big city, Pigeon. The minute I had a lead, I went after you." He eyed her then, taking in the extent of her disheveled state. His brows pinched together with a gratifying hint of distress and the burn of defensive anger sparked in his eyes. "Are you all right? That bludger didn't hurt you, did he?"

His response smoothed the edge off her anger. "I didn't give him much chance."

"That's my girl." The distress lingered in his regard for a few seconds more, then he smiled. "C'mon. Let's get you washed up and fed."

"Wait, Chaff." Hatchet-face meant to kill Macak's family. She had to do something. The wild-eyed killer wouldn't go before dark, and probably quite late to give the family a chance to go to sleep. If she got there in the early evening, she could warn the family and tell them who had Macak. She didn't want to put Chaff in danger, but she couldn't face Hatchet-face alone if things went awry. If she wanted him along, however, she needed to spin it the right way.

Chaff was watching her. Waiting.

"I got a lead on a job. Could be better than the clock shop."

He perked up. "What is it?"

"It's at that new building. The Airship Tower."

He looked skeptical. "Place that fancy will have security."

"I met a bloke last night who promised a big cut if I helped. I'd feel better having you along. I'll give you half my cut. We'd need to go early tonight though." It wasn't a lot of information and she knew he didn't like working with strangers. Would he trust her enough to go along?

One of the fancier steamcoaches, a lacquered black carriage with elegant brass accents, gave a sharp exhale on its way past, catching their attention. The coaches were supposed to be warm inside because of the boilers, never a bad thing in London. Luxury models like the one chugging past were built, so she had been told, with plush velvet seats and a convenient beverage cabinet inside for the refreshment of passengers.

What would it be like to ride in such a thing?

The only steamcoach she'd ridden in, the cheap Literati prisoner transport they had dumped her in the back of last night, lacked even a whisper of such refinement, though she had been next to the boiler. It was foolish even to fancy the idea. Those who rode in such luxury wouldn't deign to see her, which did make it easier to pick their pockets.

When she turned back to Chaff, he nodded. "I've got your back, Pigeon. We'll head that way after you've had a bite and aren't so pungent you'd blow the best cover." He put a hand on her shoulder to steer her around.

She let it stay this time. Names and teases were only so important when weighed against a meal. "I hoped you'd say that."

Maeko and Chaff stood close in the shadows, gazing up at a large gleaming building in the deepening darkness.

The Airship Tower.

They had finished construction less than a year ago, creating a haven where the wealthy could escape the squalor of the common rabble. The Lits called it neighborhood improvement. The pirates called it class separatism. Whatever they called it, it wasn't the kind of place she expected to visit and not one likely to allow her kind entrance either, even in the clean, hole-free clothes they'd gotten for her from the charitable widow who fed them lunch.

The tower had been the talk of the streets for a while. Looking through the windows validated those tales of frivolous luxury. Elegant signs, framed in elaborate brass scrollwork, directed patrons from the two-story lobby into adjacent conference rooms, the warm glow of an expensive restaurant, and a ballroom at the rear beyond the lift, with ten floors of residential flats above that. Some said that the upper flats had access to a private landing for the fancy little airships that had gained in popularity with the well-to-do.

An airship was docking now, lowering down to the roof through the soup of smog and soot. It wasn't one of the sleek new models she would have expected at such an affluent residence, but rather a stained, hulk of a thing that sported several mismatched patches on its outer hull. She watched until it dropped out of sight, then moved close to the front windows to scope out the entrance.

The problem now was how to get past security. There was no doorman. The door itself ran on steam power with a floor plate on either side that triggered it to open, the Clockwork Enterprises brand stamped upon the center of each plate. The sound of the engine kicking in to open it would draw attention.

Though she had spotted piping for gas, the lobby glowed cheerful with the light from an array of elegant brass electric lamps and two massive scrollwork chandeliers hanging in the center of the soaring ceiling. A single attendant waited at the front desk to one side of the lobby, the wood of the desk so polished that the chandeliers reflected in its surface. Two security guards watched the room, one from a corner between a tall plant and a carpeted staircase, the other standing by the lift in the center of the back wall.

"We need a distraction," Chaff muttered.

The guard by the lift left his post, stopping to say something to the guard by the stairs before he walked away and disappeared down a hallway.

She shifted her feet. "Right about now would be good."

"Ask and you shall receive," Chaff said in a hushed voice.

Maeko followed his gaze to a woman striding up to the door flanked by two men. The woman captured her attention, not only because she wore trousers and an underarm holster peeked out when her long men's coat swept back as she stepped through the door, but because she moved with the confident air of someone in charge. The two men with her, in their long wool coats and pushed down bowler caps, kept close on her heels, showing no interest in taking the lead as the unusual trio tromped into the building and made for the front desk.

As soon as they entered, the security guard at the stairs perked up and walked toward the desk on an interception course. Spotting opportunity, Maeko and Chaff locked eyes.

He smiled. "Ganbatte."

He had the most charming smile. She'd taught him the word and it had become an exclusive parting wish between them, taking the place of the customary good luck he wished his boys. It meant do your best, which she liked better than relying on luck. His Japanese accent was still dreadful, but that only made it cuter.

She grinned. "Ganbatte."

They darted through the door before it finished shutting, careful of the trip plates, and slunk around to the staircase, keeping to the far wall.

"Hold up," the guard said. "We don't need trouble here."

Maeko cringed, afraid the guard had spotted them, but a glance over her shoulder revealed that he was addressing the trio now at the counter, speaking over the desk attendant who was too busy scowling at his interruption to notice her. They scurried up the stairs, getting out of sight as fast as possible. The suite was 1001. The top floor.

A driving sense of urgency kept the pace up until they panted their way to the tenth floor. The stairs opened onto a landing. A stark white door warmed with an elaborate floral carved frame and the brass numbers 1001 on the wall beside it stood across from the lift. Was it the only flat on this floor? She urged herself forward, her gaze drawn to the fancy scrollwork door handle. She didn't belong in a place like this. It was too nice for a street rat and the tidy refinement made her nervous.

Chaff was digging for his lock picks.

She reached for the handle and pressed on the thumb latch. It sank smoothly. It was unlocked.

Chaff met her eyes and mouthed "careful."

Heart racing, she nudged the door open a crack. It glided with quiet elegance on bright brass hinges. The room beyond was dark. Pushing the door open more, she slipped in. Chaff followed and shut the door gently behind him. The pungent aroma in the room washed over her, a stench of urine, feces, and the faint stink of rot that whispered of death.

When her eyes focused in the dim candlelight flickering through from an adjacent room, she first noticed a pile of scientific journals on the table nearest the door. Myriad detailed sketches of clockwork and steam-powered devices were hung on the walls and set in frames on polished tables where most moneyed families might have artwork and flower arrangements. As her eyes skimmed over the odd items, she spotted two figures lying still on the floor, a woman and a little girl stretched out as if in sleep, the child's head resting on the woman's chest. They lay too still and a chill raced up her spine.

Could Hatchet-face be here already? Had he killed them? No. She'd been around death enough to know by the smell that these two had been dead more than a day. Hatchet-face had only escaped with her a little before dawn.

Someone else had done the deed.

I just wanted to help. It didn't matter. They died anyway.

"What do we do now?" A woman's high, frantic voice came from the next room.

Maeko ducked beside a table, a move that put her closer to the woman and child on the floor, close enough to see blood on the woman's blouse and confirm that neither breathed. She put a hand over her nose and mouth to block some of the smell and scuttled back away from them until a plush settee blocked further retreat.

"We need to get out of here, I just..." A man's voice from the other room. He sounded familiar.

Chaff, crouching beside her, took her hand. She met his eyes and he gestured toward the door with a jerk of his head.

"So do we," he whispered.

She held her breath, listening for the man to speak again. Silence ensued, broken only by the sounds of quick, nervous breathing. A plaintive meow came from a box set on the credenza along the wall near the entrance to the occupied room.

"Let's go." This was the woman again, her voice shaking.

"I need to think a minute."

Captain Garrett. As much as she despised him for betraying her trust, she wouldn't have thought him the type to be involved in murder. She looked at the still forms and shuddered. To think she had fallen asleep in the same room with him and his band of merry killers. They needed to get out of here, but she wasn't going to leave Macak with these people. First, she needed to get Chaff out of danger.

"Go," she whispered. "Start looking for a way to create a distraction so we can get through the lobby. I'll be right behind you."

He held her eyes and she thought he might argue, then he nodded and crept around to the door. He listened then slipped out, clicking it shut again behind so the people in the flat wouldn't see it open and know someone else was there.

Relieved, she crawled around the settee then stood and tiptoed to the credenza. Holding her breath, she inched the front slat up out of the box. The whir and click of tiny gears accompanied Macak out of the carrier.

His metal leg gleamed in the flicker of candlelight reflecting off a mirror on one wall.

"We need to go now," the woman insisted.

"We need to search the place," Garrett countered.

Panic spiked. She grabbed Macak and ducked behind the settee. A glance back confirmed she had left evidence of her passage by failing to replace the front slat on the box. Garrett entered the room and she ducked lower, peeking out enough to see him stop next to the credenza. She was ruined.

"What the—"

A knock on the door cut him off.

"Mr. Folesworth," a strong feminine voice called.

"Get out," Garrett hissed, hurrying back the other way.

"Open up or we're coming in!"

Maeko curled around the cat, heart pounding in time with the fist against the door. She heard rushed footsteps in another part of the suite. The front door flung open and the trio she had seen downstairs stormed in with pistols in hand followed by one of the lobby guards. They stopped and stared at the bodies on the floor, expressions turning grim as they dropped into defensive postures. Then the woman gestured to each of the men, sending them through the room in different directions. She knelt to check the bodies and Maeko began an awkward, one-armed crawl behind the settee toward the door. Macak twisted in her hands to lick her cheek with his rough little tongue.

There were sounds of a scuffle and someone shouting. Elsewhere in the suite, a door slammed.

The tower guard came back into the room pushing someone ahead of him.

Ash.

Served him right for being rude to her. She couldn't help a twinge of sympathy, though, for the terror in his eyes and admiration for the defiant set of his jaw and shoulders. He was trying hard to hide his fear.

The woman turned her gun on him and he flinched. "Who are you?"

"I don't have to tell you anything," he growled, though the tremor in his voice belied his confidence.

Maeko couldn't see the detective's face from her hiding spot, but she could hear cold promise in the woman's response.

"You don't have to, but you'll be sleeping at JAHF until you do. Looks like your associates abandoned you."

Ash lowered his gaze, the color of shame rising in his face, twisting more sympathy out of Maeko. "I wasn't supposed to be in here. They told me to wait on the airship."

The woman gave a joyless chuckle. "Guess you should have listened."

Maeko's insides squirmed. She could stay hidden and maybe they wouldn't find her before she got a chance to escape. Alternatively, she could let them catch her. It was clear Macak's owners weren't going to be rewarding her, but she did know how to get out of JAHF. Ash's family didn't look rich, but they weren't poor either. Maybe they would help her out if she helped him…and he did need help.

Before she could second-guess herself, Maeko gave Macak a little squeeze and he meowed.

With the speed of a lightning strike, the woman vaulted the settee and landed with her pistol inches from Maeko's forehead. Dread formed a solid lump in Maeko's stomach when she stared up the cold dark center of the barrel. The woman made a motion for Maeko to stand with her free hand. When she hesitated, the finger on the trigger twitched. Maeko held up one hand to show surrender and stood, moving slow so as not to alarm the woman with the twitchy trigger finger, clutching the cat to her chest. The gun rose with her, trained on her forehead. She met the woman's eyes. They looked pale gray in the dim light, cold and calculating.

"You." Surprise made Ash's voice crack and embarrassment brightened the red in his cheeks.

The stockier of the other two men stormed into the room. The woman stared where she had her pistol aimed with humorless intensity, but Maeko dared a glance at Ash then at the other man. Both looked puzzled.

"What?" the woman prompted.

"Two blokes and a bird beat feet out the back entrance and took off in an airship," the stocky man reported.

"Isn't there a guard up there?"

"A guard station. No guard."

"We're still hiring," the lobby guard defended.

"Fools." Her lip twitched into a sneer. "Did you shoot the airship?"

"Nah. I didn't want to chance it going down in the street."

The woman exhaled irritation. The last man stepped out of a dark hallway, looking them all over with disturbing nonchalance.

Maeko met the woman's eyes again. "I'd have shot it."

The woman's sneer turned into in a skeptical smirk. "You would have, would you?"

"Yes."

"Like you'd know how to shoot a gun, rat," Ash snapped.

Last time I put my neck on the line for you.

The woman holstered her weapon. "Search the place boys. See what else you can find. Our client is going to be livid when he hears about this." After the two men she'd arrived with hurried off to do her bidding, she gave Ash and the guard a calculating look. "Take the boy downstairs. I'll be there in a minute."

The guard shoved Ash ahead of him through the door.

Once they were alone, the woman gave Maeko a thorough scrutinizing. "You're not the typical London street rat." She gestured to Macak. "Is that Mr. Folesworth's cat?"

Maeko nodded, feeling the twist of anxiety at the inevitable separation from the cat she had just gotten back from Garrett. She dug her fingers into Macak's fur and he purred, gazing up at her. Tears stung her eyes.

Saving Ash had better be worth it.

"How do you play into this mess, rat?"

"I'm not a rat," she muttered.

The woman raised her brows skeptically and waited.

"I found the cat in an alley." Turning him around, she showed his metal leg. "This address is etched inside the leg. I was going to bring him here, but Captain Garrett nicked him from me. I decided to come tell Mr. Folesworth who had his cat. When I got here, the door was unlocked and..." She shrugged.

"And you thought you'd invite yourself in?" The woman narrowed her eyes when Maeko didn't answer. "Captain Garrett? Is he one of the bludgers who slipped out the back?"

She nodded.

"What can you tell me about him?"

Maeko lifted her chin, more confident without the gun in her face. "Why should I tell you anything?"

The woman's eyes narrowed more, becoming angry little slits in her face. "You need a reason other than I'm packing iron and you're not?"

Maeko nodded again, swallowing the lump of fear in her throat. If the woman thought her a rat, then perhaps she would believe that a rat had nothing to lose. It wasn't much of a bargaining chip, but it was better than nothing.

"I'm a friend of the family."

Maeko glanced at the gun and gave her a sour look. "Rubbish. You need to lie better than that."

The woman clenched her jaw. She had a hard face, all sharp planes and angles that might soften with the right hairstyle. The short men's cut she sported wasn't that style.

"I'm a private detective. I was hired by Lucian Folesworth's brother to find him and this cat." She flicked a finger at Macak and he shrank away, laying his ears back. "His wife," she glanced at the bodies, "late wife, reported them missing. Now it looks like I'm looking for a murderer as well. If you think that puts me in the mood to contend with an impudent street rat, you're mistaken."

The stockier of the two men tromped back into the room. "No sign of the inventor, Em. It looks like his study's been ransacked too."

The detective pressed one hand to her forehead.

"Em?" Maeko wrinkled her nose. "What kind of name is that?"

"It's short for Emeraude." The detective closed her eyes and rubbed at her temples now, the muscles in her jaw clenching.

"That's not much better."

The gray eyes opened, glaring down at her. "I need you to tell me what you know about the people who were here. Who's the boy?"

"I'll tell you what I know if you promise not to turn us in to the Lits." Unlikely, but it would be easier than breaking out and therefore worth a try.

"You're a cheeky little rat, aren't you?"

Maeko turned her attention to stroking the cat.

"Can't blame you. I know how it is being a girl on the streets," Em muttered.

There was remorse in those words that made Maeko want to believe her, but it was hard to imagine anyone climbing from the streets to become a detective, especially a woman.

She focused on the feel of soft fur under her fingers.

"Sounds like she's got you in a corner." The lilt of amusement in the stocky man's voice earned him a glare from Em.

The tall man stepped into the doorway of the room Garrett had been in when Maeko arrived, his narrow frame backlit by the flickering of the abandoned candle. He grinned and gave Maeko an appreciative nod. She ignored him. Best to assume they were no more her friends than the Lits were.

"All right. I won't turn you in if you tell me who the boy is, then show me where you found the cat and where you were when Captain Garrett took him away from you?"

Maeko nodded. "The boy is Ash. He's Garrett's son, I think."

"Now we're getting somewhere." Em turned her attention to the two men. "Finish checking this place over, but don't touch the bodies. We'll let the Lits do the dirty work. I'm taking the waif and the cat downstairs. Chivvy along and join us when you're done."

"Sure thing," the tall man drawled, revealing an American accent. With a nod to Em, he sauntered back through the doorway.

"You got it, boss." The stocky man tipped his hat, earning a wry smile and a shake of the head from Em before he too disappeared into another room.

"Why don't you let me carry the cat?"

Em held her arms out and Maeko turned away, clutching Macak to her chest. "I'll put him in his crate."

Em waited for Maeko to slip the cat back into his crate before gesturing to the door. "March."

With the crate in hand, Maeko marched out of the room as ordered.

Downstairs, Ash stood near the door glowering at the guard still holding one arm while the guard, in turn, glowered at the well-dressed toff standing at the front desk arguing with the desk attendant. The attendant's eyes lit on Em with a glimmer of desperate hope and the new arrival turned. A coachman hat sat low on his brow, shadowing his face. There was a flash of recognition in his eyes and he stormed toward them, giving Maeko only a passing puzzled glance.

"Detective Wilkins, what's going on? I came to check on Lucian's family and they told me I couldn't go up. Me." His incredulous tone said he was someone far too important to deny entrance, or he at least thought he was.

Em, her expression drawn with ill tidings, continued walking, gesturing for him to accompany her. At the front desk, she met the growing impatience in his eyes with unflappable somber composure.

"Mr. Jacard, I am afraid Lucian's wife and daughter are dead."

The attendant blanched.

The immediate shock on Mr. Jacard's face turned to denial and anger. "That's ludicrous. How? I can't—"

Em slapped a hand down on the desk to silence him. She spoke in a low voice. "Someone shot them in their suite. As long as Mr. Folesworth is still missing, we need to keep a low profile on this. Get the Lits down here," this to the pallid attendant who gave a jerking nod, "and have them handle the bodies as discreetly as possible. No one talks about this. The Folesworth family is on vacation." She waited for the attendant to nod again. "Mr. Jacard, I assume you can manage the business in your partner's absence."

He looked insulted. "Of course, I've done so many times, but I must see…"

"You need to wait until the Lits have had a chance to investigate the scene."

Mr. Jacard glanced at Maeko now, eyeing the crate she held. His eyes narrowed. "Is that Macak?"

"Yes. The girl found him."

An odd light sparked in his eyes. "I'll take care of him."

When he reached for the crate, Maeko drew it closer to her. Em threw a hand between them, earning an indignant scowl from Mr. Jacard.

"The cat is evidence in a murder investigation now. I can't let you take him yet. I'm sorry."

"That's ludicrous," he declared again. A favorite word? "It's just a cat."

Em's lips pressed together, her professional patience fading. "You know better, Mr. Jacard. I'll be delivering the cat to Literati offices. You can take it up with them." She scrawled a brief note for the desk attendant to pass on to the Lits. The young man accepted it and disappeared through a door behind the desk.

Her assistants arrived in the lobby then. After an exchange of abrupt nods between her and the two men, she bid Mr. Jacard good-bye, then directed Maeko and Ash outside to a coach drawn by two soot-grayed white horses. The same coach Maeko had seen outside of JAHF when she escaped with Hatchet-face. Beyond the coach, she spotted Chaff in the shadows of another building. He must have gone down the stairs as the detective was heading up the lift. She met his eyes and gave a tiny shake of her head to show that he shouldn't attempt anything. His brows pinched in distress. He stayed in the shadows, watching, eyes searching for opportunity in spite of her discouragement. He wasn't willing to give up on her, not even when he should.

She glanced away, not letting Chaff see her faint smile, and spotted Mr. Jacard watching from one corner of the tower. Staring at the crate she held, he struck a lucifer, the flame casting strange shadows over his narrow features.

She resisted Em's prodding.

Were those tears on his cheeks? Had he been close to the deceased? More than a mere business partner?

His eyes jumped up and met hers. He lit the cigarette pressed between his lips, tossed the still burning match down, and stepped back into the shadows.

She hugged the crate to her chest and climbed into the coach.

After a short ride in which Maeko, Em, and Ash sat in stubborn, pensive, and sullen silence, respectively, they pulled up behind the pub. They left Macak in the coach with Rueben, who Em tasked with questioning Ash while Maeko led her to where she found the cat. The mess from the ashbin no longer littered the ground, but the stench lingered and the bin itself still lay on its side awaiting replacement. That made it easy to show them where she had found Macak in the venting. Em stalked around the alley, searching the venting and the grime around it for clues. Amos, the stocky man, stayed with Maeko to keep her from making a break for it.

"What were you doing back here?" he asked.

Maeko looked him over once and said nothing. "Hiding from the Lits?" She shrugged.

"I thought you told Em you weren't a rat."

She ignored his teasing, turning instead to watch the detective stride back to them.

"Come with us, Amos. I want you to search the place while I talk to the owner."

"Do I get to search the ladies?" His leering grin won him a scowl from Em.

For once, Maeko agreed with her.

The detective wasn't one to be outdone, however. "If you can find a lady in this place, you go right ahead."

With that, she turned her back on Amos and opened the alley door, not troubled by the fact that it wasn't the proper entrance.

Shame on the owners for not bothering to lock it.

It was an invitation to thieves…and Literati officers looking to snag a sleeping rat. Maybe she was a rat, but did that mean she was worth less than anyone else? That was something her mother always tried to drill into her.

"Act cheap, Mae, and you'll be treated cheap."

Now that she understood how much most people looked down on prostitutes, the words rang hollow in her mind.

Setting her shoulders and clenching her teeth against a surge of fresh hurt and anger, she followed Em through the door. They entered the hallway Barman had led her down before. As they passed the first side door, Em nodded to it and Amos peeled off, ducking through it to start his search. The detective continued past the remaining doors, a hound on a scent, tracking straight through the swinging doors into the kitchen.

Heldie spun around from her cooking, still dressed every bit like a harlot.

Not fair, Maeko chastised herself.

Many women of the pirate movement adopted such attire to offend and defy proper elite society. It was rude to assume Heldie's attire screamed harlot rather than pirate when the pub expressed, at the very least, tolerance of the pirates by allowing Garrett's band to perform there.

Barman sat at the table counting coin out to an older man in the fine attire of a gentleman, perhaps a successful merchant. Both men turned as the door swung open. Barman stood and the other gent followed his example.

"What's that rat doin' back 'ere," Heldie asked, her sharp voice cracking so she had to clear her throat half-way through.

Maeko met Heldie's wide-eyed stare. The woman looked away and a creeping dark anger crawled up

Maeko's spine. Who had turned her into the Lits? Maybe it hadn't been Garrett after all. The black look Barman gave Heldie added weight to the suspicion. Em, on the other hand, appeared pleased to have Maeko's story verified by their reactions.

"Keep your mouth shut woman and cook," Barman snapped.

Under the circumstances, Maeko appreciated the sharp tone he took with Heldie, but Em stiffened, incensed by the show of male authority. She didn't seem the type to submit to any authority. Heldie scowled and spun around, returning to her task with her shoulders hunched. Barman nodded, satisfied, then looked the detective over. Coming to a decision, he turned to the other man.

"It's been a pleasure, as always. Looks like I've got some other business to attend to."

The gentleman tipped his top hat and nodded. "I'll stay for that drink next time, Barman. A good day to you all."

The man collected his coin from the table and slipped around Em, skirting through the edge of the doorway to avoid any chance of contact. Given her cross look and the way she'd set her hand on her waist, pushing the coat back to reveal the pistol she wore, Maeko couldn't blame him. Lingering silence followed then, as Barman and Em sized each other up. Heldie glanced over her shoulder at them, but turned back to her work when Maeko glared at her.

"Your name's Barman?"

"No, Ma'am. It's Grenville, actually. Folks call me Barman because it's easier to remember when they're liquored up. Who are you to be bargin' into my kitchen when I'm conductin' honest business?"

"I don't care a whit about your business," Em snapped. Her apparent disgust with lower classes was making Maeko suspect that the detective's roots were comparably humble. "I'm looking for someone. A younger gentleman, about five-foot, eleven inches, with short brown hair and brown eyes. A rather slight build, almost feminine. He wears spectacles most of the time and sometimes carries a cane. He has a wedding ring on his left hand and a distinctive ring on his right hand made up of an assortment of tiny gears. He usually sports a moustache. No beard."

Heldie dropped the spoon she was holding with a clatter and snatched up a plate of food. Eyes downcast, she walked toward the door. As she slipped by, taking the food out to a patron, Maeko noticed the whole plate trembling with the shake in her hands. Something had upset her. Was it just Barman's reprimand?

Turning her attention back to the others, she saw Barman pursing his lips in thought. After a few minutes, he shook his head.

"I see a lot of blokes through here, Ma'am. That description don't ring a bell."

"Do you remember the rat?" Em gestured in Maeko's direction and she had to fight the temptation to kick the woman in the ankle.

Not a rat.

"Indeed I do. She showed up here with a rather odd cat last night."

"Yes. The cat belongs to the gentleman I'm looking for." Barman shrugged his broad shoulders.

"Perhaps you remember the group of musicians you had here last night?"

"Captain Garrett and his bunch? They're regular entertainment around here. A great bunch of kids."

"Kids?"

"You know how it is. After you reach a certain age, they all look like kids." Barman tilted his face away then, giving her a suspicious one-eyed gaze. "Why do you ask? They aren't in any trouble, are they?"

"No," Em lied and Maeko had to give her credit for the absolute confidence with which she did it. She removed her hand from her hip, letting the jacket slide back over the gun, easing the tension in the room. "They might know something about the man I'm looking for. Do you know how I can get in touch with them?"

"You only want to ask them some questions?"

"Yes. My name is Em Wilkins. I'm a private detective hired by the man's family. If they have any information at all, it would help. He has a wife and young daughter who are very worried about him."

Tug at the heartstrings. That was Chaff's fallback if he got in to trouble and he was good at it. Still, it made Maeko feel dirty listening to the woman use the deceased to twist information out of Barman. It looked like it would work too.

"I know what it's like to lose someone," he muttered. His cheeks drooped and a shimmer of moisture gleamed in his eyes. He pursed his lips, staring at the floor a few seconds before looking up at Em again. "I know where they live out in Hammersmith. I'm sure they wouldn't mind you payin' a visit under the circumstances."

He proceeded to give her directions then introduced her to some of the more regular patrons so she could inquire if any might have seen the man she was looking for. She drew Maeko along with a tight grip on her upper arm.

With nothing else to do, Maeko listened in and watched around the room. She spotted Heldie chatting with a patron and sucking down large gulps of something out of a mug on the table. The woman stopped by the same table every time she came out with another batch of food and again on her way back into the kitchen, taking a swallow every time she passed and exchanging a word or two with the man sitting there. By the time

Em reached Heldie, her cheeks glowed with a bright flush and questioning her proved pointless given the giggling fits Heldie succumbed to a few questions in. The detective lost patience and dragged Maeko back out to the coach.

"Get in."

Maeko braced a hand on either side of the door. "Why? I did my part."

Em gave her a stern look. "Do what you're told or I'll add another lump to that one on your head. I want to ask you and the boy a few more things about Captain Garrett and his crew."

She climbed back into the coach. Someone had let Macak out of his crate. His tail went up and he leapt into her lap when she sat. She scratched his head and he pressed into the affection before curling up there. She didn't trust Em any more than she trusted anyone else, but at least she'd get to visit with the cat a little longer. Any hope of being part of his life had vanished when she'd let Em catch her. Not that she was set up to care for a cat anyway, but the idea held a certain whimsical appeal. Still, the detective's investigation involved Macak now, and two people had died. The sooner she left it all behind, the better.

"My parents didn't kill anyone," Ash declared in the silence.

"I'm sure they just dropped in for a cup of tea," Em countered.

Ash jerked toward the detective and the tall man shoved him back.

"They didn't—"

"Be quiet, boy," Em snapped. "When I want an answer,
I'll ask a question."

"The bodies were a couple days old," Maeko offered.

Em's stare was intense. "You're full of surprises, rat."

"I'm right."

"You are, but that doesn't make them innocent. They were there tonight inside the suite. Why would you assume

they hadn't been there before?"

Maeko shrugged.

Ash started to say something and Em cut him off with a sharp glare. "This is a murder investigation now, not just a missing person. Rueben's heard your story. You'll get a chance to tell it again when the Lits question you."

Ash sank into silence, his quiet burning anger heating the interior of the coach.

Macak looked up at Maeko with his bright yellow eyes and she hugged his warm body to her. Pressing her lips to his head, she murmured, "I'm sorry. I can't keep you."

Em watched her and Ash in silence as the coach moved along and a sense of dread spread within Maeko.

"Where are your parents, rat," Em asked after a time.

Maeko shrugged, falling back on the comfort of silence until the coach rolled to a stop outside of JAHF.

Amos and Reuben turned away from her glances, guilt apparent in the slouch of their shoulders and the avoidance of their eyes. Rueben ducked his long body out of the coach and started up the stairs to the building.

Maeko glared at Em. She should have lied and given an address for her parents. Why did trying not to lie always turn out for the worst? "We had a deal."

Ash looked from one to the other. "What deal?"

"Sorry, rat. It has to be this way. I can't have you two running around talking about the case while I'm working it. Besides, you're better off with the Lits than living out on the streets." Em's refusal to meet her eyes held more weight than the words themselves.

"You don't believe that."

Brushing aside the threadbare curtain that covered the coach window, Maeko saw Reuben already sauntering back down the steps with a familiar Literati officer trotting along behind in an effort to keep up with his long-legged strides. Another officer emerged from the building and started down the steps.

Em exhaled, her weary expression aging her face beyond its years. "This really is the only way. There's a lot at stake here that you can't understand."

Reuben stepped to one side. The officer was reaching for the handle on the door of the coach. Em held up the crate for Macak and Maeko urged him back inside.

The door opened.

She gave Em a cold look. "I hate you."

"I'm sure you do." Em handed the crate out to Rueben. "I would."

The young officer's jaw dropped when he looked into the coach. "You again!"

Maeko channeled all her anger into a glare for Wells as she stepped down to the pavement. General annoyance aside, she appreciated that someone like Tagmet hadn't come to collect them. Wells she could deal with.

Reuben handed the crate to the second officer then climbed back into the coach, tucking his long limbs in like a spider retreating into its den.

The officer looked puzzled. "What's this?"

The crate meowed back at him.

"Put it in the evidence room. It's part of an investigation. Someone will be by for the cat and the boy later." Em leaned forward and looked out the door past them. An ironic smirk twisted her lips. "Nice sign. Really gets the message across."

Wells glanced over his shoulder at the building. Maeko followed his gaze. A large brass sign on the side read, Literati, For a Brighter Future. Only someone had scratched an l over the r in *Brighter* so that it now read, FOR A BLIGHTER FUTURE.

"Not again." Wells groaned.

Maeko stifled a giggle. She didn't want any of them doubting the sincerity of her hatred, Em in particular.

The door of the coach closed behind them and it rattled away. Wells, keeping a tight grip on her upper arm, turned to watch the departing coach with a puzzled expression.

"She never has been one to waste time on pleasantries."

Setting aside precious silence before the draw of nagging curiosity, Maeko asked, "You know her?"

"So you do talk." The officers started guiding them up the steps.

"More than she should," Ash muttered.

Maeko turned her glare on him, but he refused to look at her.

"I know the detective as much as any officer does. She's a thorn in our sides more often than not, but she usually finds what she's looking for. Tagmet says she has black powder for blood and spits venom three feet when angry." He gave Maeko a wink and she had to fight back a grin. The image of Em in her mind developed snake eyes, a flat nose, and a long forked tongue, a transformation she thought suited the woman rather well. "I think he might be exaggerating a bit. I can say that they don't make many women like that one and I think most of us are glad of it."

He directed her through the front door. She squinted in the harsh electric lights, finding her eyes drawn to the floor where the heavyset officer had fallen under Hatchet-face's assault. No trace of the encounter remained. Wells stopped her there, sending the other officer ahead with Ash and the cat. When they were gone, he turned to her. She shifted her feet, uneasy before his searching gaze, though she liked that he hadn't called her a rat once yet. It made him likeable, the way one couldn't help liking a clumsy puppy.

"How did you get away from Dobson? He killed two of our men on his way out of this place. When I heard he'd taken you, I figured we'd start finding pieces of you around the city in a few days. Instead, I find you back in my custody apparently unharmed."

The stench of sour sweat filling her nostrils. Ropey, scarred muscles pulling her toward a deadly embrace.

A shudder passed through her. She could still see his boot smashing down on the hapless rat and feel the press of the ashbin bottom heavy against her back.

Wells furrowed his brow and his grip on her arm tightened, though she didn't get the sense that he meant to cause discomfort. The small ache pulled her out of her memory.

"You poor thing. You must have been terrified." He shook his head and then met her eyes with more of that bothersome intensity. "Tell me honestly. Did he do anything to you?"

Do anything? She thought for a second. There was a slight rise of color in the officer's face. *Oh, that kind of anything.* She shook her head. When the intensity didn't go out of his stare, she said, "I ran from him as soon as I got a chance and hid."

Wells smiled, the tension relaxing from his face, though the heightened color remained. "Clever lass. We haven't figured out how he got out yet. Did you see anything?"

Unlocking her cell had worked to confuse them. One more point for the street rat. They didn't expect a simple street girl to be resourceful enough to escape their fine facilities. The question remained as to whether she could do it more than once.

She shook her head again. "I was sleeping when he came into the cell and grabbed me. He threatened to kill me if I made any noise." *As if I would ever make noise.*

"Sorry to bring up the incident, but I had to be sure. Come along then. Your old accommodations are waiting. We should be able to get you processed and out of this place by tomorrow afternoon." He spoke as if he believed that was a good thing and started guiding her back to the cellblock. "Sadly, we lost two good men in that incident and we were already understaffed. That's how I got stuck on this duty."

Perhaps you should stop sending patrols out to pester homeless folks.

He rambled on along the same vein until he had her locked back up in the cell, dropping a few tidbits of useful information that she tucked away for later. Taking advantage of his sympathetic streak, she played up feminine fragility and talked an extra blanket out of him before he left. The cell next to hers stood empty, haunted by memories of Hatchet-face, so she curled up in the far corner on the rough camp bed, wondering what they'd done with Ash. Despite her intent to remain vigilant, the long stretch of too much excitement left her too weary to keep her eyes open.

Raised voices in the next room snatched her from a restless sleep. She didn't think it had been long since her arrival, but she couldn't be sure without a clock. The hands on the one over the door hadn't moved since she arrived. The other officer stormed into the cellblock, yanking Ash along, his face screwed up tight and red with rage. Ash balked, throwing his weight against the officer's grip, but Wells followed on his heels, prodding him in the spine with his club to get him moving again.

"My dad will make you pay for this!"

The officer shoved him none-too-gently into the neighboring cell.

Ash caught himself on the bars and spun around, an enraged dog ready to lunge at its captors. Wells bounded forward and swept the door shut. He slipped the key in and locked the cell with practiced speed.

Ash stopped and glared, having at least enough sense to realize that attacking the bars served no purpose. He glared daggers at the officers until the door swung shut behind them. When he looked at her, she turned a shoulder to him, refusing to let those lovely eyes that brought a flush to her cheeks suck her in. Too many people had taken advantage of her lately. No sense opening the door for more of the same.

"At least you smell better now."

She said nothing.

"What's the matter? Cat got your tongue?"

She sat on the camp bed and pulled her legs in to her chest, remembering the feel of soft fur warm under her fingertips. "Unfortunately, no."

He stared at her and she avoided his eyes, focusing instead on the initials J.D. carved into the wall of her cell.

"That's a barmy thing to say."

She shrugged. "Where'd they take you?"

"I tried to run," he muttered, averting his gaze.

Amateur. She eyed the bars at the front of the cell. "Do you know what time it is?"

"Late." At her exasperated look, he dug a watch out of his trouser pocket. "'Bout one thirty-seven. Why?"

Wells, in his rambling, mentioned that his shift ended at two o'clock. That meant there might be an opportunity to slip out around that time. She didn't know where the other officer went, but Wells must have been in the front office judging from how fast Rueben returned to the coach with him when they first arrived. If they were shorthanded, those two might be the only ones around. If she tried to escape and failed, they would know she could slip out and she wouldn't get another chance. If she succeeded, she could get Ash out, for a price, then beat feet out of the city and lay low for a while. A few hideouts out around Whitechapel would take her in. If she could find Macak, she would take him with her.

"My name's Ash."

"I know." She stood up and walked to the front of her cell.

"You're a little short on manners, aren't you?" He chuckled. "Actually, you're a little short all around."

She gave him a sharp glance and found her gaze drawn to green eyes sparkling with amusement at his own humor. There was also fear in them, but he did a decent job of keeping it in check. He wasn't street smart. That much was apparent in his bearing. He stood proud and rigid. There was none of the telling looseness in his posture born of experience wriggling through crowds in search of a pocket to pick and crouching in dark corners to evade Literati patrols.

Wrenching her gaze away, she turned sideways to the bars, putting her back to him, and stepped a leg through. She heard him walk to the near corner of his cell. He was silent while she pushed her way through again. It was easier the second time, perhaps because she didn't fear becoming stuck now that she had done it once. As soon as she was through, a hand closed on her arm. His grip was stronger than she would have expected and his skin rough, the calloused hand of someone who knew something of hard work.

She twisted, yanking free, and glared at him. Why did everyone think they had a right to touch her?

His eyes met hers, shining with fierce determination. "Take me with you."

If he believed she would leave him, he might be more amenable to her terms. She shook her head.

His jaw tightened. "I'll shout and they'll catch you."

She tensed. She couldn't stop him from yelling for the guards and once he did, she didn't stand much chance of getting away. The noise might provide a distraction, but it would also put the officer on alert. Chances of getting through the second door were better with stealth.

"Careful with that one, boy, she's got the luck of a devil. Devils ain't known for their kindness."

The same man lay in the shadows of the next cell, the one who had warned her about Hatchet-face. She ignored him, gazing into Ash's green eyes and willing herself not to weaken before the hope she saw there.

"Why not wait for Em to come back and get you? It's not like you're an orphan."

He gripped the bars, meeting her gaze between them with boldness she admired. For someone she doubted had ever been caught on the wrong side of the law before, he was adjusting well.

"I have to find my little brother before that woman does."

Blood and ashes! So many things he might have said she was prepared to counter or even scoff at. That wasn't one of them. She knew all too well the pain of a broken family. Maybe there was a way that helping his family could help hers.

"I'll get you out," she said. "But you have to do something for me."

His eyes narrowed. "What do you want? Quid?" He said the last with a sneer.

Maeko bristled, but what else could she say? "Yes." "However much you need, my family can manage it. Just get me out."

Too easy. She should negotiate a set price, but they didn't have that kind of time. "I'll get the key."

The chuckle from the next cell grated on her when she stepped to the door and stood silent, listening before pushing it open. She'd seen Wells pull the key from a drawer this time so she dug into that drawer and took the key back into the cellblock.

Ash's eyes lit. He exhaled in relief.

She stalked to the cell. "What? Did you think I was lying?"

"You never told me your name."

"So."

"Dad says you can't trust a person who won't tell you their name."

"He's a clever bloke." *Clever and deceitful.* She turned the key in her fingers and watched Ash. His eyes didn't track the movement of that simple item that would set him free. Instead, they held hers, waiting, expecting that she would follow through. She put the key in the lock and turned it. "You better not slow me down."

She pulled the door open and he stepped out, his presence reassuring after her escape with Hatchet-face, though the latter had been far less likely to get her caught. He hovered next to her and watched her unlock the door to her cell. Then she turned to the third cell and the dark figure reclined on the camp bed.

"You want out too?"

"No thanks, Miss. Too many blokes out there as wants me dead. I'm right fine where I am."

Chuckling sounded from the few other occupied cells. She waited, puzzled when no one else made a play for their freedom. They were a complacent bunch. Turning away, she led Ash through into the next room and set the key back in the drawer.

"Why'd you do that?"

She gave him a crooked smile. "Confuse them."

He grinned back and she snapped her gaze away.

Trust no one. Care for no one. Shrugging off sudden discomfort, she crept to the other door and listened. Nothing yet.

A soft meow drew her attention. Macak's crate sat on the shelves against the wall. She hurried over and slid up the front. The cat climbed out and pressed his head into her hand.

"What're you doing?" Ash hissed.

She skimmed the shelves and picked up an empty satchel, slinging it over one shoulder. Holding it open with one hand, she picked up the cat and tucked him inside. She could hear his purr from within.

"You're cracked," Ash remarked with conviction.

"What's the time?"

He pulled his watch out immediately this time. "1:43."

She nodded to herself. If she were right, Wells would put in one last check on the prisoners before the shift change. He was the sort who wouldn't want to leave surprises for his replacement.

Ash started to speak and she held a finger to her lips, putting her ear to the edge of the door. He shut his mouth and waited.

Yes! This time she heard footsteps approaching. Then she heard voices and her stomach turned. There was someone with him.

"Quick! Chivvy under the desk. I'll hide in the corner. You have to be silent. Not hide-and-seek silent, but street rat silent. Can you do that?"

He gave her a haughty smirk. "It'll be the bloody cat that gives us away."

She returned a warning scowl. He might think he was something special, but street rats knew their own kind and he wasn't one. "Worry about yourself."

He went to climb under the desk, bumping his shin in the process and cursing under his breath. She winced, hoping he could slip the rest of the way under without too much noise, though she appreciated his fluency in street profanity.

She could make out what Wells was saying now.

"Detective Emeraude brought them both in. She didn't say much about either, just told me to hold them and the cat until I got further orders. They must have something to do with the investigation."

Keys jingled outside the door. Ash got himself tucked away seconds before the lock clicked. She shivered, recalling how the previous escape had ended for the officers on duty.

This time would be different.

"It's a real shame what happened to Mr. Folesworth's

family," Wells was saying when he walked in. "I guess we're supposed to keep it quiet until we find him."

The Literati officer walked straight to the other door, not once turning his eyes away from his destination or bothering to switch on a light. Someone followed behind in a fine gray suit, a coachman hat shadowing his features so she could only make out a vague profile in the darkness. He struck a lucifer as he passed and she shrank back, pressing into the shadowed corner. Mr. Jacard lit his cigarette and dropped the match as he had done outside the Airship Tower. The flame guttered out on the cold linoleum and a chill raced through her.

She held her breath and crouched motionless. She almost felt bad knowing Wells would get in trouble for this, but it wasn't her fault he didn't pay better attention. This room was something to pass through on his way to the prisoners, though she suspected Mr. Jacard would be more interested if he knew Macak was in there. When Wells reached for the handle to open the cellblock door, she slunk to the door they had just come through, one hand holding the satchel steady. Seeing her make her move, Ash started maneuvering his way out from under the desk.

How amusing it would be if he became stuck there, but then she'd never get any tin from him. She didn't linger to watch though. When Wells opened the door into the cells, she opened the opposite door and ran, hoping Ash could keep up. He might be nice to look at, but good looks meant nothing when it came to escaping the Lits.

A crash behind her gave her a much-needed boost of adrenaline. She sprinted down the hall and heard first one set of feet pounding in pursuit and then a second joined the chase. Two male voices snarled out curses, Ash far more creative and diverse in his selection of expletives than Wells. It turned out that he also ran a lot faster than the officer did. By the time she reached the door to the front office, he raced along right on her heels.

"Move," he yelled in time for her to shift to one side. He slammed through the double doors alongside her.

Something struck the door above her head and careened off into the room. A glance at the offending object as it clattered to the floor revealed that Wells had launched his club at them. He wasn't eager to take a shot with his pistol, something she had counted on given his compassionate disposition, and one of the primary reasons she wanted to make her escape before the shift change. Someone like Tagmet might be more willing to fire on them, and she didn't fancy chumming up with a bullet.

They barreled into the front doors together. The doors were locked, the impact jarring through her bones and rattling her teeth, but the combined force of their full speed charge proved enough to break the lock and send them toppling down the outside stairs with the accompaniment of a panicked yowl as Macak fell from the satchel.

She twisted around in time to see the cat bolting back toward the building. Disappointment twisted in her chest. She didn't wait to see how Ash made out in the fall. Ignoring the pain of several fresh bruises, she sprang to her feet and started running, taking a route opposite the direction Hatchet-face had led her down, in case the killer still lurked in the area. Feet pounded after her again, but only one set this time. She glanced over her shoulder to see Ash gaining on her, a red mark on his cheek that would turn into a dandy of a bruise. Wells burst through the doorway and Macak, bursting out of the shadows, bolted between his feet, sending him sprawling on the steps.

Brilliantly done. Maeko stopped long enough to catch the cat when he came sprinting at her, giving him a quick kiss on the head before she tucked him back in the satchel.

She started running again. A shot rang out and something struck the building next to her. She squeaked in surprise and ducked down a side street, spotting the other officer from earlier running up alongside JAHF, his gun drawn. Another shot rang out, striking the corner of the building as they vanished around it.

"They're trying to bloody kill us!" Ash shouted behind her.

She didn't waste energy responding. Potential death was a great motivator. Keeping up the pace, she sprinted down less traveled backstreets, putting as much distance between them and JAHF as she could. Then Ash's footsteps started to fall behind, his pace slowing. He wasn't used to fleeing for his freedom...or his life. She'd gotten rather capable at route finding and running long stretches when Chaff first schooled her in the art of picking pockets. That was also when she'd learned the wisdom of selecting marks that didn't look like they could run very fast or far.

She should keep running and leave him behind. Being shot at once was a sure sign that this bollocks was over her head. Twice was too much. And yet...

I'll stick with him long enough to get my part of the bargain. Then he's on his own.

Maeko stopped and turned, watching with a mix of annoyance and grudging amusement when he staggered to a stop and bent over, supporting himself with his hands on his knees while he panted. His dark hair hung forward, obscuring his features.

"Boy...can you...run," he said between gasps.

"Because I often have to." She opened the satchel to check on Macak. He made a startling leap up to her shoulders where he wrapped himself around her neck and started purring, the metal of his false leg cold against her skin.

"Who's a brilliant kitty?" she said, stroking the fuzzy head before turning a less affectionate gaze on Ash. "Where do you live anyway?"

He straightened and scuffed across the street to lean back against a brick wall, letting his head rest back against it and closing his eyes. His hair fell back, revealing the flush of exertion in his strong features. For a short time, he stood there catching his breath. She shifted from foot to foot, listening for pursuit and debating between the wiser course of ditching him and the misguided urge to stay. The few other weary nighttime wanderers paid them little attention, hurrying along huddled down in coats and hats. A figure lay under a ragged blanket in a nearby doorway, so still they might have been dead. Not much threat there.

"I don't know if it'll be safe. That harpy is like to go searching there."

Maeko sucked back a groan. He was right. "At least you're not a complete dolt."

He opened his eyes, glowering at her under thick lashes. "Are you this rude to everyone or am I just lucky?"

"Stop whinging. Lucky, you're not." She turned away, putting fists on her hips and chewing on her lower lip. Macak stood on her shoulders and stared down the narrow street with her. After a few minutes, she started walking. Ash trotted up to walk alongside her.

"Do you know who that Mr. Jacard is?" she asked.

Ash turned to gawk at her and she felt her face flushing. "Have you been living under a rock?"

"Surviving on the streets doesn't leave a person much time to keep up on the news," she said.

"Joel Jacard, the business partner of the wealthiest businessman in London, Lucien Folesworth, founder of Clockwork Enterprises."

A wave of nausea swept over her and Macak became heavier on her shoulders. A moneyed cat indeed. This was so far over her head she might as well be a speck in the mud at the bottom of the Thames. She hid the over-whelming feeling of intimidation behind dry humor. "Well, Mr. Jacard just got a lesson in disappointment."

Ash gave a small breathless chuckle, though his faint smile didn't last long. "That cat acts like he's been with you for years."

"He's smart. He knows he can trust me."

"To sell him for parts maybe."

Maeko gave him a scathing looking, ignoring a twinge of guilt that she had briefly considered that course of action when she first found Macak. She scratched the cat's head in apology for those earlier thoughts.

"I need to get to Hammersmith and find my little brother before the detective figures out where he is."

The hopeful edge to his tone caused a sinking in her gut.

Tell him you're taking the tin and leave before you get hurt. When she opened her mouth, that wasn't what came out. "Why wasn't he with you?"

"My mum and dad are musicians. I guess you know that," he added with a charming, self-conscious grin. "They're gone a lot. Sometimes I stay home and keep an eye on the house and Sam. When I go with them, Sam stays with a mate of Dad's."

She glanced at him. "He can't stay by himself?"

"Not anymore. Dad works for an airship manufac-turer when the group isn't off playing and stuff. We both used to help him at the shop. Then, several months ago, there was an accident. Some heavy equipment fell and Sam lost a leg. After that..." He trailed off when she stopped walking and turned to her. "What's wrong?"

She remembered how Garrett had looked at Macak's fake leg with such feverish interest. She'd assumed the monetary value of the device caught his attention, but this new information changed things. Macak's leg represented the potential for a functional leg for his son. The recent visit to the pub with Em also suggested that Heldie, not Garrett, might have set the Literati on her, though that was still little more than speculation.

She chewed at a ragged fingernail. What happened to silence? Why did she have to ask so many questions?

Silly as it was, she wanted the big man who had treated her so well to be innocent of betraying her and, for whatever reason, she was intrigued by his handsome, if somewhat judgmental, son.

What about the dead bodies? Who would kill a woman and child in cold blood and why? Did Garrett have anything to do with that? Ash said no, but he might lie to protect his father. The new information about Sam, however, inclined her to believe him. Why would Garrett kill them if he only wanted information on the clockwork leg to help his younger son?

It made more sense that someone—Hatchet-face perhaps—had killed the woman and child. But how? Even if he'd gotten there before she had, those people had been dead for at least a day. Garrett and his companions hadn't arrived long before she did. They could have stumbled upon the bodies while searching for the cat's owner just as she had. Then again, they could have been there before tonight. They had gotten inside from the landing pad, so either that door had also been unlocked or they had broken in.

Macak head-butted her cheek then hopped down and wound himself around her legs.

Her gut twisted. Could she have helped Em track down the wrong people?

"You look like you don't feel well." Ash was watching her with those captivating eyes, his brow furrowing.

He looked anxious and he had good reason to be.

His family, guilty or not, was mixed up in a murder and missing person investigation that could destroy their lives. Looking at it from that perspective, he was holding up extraordinarily well.

"Do you even know how to get to Hammersmith from here?"

He glanced around at the dark buildings that lined the narrow street. She could see in his eyes that none of it was familiar long before he shook his head.

"No." He met her eyes. "Please, help me get my brother."

She didn't need this kind of trouble. "You already owe me."

"I'll make it worth your time. I promise."

Could he hold up his side of the deal? She'd be wise to give up on him, go to one of the lurks in Whitechapel and lay low for a bit. Then again, a few boys out that way had tried to show her 'what a girl is good for' once, an encounter that had ended with her well-aimed blade and the timely arrival of another youth who didn't approve of their efforts. She wasn't eager to find out if they were still hanging around the area.

If only Chaff were there to talk her out of doing something foolish. But he wasn't there and the way Ash looked at her now, not like a low street rat, but like someone who held the key to his salvation… It was strange and intoxicating being looked at that way by someone strong, educated, and handsome.

"Maeko." He looked confused, so she elaborated. "My name's Maeko. I'll help you get your brother. After that, you're on your own."

His dashing smile only reinforced the feeling of dread building within her.

Morning fog burned away before a bright sun. It shone down on the homes around the residential district of Hammersmith, bringing in an uncommonly lovely new day and making it harder to hide from patrols. Fortunately, those were lighter the farther they got from the heart of London. Unfortunately, their sprint for freedom had taken them in the opposite direction, making for a long, exhausting walk.

Every house sported a tiny front garden patio in various states of upkeep, each with some sort of fence around it. Some of the brick and wrought iron fences were tall, intended to keep people out, like reverse prisons, while others were too low to serve for more than decoration. The street's rough and rutted surface held pools of water from the recent rain. Enough dirt had transferred onto the pedestrian pavements that they blended with the street itself, making the low curb more of a tripping hazard than a defining separation.

Since the Literati had taken charge of local government operations, some street development and sewer maintenance was cut back in favor of cleaning criminals off the street, which mostly meant the homeless population because they were easier to apprehend than the truly dangerous ones. This effort resulted in the more able-bodied homeless seeking refuge with pirates, increasing the rebel numbers while neglected streets became rutted mires and sickness ran rampant through poor districts. At least this street wasn't the sucking sludge she had to slog through in some of the slums and Macak, who'd grown weary of the satchel, padded along with an almost magical ability to find dry spots in the damp.

Maeko trudged along the mid-morning street in a blur of exhaustion. With her new used clothes, she stood out less and local traffic, which had died down since the early morning rush, paid little attention to them. She returned the favor, distracted by the ache in her feet and the vast emptiness gnawing at her stomach, reminding her that she hadn't eaten since around noon the previous day. The need for sleep pressed ever more insistent, tugging heavy at her eyelids. How long had it been since she'd had a decent sleep?

Her foot caught the edge of a rut and she stumbled. Someone caught her arm. She started, expecting an officer. When she looked up into Ash's pale green eyes, she relaxed, though her pulse would take some time to slow down again.

"You all right?"

He'd been so obliging, following along and mimicking everything she did to get them through more heavily patrolled areas of the city, that she'd almost forgotten about him.

"I'm fine." She glanced at the hand still holding her arm and he flushed, snatching it away. "Thanks."

"Sure." He took a small step out to one side. "You seem to be fading."

She shrugged off his awkward attention. "I haven't had a good kip or much to eat in the last few days."

"I'm sure Mrs. Blackwood will let us stay for a while. We can rest and get some food there."

Rather than express her cynical view on the likelihood of that, she turned to the task of putting one foot in front of the other until they reached a part of the neighborhood where his strides loosened out and the tension in his shoulders began to release.

"Are we getting close?"

He nodded.

"Splendid," she muttered. "You lead. I'll sleepwalk for a bit."

His grin was tentative, as if he thought she might be joking but wouldn't be surprised to find her capable of snatching a brief kip while walking. He accepted the lead at her gesture, but took to casting frequent glances over his shoulder, perhaps to check if she had indeed fallen asleep or, more likely, to make sure she didn't slip away.

He didn't trust her outright. That was something she couldn't help liking about him, in addition to his eyes and his smile. Only a complete fool trusted so fast and she took comfort in knowing she wasn't stuck with one of those. Fools made noise. Fools got you caught in bad situations. Fools trusted without thinking.

He glanced over his shoulder again and caught her staring at him. He grimaced, his brows pinching together. "What now?"

Had she said something aloud, perhaps something about fools? "What do you mean?"

"You were looking at me like you wanted to skin me alive or something equally fun."

"Oh. Was I? I was thinking about someone else," she evaded, her cheeks warming.

"I'm glad to hear that. I might be more comfortable if you walked beside me for now." He regarded her with wary scrutiny, and she almost smiled at that, but she didn't want him reading anything into it.

Don't get him thinking you like him. That would be foolish, true or not. "If it'll move things along."

Rather than make her speed up to join him, he slowed his pace until she started to pass him and then resumed normal speed. Chaff never would have been so polite, but Chaff trusted her to manage herself. She wasn't sure if she should appreciate the consideration or take offense at it.

She grinned. Dear Chaff. He would think she'd gone barmy if he knew what she was up to now, and she would be tempted to agree.

"Why did you change your mind?"

A sparkle of nerves greeted his question. "About what?"

"I got the feeling you meant to ditch me back there in the city. Why'd you change your mind?"

"I wasn't going to ditch you. I just wanted to get clear of the Lits."

"Liar. I suppose it's the money I promised you."

She didn't argue. It wasn't the only reason, but it was the only one he needed to know about. "You work?"

He gave her a curious look.

"Your hands are rough," she explained.

He flushed and rubbed at a callous on one thumb. "It's from helping my dad work on the airships."

"That's right." That explained his rough hands and the upper body strength.

He touched her arm to get her attention and stopped. "There's the house."

The house he pointed at was a charming cream-colored residence on the opposite side of the street with two overflowing flower baskets providing a burst of cheery color on either side of the door. That wasn't what seized her attention, however. A familiar coach drawn by two dirty white horses rattled down the street toward them. Another coach rolled past them heading in the opposite direction, hiding them from the detective's coach long enough to duck out of sight.

"Into the bushes. Quick!"

Ash's gaze tracked to the coach. He blanched, leapt over the low iron fence around the yard next to them, and crouched in the bushes along the front of the house. She followed, Macak on her heels, and tucked herself in next to Ash. He smelled pleasant, like clean wood shavings and home-cooked food, even after all the running they had done. Shifting a little closer to take advantage of the comfort of another warm body, she tucked a somewhat resistant Macak into the satchel and settled in to watch the coach.

It pulled up in front of the cream-colored house. Em stepped out and strode up to the front door with her two henchmen shadowing her. Did the detective feel half as tired as she did? Had she taken time to sleep and eat? It seemed unlikely if she done enough investigating to locate Ash's brother and get there ahead of them.

Em rapped the door, the crack of boney knuckles on the wood carrying across the street. The door opened. Whoever answered remained inside, just out of view. After a few minutes of conversation too quiet for them to hear, the three entered the house. Ash leaned far forward now, poised as if he meant to go after them. She placed a hand on his arm and he sank back a little, but she could feel his muscles tremble under her fingers.

Several tense minutes later, Em and the two men emerged with a young boy hobbling along between them. The stiff swing of his right leg suggested some manner of false appendage hidden under his trousers.

"That's Sam," Ash hissed.

"Get your hands off my son!"

Ash sucked in a quick breath. Tension poured off him, rattling her nerves. The detective and her companions turned to face a familiar man walking down the pavement toward them. Garrett stopped a few houses away, keeping well out of range. Maeko could see him around the back of the coach. Sam started toward him, making it only a couple of halting steps before Em caught his shirt collar and drew him stumbling back.

Ash began to move and Maeko grabbed his arm. Turning a fiery glare on her, he yanked his arm away and she pounced, grabbing hold with both hands this time when he started to leave the cover of the bushes. Stiff foliage scratched at her arms, but she held on, throwing herself back against his superior weight. When he glared at her again, a crazed fury lighting his eyes, she gave him her best pleading look. Chaff insisted that look could melt a glacier. In this case, it at least made Ash hesitate.

"My dad doesn't even know where I am. I have to let him know I'm all right."

"All evidence points at your dad's guilt right now. If all three of you get hauled in, you won't be any help to him at all," she whispered, willing him to see the sense in her words.

He lowered his gaze, a tortured look twisting his face, sorrow and rage creating a storm in his pale eyes. Finally, he gave a sharp nod and crouched beside her. "You're right. Free, we can try to find a way to prove his innocence."

We can what? Panic gripped her. "I didn't mean..." She trailed off when Em's voice rang out.

"Captain Garrett, I presume." The detective's tone was acidic with false civility. "Why don't you join us? We can all go for a little ride downtown together. Your other boy is already there."

"You can't just take my sons."

She patted a pocket on her long coat. "According to this piece of paper in my pocket, I can arrest and detain any and all persons who might have information relating to this investigation."

"They're only kids," Garrett growled.

"No. They're *your* kids," Em countered. "Now let's go."

"I don't think so." Garrett backed up several steps. He glanced over one shoulder then honed in on Sam with a despairing look. He knew he couldn't get to the boy and the knowledge tore at him.

Amos took hold of Sam, moving the boy out of the way, and Em flipped her coat back, reaching for the pistol.

"Go now." Ash hissed under his breath. "Run."

Garrett took a few more steps back.

Ash leaned forward again.

Tension built to a painful pressure in Maeko's chest.

I should let him go. She glanced at Ash. His hands clenched to fists by his sides, the muscles in his jaw tightened and there was a shine of desperation in his eyes.

"Stay here. Be ready to run," Maeko whispered.

She handed him the satchel then pulled a small knife out of a pocket sewn into her shoe and slipped out of the bushes. When she glanced back to make sure he wasn't following, Ash was staring at her as if she were deranged, his mouth open as though he meant to say something but couldn't find the words.

Perhaps I have gone barmy.

Amos, Reuben, and the coachman were watching the developing drama between Em and Garrett. Em had the pistol out now, aimed at Garrett. Maeko slunk across the street toward the carriage, thankful for the lack of traffic. Sam lurched forward, grabbing for Em's arm and Amos pulled him further away.

"Last chance," Em warned.

The click of the pistol cocking was loud, like the tick of a clock when time is running out.

Maeko's skin prickled in anticipation of a gunshot. She scurried over to the front of the coach. The horses shifted restlessly in their traces, reacting to the tension in the air. What would they do if a gun fired? Her gaze dropped to their iron-shod hooves and her throat tightened. She crept up between them. One horse snorted, his nostrils flaring and the whites of his eyes showing. She closed her eyes for a second, breathing in the smells of salty sweat and hay.

Please don't panic.

Somehow, the idea of being crushed to pulp under the muddy hooves of frightened horses ranked right up with being stuck under an ashbin on her list of ways she didn't want to die. The blasted beasts were unpredictable as best she could tell and frightfully strong.

Using the sharp little blade, she hacked at their harnesses, cutting them free of the coach. The leather was old and cracking, easy to cut. Fear of being seen made prickles run up and down her spine. She worked as fast as she dared, a cool sweat breaking out on her scalp and her heart drumming in her ears.

She set the center pole down and glanced up at the coachman as she stepped over it. He still watched the drama. The nearest horse's tail swept out, catching her with a stinging lash across the face. Her toe caught the pole, knocking it toward one horse and the animal bunched, ready to bolt. She held her breath. When they didn't move, she stepped clear and slunk back toward the hiding place. A gunshot blasted out. Her heart jumped and she dove in beside a low brick wall, spinning around to watch.

The horses tensed, their heads jerking up. One rose in a half rear, but they didn't run.

The shot took Garrett in the upper leg and he reeled back with the impact. He spun and started a clumsy, uneven sprint toward the nearest cross street.

"Get him," Em shouted.

Rueben started after Garrett. Sam fought to get away now with desperate ferocity considering his size and handicap. Em turned to help Amos with him, catching one flailing fist before it could club Amos in the nose.

Snarling to herself, Maeko yanked off a shoe and threw it, striking the near horse in the hip. The animal reared again and lunged free of the coach. The other horse followed. In that at least, horses were predictable. If one moved, the other would try to follow. Without the carriage holding them back, they bolted, their shod hooves splashing up sprays of mud as they sprinted down the street.

Reuben spun around at the coachman's cry of alarm forgetting his quarry. Em held fast to Sam's left arm, her head snapping around toward the sound. Her face brightened to an almost luminescent red. Then her gaze tracked to the discarded shoe lying where the horses should have been standing hitched and scanned across the street.

It was time to move.

Maeko leapt up from her hiding place and began to run, lamenting her shoe. Damp grit-coated pavement ground against the foot through her threadbare sock. Ash leapt over the fence when she sprinted past and fell in beside her. She could hear Em yelling for someone to get the horses, to go after them, to hold onto Sam, to go after Garrett. In the end, all the detective could manage was a final hoarse cry of frustration.

Another win for the street rat.

What mattered most now was getting away. It would be nice, however, if Ash with Macak and Garrett also benefited from the loss of her shoe. Sam was a hopeless cause for now. Even his father and brother had to realize that.

She ran through the neighborhood until her foot stung with every step and she was stumbling with fatigue, then she jumped a low wall around the front of a quiet tan house and slumped to the ground there.

Several seconds later, Ash landed beside her, bumping her shoulder with his heel as he came over. She was too tired to complain. Macak, however, vocalized displeasure from within the satchel when Ash tossed it back to her. She let the cat out to quiet him then glanced at her companion.

His face fell, sinking into utter misery, and he slumped back against the cool stone wall, drawing his knees to his chest. He squeezed his eyes shut, running his hands into his hair and clenching them into fists. The muscles in his jaw jumped when he ground his teeth. He didn't say a word or make any sound beyond his labored breathing from the run, but the silence made his pain more potent.

It was strange to watch this intense display of emotion, the same way it was awkward to watch someone cry, but it also sparked fierce jealousy. A hunger really, for the kind of relationship he had with his father and brother. She didn't think anyone felt that strongly about her. Chaff might miss her if she disappeared forever, though she didn't imagine he'd lose that much sleep over it. After all, Chaff advised that you shouldn't get too fond of a mate on the streets because you never knew when they'd get nicked or end up holding up a stone. She tried to follow that advice. It was easy, except when it came to Chaff.

You're a rat. No one cares about rats.

She would never have what Ash had. Her family was forever broken. She couldn't watch that happen to his.

"Did the..." Ash's voice caught and he swallowed hard a few times before trying again. "I couldn't see past the coach. Did she shoot him?"

Maeko took a few deep breaths, as much to slow her breathing as to take control of her emotions before answering. "She hit him in the leg."

He grimaced. "Did he get away?"

Why did he think she had the answers to everything? "I didn't see. I was too busy running."

Ash clenched his teeth, his breath hitching while he
struggled to maintain composure.

She made her tone gentle. "If he did, he probably
won't get far."

Ash stood and climbed out from behind the wall to
stalk back into the street. She followed, scuffing along
behind and trying to ignore the growling of her stomach.
Perhaps that hadn't been the right thing to say. The truth
rarely was.

"Where are they going to take Sam? JAHF?"

She forced a brief jog to catch up, limping on her
sore foot. Macak trotted along with them, looking much
too calm for the situation. "No. That's just where they
take us at night. At this hour, they'll take him straight
to a stray house."

He spun and she staggered back a few steps, startled
by the rage that darkened his features. "A what?"

Macak leapt up onto her shoulders and stared
at Ash. "One of the Literati orphanages. They keep
orphans and street rats there until they decide which
workhouse or reform facility is best for them. They
won't hurt him."

"He'll be terrified. I can't leave him. He's my responsibility. How do we find him?"

This was getting too dangerous, but they did have
a deal and he needed the help. She dug at the dirt with
the toe of her remaining shoe. "I know someone who
could help, but," she gave him the pleading look again,
since it had worked well enough last time, "I can't keep
up this way. If you want my help, you have to let me get
some food and sleep."

His arm swept up so fast that she flinched and
Macak dug in to keep his balance. Tiny pinpricks on her
shoulders.

Ash pointed back the way they had come. "My dad is out there somewhere shot in the leg and my brother is in that tramp's custody and you want to stop for food!"

"Yes, please. And sleep. You want my help or not?"

His eyes narrowed and she felt her temper rising up through the weariness, ready to fight him or desert him if he didn't give. Then he looked down. She followed his gaze and saw that her hands were shaking. She drew them to her chest and clenched them together to still them. His gaze dropped further, to her shoeless foot, and he deflated. He held his hands out in front of him then, staring at his palms as if they might hold the answers.

"All right." He glanced back the way they had come once more, then shook his head and turned away. "We're not far from my house, but that detective tramp and her brutes might go there."

"Not right away. It's too obvious and it'll take them a while to repair the harnesses." She stared at his back and chewed her lip. It was daft to feel guilt for being tired and hungry, but she did. "I'm sorry we were too late."

His back stiffened and he started walking again, trusting that she would follow. With the promise of food and rest hanging over her, it made little sense not to. Wading through a sludge of exhaustion and misery, she trudged along after him, Macak draped around her shoulders like a fuzzy shawl.

"Maybe it wouldn't be that bad."

Ash didn't look back. "What?"

"If Em caught your dad, maybe he could convince her he's not guilty."

Ash shook his head. "No. She's working with the Lits."

"So?"

"Pirate," he said, as if that explained everything.

"Lots of folks are pirates."

"Yeah, but lots of folks don't know the things he knows."

Maeko chewed on that thought. Just how important was his father to the pirate movement? Perhaps it was better not to know. She changed the subject. "Why would someone kill a woman and her daughter like that?"

"Could have been pirates."

Maeko stared hard at his back, wishing she could see his face to figure out if he were serious. "Your parents are pirates."

"Not like them. Some pirates are too extreme. They take things too far."

"But why would they do something like that?"

He glanced over his shoulder now, taking her measure with a gaze. "You really don't keep up on things, do you?"

She ground her teeth to keep from saying something rude. She despised feeling simple. Who had time for other people's problems when staying alive from one day to the next was a full-time job?

When she didn't answer, he explained. "Lucian Folesworth is Literati. He helped fund the Airship Tower and several other Literati projects. Basically, Clockwork Enterprises is supporting the Lits. That's reason enough for some people to want him dead and they wouldn't think twice about taking down anyone who got in their way."

"So bad pirates did it?" How ludicrous did that sound? *There, Mr. Jacard, now you have me using that word.*

"Maybe."

"If not them, then who?"

"I'm working on it." Ash held up a hand and stopped to scan the area. After watching for a few minutes, he started to cross the street, motioning for her to follow. They hurried to the door of a little blue house. The door was unlocked, something that brought another creative string of curses from him. He stormed in and straight to the small kitchen.

"You may not be a street rat, but you can sure swear like one," she observed, scanning the cozy accommodations while he dug around in the cupboards.

Macak hopped down to investigate, wandering about to the soft click and whir of clockwork gears. The furnishings weren't fancy, but the little bit of clutter on a scratched-up table surrounded by a well-worn brown couch and two chairs gave a comfortable feel to the front room that she found pleasant. She wasn't sure what she'd expected from a pirate household, but it wasn't this common, relaxed setting. It was normal. It was a place a family could be happy together. Something she knew nothing about.

"Do you realize you sounded impressed when you said that?" Ash asked, his voice muffled by the cupboard.

"I was." She ignored another noisy growl from her stomach. Under different circumstances, she would have joined his search. Since this actually was his house and not one she'd broken into, it felt inappropriate to rummage around like a thief.

"Dad says I shouldn't do it."

"Why not?"

He started pulling out several items, setting them in a row on the counter, and it took a considerable act of will not to pounce on the food like a ravenous mongrel.

"It isn't polite. Here."

She accepted the food he offered and turned to eating, no longer interested in the ethics of bad language. Macak joined her, accepting offered bites only if she set them beside her and pretended not to notice him taking them. When they finished, Ash led her to one of the back rooms. Two narrow tousled beds tucked against the walls, the floor between them littered with clothing. A room shared by two boys with little regard for cleanliness. She could imagine their mother scolding them over it to no effect.

"You can use Sam's bed if you want."

He gestured toward one of the beds, then stood staring at it for a long moment in angst-filled silence. She stared at it too, but for a different reason.

"I can't sleep there. I'd never wake up."

"Would you rather sleep on the floor?" His tone held cutting sarcasm.

With all seriousness, she asked, "Can I?"

The momentary bitterness faded. He shook his head and shrugged. "Suit yourself. You're welcome to the blankets and pillow if you want."

Afternoon sunlight filtered in through the closed curtains, providing her enough light to make up a quick bed for herself on the floor. Ash stood watching, his hands and feet in constant restless motion.

When she was satisfied, she sat on the floor in the nest of blankets, feeling awkward before his uneasy gaze. "What's wrong?"

"It's strange, having a girl in my room. It's not proper. Dad would be peeved."

"It's not that strange." She'd spent most of her life camped out in various hideouts with boys around. Most of the boys knew she had the protection of Chaff and several others who were happy to keep watch over her to please him and because they respected her skill as a pickpocket. Those who didn't learned fast. Still, she preferred a room to herself when given the option.

"Where do you usually sleep?" He sat cross-legged on his bed. Shadows obscured his features, his pale eyes shining bright in the dim.

She lowered her gaze and began to pick at a loose

thread on one blanket. "Wherever. Lurks, alleys, boxes, the floor of a shop or pub when I can. Who else would go after Mr. Folesworth?"

Ash was silent for a time and she thought he might try to steer the conversation back to her, but his gaze moved to his brother's empty bed. "Someone who stood to gain from his death I suppose. His company is worth a fortune."

"Well, it wasn't his wife or daughter."

Ash nodded and gave her a critical look. "How old are you?"

"I was almost seven when I hooked up with Chaff." At his puzzled look, she added, "My mentor."

He looked more confused.

"Chaff's a nickname," she explained. When he nodded, she went on. "That was close to ten years ago. 16 maybe."

"Maybe? Don't you celebrate your birthday?"

"Street rat," she pointed to herself. "When you don't know where your next meal is coming from, birthdays lose importance. Chaff and I do pick a day each summer when we have a little extra coin to get a special treat. We call it our still kickin' and pickin' day." She grinned, remembering the sticky sweets they'd shared last year before trying to wipe the sticky off their fingers into each other's faces in what turned into a grand wrestling match. Chaff won, but she'd given him a good fight.

"You spend a lot of time with this Chaff bloke."

"He's a kidsman now. I work for him, though it rarely feels that way. He's not that demanding. Well, not of me." Why was that? Was it just because she was a girl or was there more to the special consideration? She began to pick at a tear in her new trousers until Macak came and kneaded the blankets to get her attention.

"How'd you end up on the streets?"

The few feet between them became miles. Maeko pulled a blanket tight around her shoulders and focused on petting Macak. That wasn't a story she told to people. Chaff knew. No one else did. There was no way she was going to tell Ash. She barely knew him. "The usual way. I don't know who my dad is. Mum worked at a brothel. Something happened to her."

Men charge into their rooms in the brothel, their feet pounding on the floorboards like thunder. Her mother snaps at her, ordering her to hide under the bed and stay there no matter what happens. She does so, shoving her fingers into her ears to drown out her mother's cries and shaking so hard she is sure they will hear her body rattling the floorboards. It seems an eternity before they finally leave. She calls for her mother. The only answer is a choked sobbing. She crawls out and finds her mother curled on the floor, her dress torn, her hands pressed over her face. Blood runs between her fingers, so much blood.

Maeko shuddered and looked up at Ash struggling to escape the crushing power of memories she tried to keep locked away.

"What happened?" His voice was a whisper, the natural lure of morbid curiosity taking hold.

She learned that you never turn down a crime boss.

No one came to help that day, not until the men were good and gone. She hated them for it—all the women at the brothel who helped raise her. She hated her mother too, for making the man angry, for staying in that place and forcing her to live there. She didn't understand then. She only partly understood now, but she didn't hate her anymore.

She stared at the floor where a pair of boy's trousers lay heaped in a pile with two shirts and a lone sock that sported a hole in the toe. He slid the pile self-consciously under the bed with one foot.

"It's all right if you don't want to talk about it."

She nodded. She couldn't bring herself to meet his eyes now and risk seeing judgment there. The illegitimate child of a toffer turned to the streets. It wouldn't surprise her if he threw her out in disgust. Only he still needed her to find his brother, so he would tolerate her presence for now.

What to say? "Do your folks take you places in the airship?"

"Sure. Sometimes. The band pooled their money to buy it so they could play in other towns. I get to help Dad keep it running. It's a lot of fun when we get to ride along. The city looks different from up there. Better somehow."

"Sounds wonderful." Macak curled up next to her, his soft purr soothing. "You know a lot of stuff, Ash. You may not have street smarts, but you're smart in other ways."

"Thanks," he pretended intense interest in a protruding thread on his bedcover.

Maeko gave herself a mental pat on the back for making
him uncomfortable.

Ash cleared his throat. "You know, with your street smarts and my other smarts, I bet we could find Mr. Folesworth and prove my dad innocent."

"You think so." She let plenty of skepticism into her voice.

He ignored it, his grin bringing enthusiastic energy into the room. "I do, and I bet there'd be one bloody splendid reward if we pulled it off. We could start back where you found Macak."

Good plan. She knew he was trying to manipulate her into offering further help. He might also be right, but that didn't make it a good idea. Besides, they would never be partners the way she and Chaff were. They came from different worlds. She was out of place here.

"Maybe." Turning her back on his hopeful smile, she curled on the floor and tugged a blanket up over her ear. Macak hopped over, settled in against her chest, and licked her face. Annoying, and yet somehow comforting.

"You sleep," Ash muttered. "I'll keep an eye out. I couldn't sleep right now."

She made a sound of assent and squeezed her eyes shut against the ache of aloneness in her chest.

She woke sometime later to a soft paw batting at her nose. When she opened her eyes, Macak's face filled her vision, his nose almost touching hers. She started to speak and he put his paw on her lips. Elsewhere in the house, she heard a door creak open.

So smart.

She scratched the cat behind the ears and sat up, getting her bearings. Judging from the darkness that filled the room, she had slept away the remains of the day and a good portion of the evening. For the first time in days, she felt well rested. A quick glance at the sleeping figure on the bed confirmed that Ash wasn't the one who'd made the door creak. She froze. If it wasn't him...

There was someone else in the house.

She threw the blanket off and got up, creeping out of the bedroom. Someone rummaged around in drawers in the kitchen, then proceeded out into the hall with an eerie shuffling walk. Just when she decided it might be better to hide, the intruder struck a lucifer. In the brief flare of light, she and Garrett stared at each other. He looked confused, his eyes glossed over with exhaustion and pain.

"What the hell are you doing in my house?" His voice came out slow and thick, as if speaking took considerable effort.

"Did you send the Lits for me after you nicked Macak?"

It took him a moment to gather his thoughts and the match guttered out. He struck another and used it to light the candle he carried, holding it up near enough to her face that she could feel its warmth. She took a step back.

"No. And I didn't *nick* the cat. It was never yours." He sagged against the wall and exhaled. "I only wanted to help my son."

She nodded, hoping she wasn't accepting his explanation too easily. "What about the woman and the little girl. Did you kill them?"

"How do you even know about that?"

She waited for his answer, ready to abandon him to his suffering if he gave the wrong one. After all, she'd already stuck around longer than intended.

He grimaced, his eyes squeezing shut, and shook his head then pressed his free hand to the wall as if the motion had unbalanced him. "No. We didn't kill anyone. We went there hoping to talk to the cat's owner about the clockwork leg." He opened his eyes, starting almost as bad as she did when Macak landed on her shoulders. His eyes narrowed at the cat and it took him a minute to continue. "They were dead when we got there."

Knots of anxiety freed up in her gut. "I thought so." More questions popped to mind, however, refreshing the tension burning through her nerves. "But why did you go inside? How did you get in?"

"The door was cracked. Jack thought we should poke around, see if we could find out more about the leg. He has a bit of a nefarious past, something I'm sure you can relate to."

She assumed Jack was another of the band members and while she wasn't sure she knew what nefarious meant, she didn't think it was complementary. "You're a pirate. Why should I believe you?"

"Is Ash here?" He took a step toward her and staggered, bracing himself against the wall again. A dark stain had spread across his trousers where Em shot him, glistening wet in the candlelight.

"I'm here, Dad."

Relief washed away some of the lines of strain in Garrett's face when Ash emerged from the darkness. He slipped an arm around his father's waist, giving him his shoulders for support. They made a slow trek over to the brown couch and Garrett groaned when Ash lowered him down. Then he stood and stared at his father, his face drawn with worry.

Garrett's gaze moved from Maeko to his son. "I thought you were arrested. How'd you end up here with her?"

"That bloody detective tramp," Ash growled and Garrett gave him a stern look that he ignored. "She threw Maeko and me in JAHF. Maeko was cracking brilliant, though. She helped me get out of there." Ash glanced at her with a look full of gratitude and admiration.

Praise wasn't what she expected after telling him where she came from. She shifted, uncomfortable, and turned her attention to his father to avoid his eyes. At least Ash made the effort to say her name right.

"You should have stayed on the airship."

Ash hung his head, chastised.

Garrett sighed. "No matter now. We have other problems. That woman has your brother."

Ash's expression soured and he swallowed hard, his teeth grinding together.

Maeko took a step closer. "We know. We went after him and got there when Em was taking him away. I'm the one who unhitched the horses."

Garrett's head snapped up. "You should have stayed out of it. You could have been hurt."

What do you care? "If you'd have run when you should've I wouldn't have had to do it."

Garrett scowled, not conceding, but wise enough not to waste energy arguing with her. "Em, she's the detective?"

Maeko nodded.

"And she thinks we killed those people?"

She nodded again.

"We need to get out of here." He started to stand and fell back, clutching at the injured leg.

"You need a doctor." Ash gripped his father's shoulder, his face now almost as pale as Garrett's.

"No. I can't take that chance. The detective knows I'm injured. She might have Lits watching the hospitals. I need to get to Chelsea. There's a woman there, a pirate supporter. She treats us when we can't risk taking someone to the hospitals. She can help."

The room lurched and Maeko had to swallow against the sudden urge to heave up her last meal. She knew that woman too well. She'd been spying on her mother for years. She provided illegal medical services to the pirates and ran a laundry as a cover, all to pay off her debt to the mysterious man who had paid her medical bills after the attack in the brothel.

I can't do this. I should take the tin he owes me and leave. Maeko cleared her throat and two sets of expectant eyes turned to her. Macak purred in her ear. I really am cracked. "We better get moving then. Got any shoes I can borrow?"

Garrett sent Maeko to sort through his wife's shoes to replace the one she'd thrown at the horse. She selected out a pair and stuffed a sock in each toe to make them snug then stashed her lock picks in the satchel. When she returned to the living room, Garrett was drinking something that smelled of strong liquor. After several long swallows, he nodded, implying readiness to move on. He didn't look ready, but the longer they stayed, the more likely they'd get unwanted company. She peeked out into the street to look for any sign of the Lits or the detective. Satisfied that they had nothing to fear, she nodded back to them and Ash helped his father up, providing support while they headed out into the street. She ached to get back to the inner city where it was easier to become lost in a pinch, but Garrett's injury forced a slow pace and a different destination.

A destination she wasn't ready to go to, but she didn't have to go inside. She would make sure they made it to the house and would stay outside so her mother couldn't see her.

She glanced at the cat trotting beside her, then over her shoulder at Ash. "You're a lousy lookout. If not for Macak, we wouldn't have known someone was in the house."

"Sorry," he muttered, grunting when Garrett stumbled into him.

It made her queasy to watch the injured man stagger along, so she faced front again.

"I'm not used to having to be on watch in my own house" Ash said. "Besides, you looked so good sleeping there…"

He trailed off and she shot another look over her shoulder at him. He was staring at her back, wide-eyed like a cornered cat. His face flushed.

"Comfortable, I mean. You looked comfortable," he amended.

"You looked rather *comfortable* yourself, keeping watch so vigilantly." She winked before turning away again. At least she'd distracted them both from the reality of Garret's circumstances for a few moments. She didn't know much about gunshot wounds, but she'd seen enough knife wounds on the streets to know it wasn't good and the longer it went untreated, the higher the risk that he would die of blood loss or some other complication. They needed to keep him functioning a little longer.

"Captain Garrett, who, other than pirates, would gain the most from Mr. Folesworth's death?"

"If they weren't dead, I'd say his wife and child." Garrett paused, breathing hard. "His business partner or his brother would come next, but…" Another long pause. "…Clockwork Enterprises was in negotiation for weapons development with Literati law enforcement."

There came a scuffing of feet and a groan behind her. She turned in time to see Ash topple to his knees as he tried to catch his father, whose injured leg had given out. Jumping in, she caught Garrett's shoulder and helped him get his balance on one knee before they all ended up face down in the street. Ash stood, wincing when he brushed dirt off the knees of his trousers. Maeko waited, chewing at her lip while she supported Garret who knelt there, head hanging, his breath coming in hard gasps like the sharp exhales of a steamcycle. When they went to help him to his feet, he staggered again, his face ghastly pale. Fresh blood seeped out, glistening wet on his trouser leg.

As soon as Ash had him up and leaning on his shoulders again, she scanned the area.

"He can't walk much more," she muttered to herself. Turning to Garret, she said, "If you can make it a little farther, we can find a hansom to take us the rest of the way. Do you have enough for fare?"

Garrett nodded, swaying on his feet so that Ash had to slip an arm around his waist to keep him upright. His breathing was heavy and strained. She hoped that was from pain and not the loss of too much blood. Either way, they needed to get him help fast.

She forced a positive tone. "Splendid! Why don't you give it to Ash now so we don't have to mess with it later?"

Garrett mumbled something and Ash dug into his father's right pocket, pulling out a small wad of cash. To her surprise, he held it out to her. After a few seconds hesitation that Ash didn't seem to notice, she accepted it, taking a few seconds to count it before stuffing it in a pocket.

"That should do. Try to hide the injury from the driver. We don't need questions."

Ash nodded and waved her on. His brow furrowed with worry and his eyes shimmered in the reaching light from a gas-lamp across the street with a deep desolation she couldn't pretend to fathom. He'd become a fugitive, had watched his brother be taken into custody and his father shot, and was now rushing to get help from the pirate underground, all in less than a day. His family might not be rich, but she got the feeling Ash led a comfortable life before this. He was getting a rough indoctrination into true adversity.

Chumming with pirates would get them there eventually. The thought didn't offer much comfort.

She marched on, keeping her pace slow and doing her best to ignore the nagging urge to run away from the whole mess. "Better weapons would give the Lits an advantage. That would make him even more unpopular with pirates," she speculated, resuming the earlier conversation. It was a good time to ask him about the situation. The conversation kept him functioning and he was compromised enough to divulge things he might not share in a more lucid state.

"Except it fell through." Garrett said, each word dragged out between labored breaths. "His partner initiated the deal, but Folesworth ultimately decided he didn't want his

company used for weapon manufacture."

That information changed some things.

"That would make him a target for the Literati," Ash suggested.

"Or a thwarted business partner," Maeko added.

The landing area door had been ajar, suggesting a careless or hasty departure, but exiting that way would require an airship. Not many pirates, Ash's family being an exception, had access to an airship. The small, sleek airships that had become popular with the wealthy were more common, which pointed to someone of privilege. It was a key bit of information the detective didn't have. If only she were willing to talk to them without dropping them in JAHF or an orphanage.

She glanced over her shoulder. Garrett leaned on Ash, his head hanging low, his limping gate deteriorated to a dragging shuffle. Ash met her eyes, pleading, begging with a look for her to do something.

They had reached a busier street. She tucked Macak into the satchel, then hurried out ahead to flag down a hansom, telling the driver they needed to get her friend's besotted father home. Ash struggled to get Garrett up into the seat and keep his injury hidden from the driver. The man shook his head in disgust and waited while she hurried to help. The off-hour fare would use up all of their money, but they couldn't keep walking.

They sat silent for the start of the ride, Ash keeping diligent tabs on his father's condition and holding pressure on the wound now that they were in a position to do so. While he was preoccupied with that, she chewed at her ragged fingernails.

Things had gotten too complicated. As a pickpocket and thief, she had an honorary, if anonymous, place on the list of Literati's least favorite people. Breaking out of JAHF twice and getting involved with pirates wasn't going to improve that. The pirate movement didn't notice her kind any more than anyone else did. All they cared about was an end to the stranglehold the wealthy Literati had on London society that served to widen the gap between the upper classes and everyone below them. For anyone surviving on the sidelines of the criminal underworld, life would be hard regardless of who ran things.

She should have left Ash at JAHF. No matter how handsome he was or what he could offer in return. Now she was heading to the home of a mother who had wanted to get rid of her. She'd hoped to avoid this encounter until she could pay her mother's debt and prove her worth. What kind of welcome would she get showing up now with a heap of trouble instead?

Ash put a hand on her arm, pushing it away from her mouth with surprising force. "You're going to have to start gnawing on your fingers soon. What's wrong?"

"Nothing." She spit a shred of nail out the side of

the hansom then flushed at how crude she must appear
to him. Then again, what did it matter? She would be
invisible to him if circumstance hadn't forced them
together.

"It's the pirate thing, isn't it?"

She gave him a sideways glance. "Why do you say
that?"

"Because the closer we get to Chelsea, the more you
look like you're going to heave."

She resumed chewing at her nails and stared at the
working haunches of the dappled gray horse pulling
them along.

"I'd think you'd prefer them to the Lits."

She tore off a piece of another fingernail and spit
it out to the side, determined not to let his presence
influence her behavior. Her skin still prickled with the
knowledge that he was watching. With a heavy exhale,
she looked at Garrett. Red was spreading through the
dirty white linen pressed to his wound. Walking had
worsened the bleeding.

Schooling her expression to hide anxiety, she answered Ash. "I'd prefer neither. I've always been an
anonymous nuisance to the Lits. They know my face
now. This mess has made me popular with all the wrong
blokes. I'm not chuffed about diving in deeper."

It was the bleeding cat. If only she hadn't come upon
Macak, hadn't picked him up and taken him with her.
The cat licking her hand in the alley, as he was doing
now, his head poked out of the top of the satchel, had
started the whole bollocks. Still...he was only a cat. It
wasn't fair to judge him for that.

"You could always leave."

She scowled at Ash, catching the slight movement of
his jaw as he chewed at the inside of his lip. "Is that what
you want? You want me to leave you to your fate, let you
and your father figure this out? Let you try to find Sam

on your own? I'm happy to accommodate. Just give me what you owe me."

He narrowed his eyes, his hands half closing into fists. "Could you do that? Just abandon us and not look back?"

"Yes." The sting of guilt when he turned away made a lie of her words, but she would let him believe it. Nothing good would come of liking him. Maybe, if she treated him bad enough, he would get tired of her attitude and tell her to go. No matter how she fancied him, he wasn't her kind. When this was over, he would realize that or someone would point it out to him fast enough.

She went back to chewing her nails and watched the gears in the meter spin, like looking down from above on dancers in belled gowns. The Clockwork Enterprises brand gleamed in bright brass below the ticking numbers, a brand she saw on everything from the cycling liquor dispensers in some pubs to the engine compartments on luxury steamcoaches. All part of a world far removed from hers. A world enmeshed in political schemes and conspiracies she knew nothing about. She was a fool to think she could solve this bollocks.

"I wasn't joking. You won't have any fingernails left if you keep that up."

A quick glower sent Ash back to tending his father. She turned to petting Macak with one hand and fidgeting with the small tear in her trousers with the other. By the time they arrived at the house, the tear had expanded by at least an inch and she had begun to wonder if she might not vomit after all. A glance at Garrett once they were out of the hansom—his face pale as death now and dark shadows under his eyes—compelled her to the door. She raised a shaking hand to knock and held it there, hovering inches away from the flaking white paint.

They were here now. She should leave and let them deal with the rest.

Ash put a hand on her shoulder and gave it a squeeze, offering encouragement despite her cold words on the way there. A warm flush of shame rose into her cheeks. She knocked.

"We ain't open." The voice was female with a heavy cockney accent. "Yer launderin' can wait 'til daylight."

She lifted her hand to knock again. The door jerked open. A buxom woman with thick gold hair stood in the doorway. She scanned the trio, her eyes widening when they went to Garrett's leg.

"I think ye have the wrong place. The docs over five blocks east."

"The flags at half-mast," Garrett rasped.

The woman pursed her lips and stared hard at him then shook her head. "Daft fools, comin' to the front door in a 'ansom." She snarled something crude sounding under her breath. "I should send ye packin'."

"Please," Maeko stuck a foot in the door to stop her shutting it. "Is Tomoe-san here?"

The woman looked hard at Maeko. Her eyes widened. "Oh my." She caught Maeko's arm and pulled her in as she turned toward the interior of the house. "Tomie, I think ye better have a peep at this 'un!"

Maeko stumbled through the door, Ash and his father crowding her further in when the woman urged them through and shut the door behind.

No. It wasn't supposed to happen like this.

Simple wood furniture, piled high with clothing draped over or stacked upon every available surface, filled the cramped interior of the house. Shuttered front windows and a single flickering gas lamp made it darker than it needed to be inside. Fading aromas of a recent meal made Maeko's stomach growl when she entered. Another woman stood in the shadows, outside the ring of light from the lamp. There was a twisting in Maeko's chest and she strained her eyes to see into the dark while Ash helped his father inside and the painted woman shut the door behind them.

"Do I know you?" The woman spoke with the meticulous pronunciation of a foreigner, and her voice made Maeko's skin go cold. She took a step into the light and stared at Maeko, then one hand went to her lips, tears springing to her eyes. "Maeko," she breathed.

Everyone behind Maeko disappeared from her awareness. Her throat clenched. She stared at the woman with her long black hair wrapped up in an elegant bun, the beauty she had once been still visible despite numerous puckered scars that crisscrossed her pale face. This woman hadn't wanted her, had intended to send her to an orphanage after the attack that ended their life in the brothel. The rejection still hurt. Anger welled in Maeko like a rising storm, leaving her at a loss for words.

Her mother, Tomoe, took several hesitant steps closer, staring at her with wide-eyed wonder. A few tears crept unimpeded down her cheeks. "Maeko, is it really you?"

She reached toward Maeko's face and Maeko jerked back, bumping into the table behind her. A pile of clothes toppled, hitting the floor with a soft thud.

"Don't," Maeko warned, terrified of the contact that would make the encounter undeniably real. She wasn't ready.

Tomoe drew her hand back. Her lower lip trembled and more tears spilled forth. She swallowed several times.

Maeko spun, intending to flee, but too many people blocked the exit. She met Ash's eyes, full of confusion. Her gaze darted away, going to the blood-soaked leg of

Garrett's trousers, the soft rasp of his shallow breaths becoming too loud in her ears.

This was a mistake.

She forced herself to turn again, staring hard at a table to her mother's left while she spoke. "That man needs your help."

A crash made them both start. Behind her, the blond woman was helping Ash support his father back to his feet next to an overturned table. Tomoe rushed to them, skirting wide around Maeko so as not to come in contact with her estranged offspring. The obvious avoidance brought the sting of tears to Maeko's eyes. She shrank from the pain, detaching from it, and stared at the group by the door as if watching strangers through a window.

Ash flinched when he noticed her mother's scars but promptly turned his attention back to his father. Maeko stepped out of the way so Tomoe could guide them to a camp bed tucked against the wall in the back of the room. They sat Garrett down and Tomoe ordered him to lay back in a tone that would brook no argument. The blond woman lit two lanterns around the bed. Ash came to stand beside Maeko where he too would be out of the way. They watched in uncomfortable silence while her mother took a pair of fabric shears to Garrett's trousers, cutting away blood-soaked material around the wound so she could inspect the damage. She worked with confidence born of much practice.

Now Ash looked like the one about to heave, his face turning as pale as fresh snow. She took his hand and squeezed it, as much to steady herself as to comfort him. He glanced at her, flashing a tremulous smile, then looked from her to Tomoe and back, his smile fading.

"She's your mum?" he asked in a puzzled whisper.

Maeko gave a sharp nod, almost yanking her hand away, but he didn't deserve her anger. The whole situation felt surreal. Any moment now, she would wake in a lurk somewhere amidst relative strangers she had never cared enough about to love or hate.

"I thought she was dead. Why didn't you tell me?"

"You assumed that. Besides, I wasn't sure I was going to come in with you." *I shouldn't have come.*

"I'm glad you did." Still holding her hand, he turned his attention back to his father.

Tomoe turned to the blond woman. "Lottie-san. Fetch Doctor Barker. Tell him I need him in a professional capacity."

"I'm on my way." The other woman shifted a pile of clothing to pull a shawl out.

"Now!" Tomoe snapped her fingers.

Lottie jumped into action, wrapping the shawl around her bare shoulders while she rushed out the door.

"You." Tomoe pointed to Ash. "Bring that lamp over."

Ash took his hand away to do as bid and Maeko met her mother's eyes, seeing the pain of deep sorrow etched in her scarred features.

How dare she look hurt when she had been the one planning to abandon Maeko to an orphanage?

Sucking back anger, Maeko stormed out the back door to a tiny terrace. Cool night air struck her, lonely and desolate darkness greeting her with indifference. She fell back against the house, sinking down alongside an empty washtub and let Macak out. The cat climbed onto her lap, placed a paw on either side of her neck, one warm and alive, the other chilly brass, and pressed his head against her neck. Maeko wrapped her arms around him and the tears broke free. She placed one hand over her mouth to muffle her sobs. A thousand bands of iron twisted in her chest, constricting. Blades of pain cut at her throat and tears burned in her eyes like hot brands, forcing their way free.

How could it hurt so much after all this time? She always told herself that if she ran into her mother before she was ready, she would pretend not to recognize her and walk away. Had she been a fool to believe herself that strong?

Muffled voices crept out through poorly sealed door seams. Another voice joined them after a time, a gruff male voice. The doctor.

Tears gave way to hollow misery. Maeko stared into the gloomy night, watching stars through breaks in the cloud cover making unhurried progress across the sky. Macak curled in her lap, his warm body contrasting the cold that bit at her fingers and toes and numbed her cheeks.

After a long while, the door creaked open and Tomoe came out, pausing to light the lantern hanging by the door. Maeko hung her head, letting long hair fall forward to hide her face from the light. Tomoe stood for several minutes, staring at Macak with his unusual leg, then she sat beside them. Maeko shifted a few inches away, pressing against the washtub. Tomoe clenched her pale hands in her lap. The few inches between them might as well have been miles.

"Samishi katta desu."

Maeko's throat tightened and she clenched her teeth against the threat of more tears. *I missed you too, but that doesn't make it all better.* She clung to silence, bearing the pain of rejection up like a shield between them.

Tomoe drew her legs in and wrapped her arms around them. "You are nearly as tall as me now," she murmured.

Maeko stared at her own hands, at the pathetic remains of her ragged nails. How tiny she felt. She ground her teeth. This wasn't going to work. She wanted no apologies, no explanations. She couldn't forgive. Not yet. "Don't worry, I'm leaving."

She moved Macak off her lap and started to get up, but her mother shot a hand out, pausing shy of touching her arm.

"Please. Do not go yet."

Maeko hesitated. She would have to walk around Tomoe to leave. If her mother wanted her to stay, how hard would she try to keep her there?

Macak pressed his head into Tomoe's outstretched hand and purred, then gazed up at Maeko. She stared at him and he gave a slow blink, patient, content, trusting. She sank back down.

Tomoe drew in a trembling breath and scratched Macak's head. "All these years I thought you were dead, Mae. It is hard to see you now, so long after I had come to terms with that. Harder still to see you involved in affairs that could get you killed." Maeko started to speak, intending to point out that she was less involved than Tomoe herself, but her mother shook her head, touching a finger to her lips to silence her. Maeko pressed her lips together and remained silent. Tomoe continued, her English still so carefully enunciated despite all her years in London. "But I am glad I did not have to put you in an orphanage. I am glad you are alive. I only wish I had known before now."

"You didn't want me." Maeko almost choked on the words, surprised by how much they hurt. Macak curled between them, his warm body connecting them.

Tomoe lifted one trembling hand to touch a scar on the side of her chin, a white puckered line that tugged down on her lip. "Do you know why I refused him my services?" Her voice shook and she swiped at the tears now running down her cheeks. More followed.

Maeko didn't have to ask whom she meant. She stared into the dark, afraid to do so much as breathe for fear that it would bring more tears.

"I attracted enough business to the brothel that

Byron allowed me to turn clients down if I had good reason. When that crime boss came to seek my services, you were already blossoming into such a beautiful little girl. I didn't want him and his kind around you. I told him no. I told him he must find another woman to satisfy his desires. I even recommended someone. He left without a word and I thought it done. The next day, he sent his boys back to show me why no one ever refused him. Afterward..."

She closed her eyes and swallowed, fighting down the same memories Maeko struggled to keep at bay. Screams from the past filled Maeko's head, screams she couldn't drown out any better now than she had been able to as a child hiding under her mother's bed with her eyes squeezed shut, small hands pressed over her ears. Her breathing sped up with remembered horror.

Tomoe opened her eyes again. "I was terrified they would come back before I could get away from there. I did not know if I could trust the man who paid for my surgery. I thought sending you to an orphanage was the only way I could keep you away from them. Then you disappeared. I thought I waited too long. I thought they had taken you and I knew in my heart that you were lost to me. When I thought of what they might do to you, I could only pray you were dead." Her voice cracked on the last word and she buried her face in her hands, her shoulders shaking with soft sobs.

Maeko stared at a rusty dent in the washtub. What was she supposed to say? Was there a point in telling Tomoe that she'd been trying to earn money to pay off her debt so she could be free of this? Did she want to be free?

She moved a hand to stroke Macak. Tomoe had done the same and their hands touched. They both retreated, closing in on themselves, leaving Macak to gaze on in forlorn puzzlement.

After so many years, it wasn't easy to hear that her mother hadn't wanted to send her away, that she might have been wrong to run away and resent her as she had for so long. It also raised many difficult questions. Might her life have been better if she had come back sooner? Might she be the one with a roof over her head helping Tomoe instead of Lottie? Would that be better than where she was now?

The last was an interesting question. She might not have blood family around her, but she did have the strange and honorable camaraderie of the streets. A whole circle of thieves and other petty criminals who, although they might not call one another friend, would always watch each other's back. Chaff helped her find that and, in some ways, she had more in him alone than her mother had here, forced into service playing doctor to a band of rebels and hiding behind the façade of a laundress.

She let her head fall back against the house and closed her eyes. In a way, she missed being invisible to the world. When no one cared about you, you could pretend not to care about anyone. It was easier, sometimes miserable and lonely, but easier.

After a time, Tomoe sat up again, wiping her cheeks dry with her hands. "Where do you live?"

"On the streets with all the other castaways," Maeko snapped.

Guilt made a sick hollow in her chest when Tomoe flinched and looked as if she might cry again. Maeko couldn't bear the tears. *Perhaps we should talk about something else.* "How's Captain Garrett?"

"Barker-sensei treats him." Tomoe paused to sniffle, staring at her worn shoes. "The bullet is near the back of the leg. He put him out with chloroform and is removing it now. When he is done, I will tend him." The words were spoken matter of fact. She wouldn't do it because she felt like she had to or even because she wanted to, but because it was what she did.

"Do you want to be a pirate?"

Tomoe started to shake her head then settled for a small shrug. "I use the skills I have to help those who need them."

No mention of the debt that forced that role upon her. It hung unspoken between them. Tomoe choosing to hide it and Maeko unwilling to admit that she knew. "Will he be okay?"

"I believe so. He is strong and healthy." Tomoe started to stroke Macak who had settled into his place between them, purring. "This Asher, this is his son?"

"Yes." Maeko turned away a little and started to pick at the tear in her trousers again.

"I can fix that."

She stopped picking.

"He is handsome."

Maeko shrugged, an irritating flush rising in her cheeks. "I don't need you trying to be my mate."

Her mother reached out and ran her fingers through Maeko's hair. "I never stopped loving you, Mae."

She jerked her head away. "You don't know me."

Tomoe's hand sank back to Macak. Her lips pressed together in a tight line for a moment as they stared at each other. "No. It is clear that I do not."

The door opened and Ash leaned out.

She ignored him. "Do you have scissors I can use? I need to cut my hair."

Ash gave her a dubious look. "If you're trying to pass as a bloke, it won't work."

They both looked up at him and Maeko set her jaw, defiant. "Why not?"

"You're too pretty."

Heat burned in her cheeks. She stared at him, appalled that he would say such a thing so openly. Then again, she wasn't a child anymore. It was disconcerting how that reality got confused in her mother's presence.

Tomoe stood to go inside. Maeko also stood, half-hiding behind her mother to conceal the flush in her face.

Ash winked at her, his mood improved now that his father was out of immediate danger, and turned his attention to Tomoe. "Doctor Barker's finished. He said it went well."

"Good." Tomoe put a hand on Ash's shoulder and turned him into the house, following him with Maeko slinking along behind like a shy toddler.

Macak trotted in with them, tail and head high as if he had always belonged.

Lottie screeched when they entered and lashed out at the cat with her shawl. "Eek! Filthy beast! Out with ye!"

Not one to be discouraged, Macak ducked around Maeko. He bounded to a table then to her shoulders, crouching close to her neck and giving Lottie an offended look that matched the one Maeko was giving her.

Tomoe glanced over her shoulder at them. The tiniest hint of a smile touched her lips. "Let it be, Lottie-san. It is a guest."

Before Maeko could battle down years of resentment enough to express gratitude, Tomoe disengaged and went to see the doctor to the door. They stood there for a while discussing Garrett's continued care. Lottie adjusted a blanket over Garrett who slept, probably still under the influence of the chloroform. Maeko could smell the faint sweet, chemical aroma lingering in the room, reminding her of the day her mother received her scars. That doctor had worked for a long time, each stitch digging Tomoe deeper into debt.

The door clicked shut behind the doctor and her mother came back to them after a few minutes holding the scissors. She eyed Maeko. "Do you want me to cut it for you?"

Maeko shook her head. "I do it all the time." Though it did turn out better when Chaff helped, she didn't think she could bear her mother doing it. "I don't need help, but a mirror would make it easier."

Tomoe showed her to a tiny bedroom with a vanity tucked in the narrow space along one wall. The mirror had black cloth draped over it. Maeko moved the fabric and sat in the crooked little chair. She winced when the first heavy batch of severed black locks dropped to the floor then struggled to get a good angle for the next cut. She caught Ash's eyes in the mirror. He held a hand out.

She handed him the scissors, trying not to see the hurt in Tomoe's eyes when she did so. Her face grew warm and her pulse quickened when his fingers touched her hair, careful not to pull. He was gentle and precise and, if she wasn't mistaking, there was a slight flush in his cheeks.

Macak sat on the vanity and watched with bright-eyed interest, taking an occasional swipe at the hand wielding the scissors as if objecting to her decision.

Tomoe stood in the edge of doorway, still as a statue. "Where do you go now?"

What right did she have to ask? Maeko chewed her lip before answering to be sure she had her quick temper under control. "We're going to get Ash's brother out of the orphanage." *Anything to get away from here.*

Her mother wrung her hands and Maeko could already hear the many arguments she was certain to make against the idea. They were arguments she'd heard enough as a child that she had them memorized even now. It's too dangerous. You're too small. Let the adults handle it. Let the men handle it.

Tomoe said none of those things. She nodded to herself and said, "Be careful."

Maeko stared at the mirror, confused by her response to Ash cutting her hair and absurdly disappointed at her mother's lack of argument. So much pent up emotion wanted for an outlet.

Ash broke the silence, distracting them all by recounting the events that brought them to this point. He glorified Maeko's role in the escape from JAHF so much she blushed. Her mother laughed tentatively, almost as though afraid to find the story entertaining. It occurred to Maeko then that cutting her hair might have been a bad idea with him around. It was now too short to hide her blush behind.

Once he was done cutting, Ash gave her a scrutinizing look and shrugged.

She bristled. "What does that mean?"

"Means it's different."

She stuck her tongue out at him and popped up from the chair. Her head felt light without the heavy length weighing it down. What a shame it would be if it just up and floated away, leaving her body stumbling about, running into everything.

Swallowing a giggle, she met Ash's eyes. "We'd better get going."

"It is not sunup yet," Tomoe protested, a hint of desperation in her voice. "Sleep here and I will mend those trousers."

Maeko almost objected, she didn't want to stay, but Ash looked tired and she was weary despite the rest she'd gotten at his house. She nodded. Tomoe gave her a blanket to wrap around herself and ushered Ash from the room. Maeko came out in her blanket wrap to find Ash already asleep on the floor near his father. Tomoe took the torn trousers and gestured to a small couch. Maeko curled up on it, Macak making himself at home on her chest after much kneading and licking. His little body made a better heater than hot coals.

She dozed some, but mostly she watched Ash and Garret, and her mother. She pretended sleep when

Tomoe brought the trousers over, setting them on one arm of the settee and giving Macak a quick scratch on the head. Pretend sleep led to true sleep. When she opened her eyes again, late morning light filtered in through the shutters, illuminating swirling dust motes. She ousted Macak from a bath. He huffed at her for the interruption. She grinned and scratched his head, then yanked on her trousers and prodded Ash awake with the toe of one shoe.

He struggled to his feet and stood rubbing his eyes.

Maeko's stomach grumbled. She ignored it, unwilling to ask any more of her mother than she had to. She frowned at the still form of the injured pirate musician under the blankets on the cot, then turned to Tomoe. "I don't know when we'll be able to take him back to their house. Can he stay here until it's safe? Macak too?"

Tomoe watched the sleeping man for a few seconds. Her gaze wandered to Ash. He chewed at the inside of his lip, waiting for her answer. After several more long seconds, she turned to Maeko.

"They are both a risk," she said, giving Macak's leg a meaningful glance, "but they may stay. Garret-san will need to pay for his keep at some point," she added to Ash.

"That's not a problem," he blurted.

Tomoe nodded and held Maeko's eyes. "Be careful. You have survived this long on your own, so I will not try to stop you, but I must speak. You should not be involved in these things. These are political battles, the makings of revolution. Do not become mixed up in the affairs of pirates."

Maeko frowned. "You're in too deep to be telling me that, aren't you?"

"I knew you would not listen." The tremulous hint of a fond smile tugged up the corners of her mouth. "Do not become lost to me again."

Maeko blinked her eyes against the sudden sting of tears. She stepped around her mother and strode toward the door, wiping at her eyes, then stopped and turned back when she noticed that Ash hadn't followed. He gave her a dark look and turned to Tomoe.

"Thank you," he nodded to his father, "for taking care of him."

Tomoe swallowed hard against tears that brimmed in her eyes. "I expect you will return the favor." She indicated Maeko with a small wave of one hand.

Maeko bristled at the implication that she needed someone to look out for her, but she kept her mouth shut.

"I'll do my best."

"Arigato... Thank you, Ash-san."

He nodded and hurried after Maeko.

With a long walk ahead of them and a tempest of emotions to outrun, she set a brisk pace. When things went wrong, she and Chaff had a standing agreement to find each other at the Cheapside lurk at night or the nearby marketplace during the day. If he hadn't gotten himself into trouble trying to find her, there was a good chance he would be at the marketplace. Since he'd gotten away from the new Literati orphanage once, he would know how best to get to Ash's brother. He was her one constant in this life, and right now she needed someone she could count on.

"If your mum's alive, why are you living on the streets?"

"It's complicated," she snapped.

He stared at the ground in front of them, his lips curving down hard.

She tried for a less bitter tone. "You saw the scars?"

He nodded.

"She was attacked by some men and hurt bad enough that she couldn't work at the brothel anymore. No one pays for a woman with scars like that. The brothel owner let her do odd jobs around the place in exchange for a room while she healed, but that didn't help with the medical bills. One day I overheard her telling another woman there that she was going to give me up to an orphanage."

She chewed at her lip, remembering her mother's stitched face the last time she had seen her. The solemn resolve in her expression, the distance she forced between them like scar tissue Maeko couldn't see, but she felt it building. The rejection still stung, like the prick of a thousand angry bees.

"So you decided to run," he prompted.

"Better that than to end up in a Literati workhouse."

"Don't you think you were a little hard on her back there?"

Maeko gave him a look of warning. "It's not your concern."

He glared back. "Is money all you care about?"

Maeko increased the pace. She didn't have to explain herself to him. Theirs was only a business arrangement.

They ducked into crowds a few times along the way when Lit officers on steamcycles passed by. Ash followed her direction without question, which gave her some hope for their chances of getting through this without too much more trouble.

"Do you think the detective believes my parents killed those people?" he asked after a noisy steam-collector rumbled past.

The edge of hopelessness in his voice diffused her temper. Unable to come up with a reassuring lie, she nodded.

"They'd never do something like that," he defended. "Not even to someone who deserved it."

She already believed that of the man who treated her so kindly in the pub, before making off with the cat, of course. To have Ash confirm it with such certainty banished any lingering doubts. "I'm not sure it was pirates at all. If what your dad said about Mr. Folesworth denying the weapons development is true, the pirates would want him in charge of Clockwork Enterprises rather than let it fall into the hands of his partner."

"His partner might be a target too."

"Maybe, but if the landing pad door wasn't shut, it's likely that someone made a quick exit that way."

He caught on quickly. "Which would mean someone with access to a decent airship. One that wouldn't look out of place up there like ours. You're smarter than you let on." He flashed her a quick smile. "If you're right, we might find allies in the pirate community. After we get Sam, we should ask around where you found Macak. I doubt the cat ended up there on his own. Barman might have seen something."

She nodded. It was a place to start, but not suspecting pirates meant Lits, Lits who would be more than happy to pin the crime on pirates like Ash's father. The detective might have information that could help, but they didn't know how deep her affiliation with the Lits went, which meant they couldn't trust her. This was far more complex and dangerous than she could have imagined. It was time to disown the mess and yet... Ash had an education and the advantage of his more privileged upbringing, as well as some connection to the pirates, but he didn't have the underworld knowledge or street smarts to dig into this alone. He'd get himself killed.

"Can I ask you something?"

Fresh tension tightened her shoulders. *What now?*

"Do you go through a lot of shoes?"

She laughed with amusement and with genuine relief. "I don't usually cover this much distance in so few days, and throwing them at horses is a new thing."

"It was a brilliant throw."

She grinned at his praise. "It was good, wasn't it? Too bad about the shoe."

Cheapside afternoon markets were crowded, which increased the chances of Chaff being around, but made it harder to pick out one individual in the crowd. On the other hand, it also reduced the chances of the occasional

Literati patrol picking them out of the bustle. There was no doubt they were both on wanted lists now. Being smaller than average for her age, Maeko had an advantage when it came to vanishing in crowds. With Ash there, however, she had to take more care. He wasn't large, but he wasn't slight enough to disappear behind a slender man. Women were easier to hide behind with bustled skirts and parasols broadening their profiles, but they also tended to frequent the area less due to an abundance of shops catering to a male clientele.

A wild array of aromas from food vendors selling sandwiches, meat puddings, and even cold sweet ice cream along the pedestrian pavements made her stomach growl. Now wasn't the time to let such things distract her, though, especially given their lack of tin.

Glancing over her shoulder, she discovered with a prickle of alarm that Ash had vanished. She scanned the crowd, leaning this way and that to peer around people, and finally spotted him off to one side among a group staring up at the massive new steam-powered clock above the watchmaker's shop. Under the clock was a board made up of metal plates with numbers and letters on them that flipped periodically to display various tidbits of news.

LITERATI STREET CLEANUP PROGRAM AN OVERWHELMING SUCCESS

She snorted at that. *Brilliant job locking up scary old homeless folks and orphans. A blighter future indeed.*

The clacking of the plates as the headline changed drowned out the ticking of the massive clock.

CLOCKWORK ENTERPRISES BREAKS GROUND ON TWO NEW FACTORIES

Maeko stalked up behind Ash and waited, watching the machinery above for the right moment.

"Stick close," she snapped when the steam clock blasted out a loud exhale.

He jumped and spun, then smiled and pointed at the news board. "How does that thing work?"

"I don't know. But on the streets, we call such things orphan bait."

He looked up at the clock then back at her, puzzled. "Why?"

"Lit officers stake out distractions like that. When a street rat stops to gawp, the Lits slip in, cuff and bag them, and take them away." She frowned a warning and turned to the task of finding Chaff, trying not to giggle at his sheepish look when he followed her away from the display.

"I wasn't gawping," he muttered.

Selecting a cluster of foreigners with several women in their midst to follow, Maeko worked them along the street, scanning for a familiar face. Not an easy task when most people were taller than she was. A few familiar faces made brief appearances in the crowd, rivals and acquaintances working the streets, none of whom she would consider friends, though a few might be useful for tracking down Chaff if she didn't spot him soon.

The group they followed made an abrupt turn at a jeweler's shop. As they moved out of the path, she spotted Chaff just past a tailor's shop, hovering menacingly over another kidsman who wasn't supposed to be on their turf, which was probably why he looked ready to tear the bloke apart. She moved in, keeping an eye out for Lits and weaving through the crowd in an effort to get close enough to eavesdrop.

"Have you seen her or not?" There was an edge of breaking patience in Chaff's voice. "You've no business being here and I'll drag you back where you belong by your ears unless you have something for me."

The man's eyes darted about. He knew Chaff rarely lost a fight and he wanted a way out. His gaze lit upon her then and his eyes widened. He grinned and looked at Chaff.

"I've seen her." He pointed past Chaff with his chin. "She's right there."

Chaff turned with the fluid movement of a serpent, which was appropriate somehow. He might not spit venom, but he could strike fast. The other kidsman took advantage of the moment and bolted away.

Chaff's tight angry look relaxed instantly to one of relief and pleasure that made her feel a little short of breath.

"Blimey, is that my Mayko? Nice churches, Pigeon." He gave a nod to the oversized shoes, following it up with a teasing wink.

Pleasure took back seat to a flash of irritation. "I'm not your anything, especially if you refuse to say my name right," she grumbled.

At her tone, Ash puffed up beside her, a strutting peacock ready to defend its territory. It might have been funny and a bit flattering if she didn't know how dangerous Chaff could be. He'd made a tidy sum prize fighting when pickings were slim and she'd seen him pressed into street scraps often enough, many times in her defense. The lucky ones he let limp home.

Chaff grinned, his eyes sparkling with satisfaction at managing to get under her skin so fast. Then he turned to Ash, picking him apart with a quick glance to evaluate all the details important to a street rat. Strength, speed, intellect, street smarts, wealth, all things Chaff could gauge in a heartbeat with uncanny accuracy from a person's attire and bearing. After a few seconds, he shrugged, openly insulting Ash by implying with the gesture that he wasn't worth his time.

He turned back to her, tilting his head to one side in a gesture that reminded her of a large puppy eyeing a toy... or a hawk eyeing its prey. Odd that the two images were so similar and yet one was much more sinister. "Not sure about that particular haircut on you. It does help you blend in though. I approve of that."

"I wasn't looking for your approval, great one," she teased in a more playful tone, hoping it would deflect the building tension she sensed in Ash.

Benny was gazing up at her with that open admiration of a child not yet jaded by life on the streets. "I think it's splendid!"

Despite her change in attitude toward Chaff, Ash gave the taller boy an icy look. Though younger and shorter, he had that muscular build that might give him the misguided impression he could overpower the lean street rat. She doubted that little bit of extra mass would matter in a fight. Chaff could fight like a wildcat, all speed and sharp pointy bits. If they weren't in a hurry, she would let Ash learn that lesson the hard way. It would be good for him to gain some respect for the education of the streets and she didn't think Chaff would really hurt him, not so long as he was in her company, but they didn't have time.

Stepping forward to put herself between the two, she faced Chaff and said, "I need your help."

Chaff lowered his blue-eyed gaze to her and the forward aggression in his stance faded some. He met her eyes, his expression turning serious when she returned a solemn regard. It was rare for her to request his help outright. She often managed to get it through clever manipulation when she did want it, making something of a game of wits out of it. The uncharacteristic approach gave him something to think about other than the strange boy encroaching on his turf. Since she was one of many youths working the streets for him, she was, in a sense, his turf.

"What for?"

There was no way to ease into the subject without wasting time. "To help get Ash's brother out of an orphanage."

He frowned and shifted back from her, resistance giving a frosty edge to his gaze. "You don't want much. Why should *I* care what happens to *his* kin?"

She could feel the pressure of Ash's anger rising behind her like an approaching storm. *Boys!* "Because I do," she answered, soft and sincere.

There was a small inhale of surprise from behind her. Chaff started to look up at Ash and she took another quick step forward, catching his attention again and holding it. She gave him her soft-eyed pleading look, an art form it had taken her years to perfect. "I've been a meal ticket for you for years. Isn't that worth something?"

Her world lurched out of balance when his expression warmed, a fond smile tugging at the corners of his mouth. "You've never been just a meal ticket. I wouldn't be here without you." The resistance in his eyes faded away. "I'll do what I can to help if that's really what *you* want, Pigeon."

The nickname didn't sound so bad when he infused it with such warmth and gratitude. She couldn't recall him ever speaking to her in quite that tone before. It was powerful, a spell to counter her pleading eyes, though she wasn't about to acknowledge the giddy melting sensation he'd caused in her middle.

Focusing her thoughts on her feet and the way the ground felt solid beneath them, she gave an earnest nod.

The odd moment passed. Chaff turned serious, or at least as serious as he ever got. "Right then. I s'pose he was nicked recently?"

"Yesterday."

"Daytime?"

She nodded.

"He'll be in the new building near Tyburn. If you want to get him tonight, we should get there by dark, which means we need to chivvy along. You have tin for an omnibus?"

She shook her head and glanced over her shoulder at Ash who did the same. "Please, Chaff, can't you take the hit this time? I'll pay you back. You know I'm good for it."

He pulled out his pant pockets, showing that they were empty, and shrugged. The wicked light flickering to life in his eyes told her he was hiding something. "Looks like you've got a predicament."

He couldn't handle being too nice, not when he didn't want to be involved in something in the first place. Maybe that was why she got snippy with him so much, a kind of pre-emptive strike at the rotten devil inside him, though she rather liked that devil most times, just not when it worked against her.

She turned around to scan the pedestrians. She could feel Ash's eyes on her and did her best to ignore him. Foolish as it was, she had hoped this wouldn't come up while he was around.

This is who I am. It's how I survive. If he doesn't like it, that's his problem.

She set her jaw and continued studying the bustle of people.

The best thing about Cheapside was all the foreigners it attracted. That made it easy to find unsuspecting marks. She didn't like leaving the two boys alone together. There was little chance of them playing nice without her there and she didn't doubt that Chaff would take the opportunity to taunt Ash. With that in mind, she searched for a mark that wouldn't take her too far away.

When Chaff first took her under his wing, he'd been stealing and recruiting for a kidsman who managed a small ring of child thieves. To his credit, he never presented her to that man, fearing he would put her to work doing something other than thieving. He chose to protect her from that ilk, sneaking her into various lurks to make sure she didn't die of exposure or hunger while he taught her the ropes. She'd been a quick study, taking to the art of picking pockets as if she had done it all her life. With her help and that of a few other skilled youths, he liberated himself from that kidsman a few years later. Now he ran his own group of thieves, which was why she doubted he was penniless, but it was too much work to argue when a quick foray could solve the problem.

She spotted her mark, a dapper toff focused on the lady he was escorting through a tight crowd. With his attention on her and the jostle of the crowd to help, he would be an easy mark for an accomplished thief. The thrill of the hunt made her nerves dance.

She glanced in Ash's direction, avoiding his eyes. "Wait here."

Behind her, she heard him ask Chaff where she was going, setting aside earlier tensions before the pressure of curiosity. Chaff told him to watch and learn because a cracking fine wirer was going to work.

She smiled at that. Did Ash even know what a fine wirer was?

She wound her way into the crowd with practiced ease. Her heart drummed a rhythm in her ears, a familiar music that helped her keep a steady, calm cadence to her movements. Without drawing attention, she maneuvered close to the couple, spotting the faint bulge of a wallet in his left pocket when another passer brushed his coat back from his hip.

With a quick maneuver, she bumped another bloke, making him stumble into the mark's lady. When the toff stepped a leg back for balance, reaching out to catch his female companion and keep her from falling, Maeko slipped in, dipping a hand in under the coat and into his pocket. The wallet was in hand and tucked into her trousers by the time he turned. She pretended to be catching herself from a trip over his back flung leg, using his fine frock coat to get her balance and then held up her hands in a show of apology.

"Sorry, Sir."

He nodded once, distracted, and turned back to his lady who swooned as only a wellborn lady in a tightly laced bodice could.

Maeko worked her way out of the crowd and back to where the three boys waited. When she got to them, she grinned and chucked the wallet at Chaff who snatched it out of the air, beaming with pride. In stark contrast, Ash's face had become a tempest of black emotion. Uncertainty fluttered in her chest, wiping away her grin.

Chaff peeked into the wallet, nodded, and tucked it away. "Top mark, Pigeon," he praised. "Let's leg it before we attract attention."

She fell in on his heels as they made for an omnibus. Ash stomped along beside her.

She gave him a nervous glance. "What's wrong?"

"You stole that bloke's wallet," he growled under his breath, wary of the people around them.

The judgment in his tone made her bristle. "So."

"So? What if that was all the tin he had to feed his family?"

She glared at him. The burn of shame rose in her cheeks and it fed her anger. She'd never felt guilty for nicking a bit of coin before, especially from someone so obviously well off. On the contrary, every successful theft was a source of pride, an accomplishment… and another day or two that she wouldn't go hungry. Those skills helped her stay out of the hands of men who would use her for far more unsavory things and every good mark let her stash more away toward her mother's debt.

"How dare you judge me," she snapped under her breath. "You have no idea what it's like to survive on the streets."

"But you don't have to, you have family."

"I have no family," she hissed, her voice cracking. The recent encounter with her mother twisted like a knife in her chest.

He started to respond, but trailed off when Chaff stopped and spun around to face them a few feet short of the omnibus.

He cocked his head, his beautiful blue eyes boring into Ash with the calm, cold burn of protective fury she had seen so many times. "I'm not sure who you think you are, but you're hounding the wrong bird." He gave Ash a disgusted sneer, then slugged him in the jaw.

To her surprise, Ash didn't fall. He could take a hit. He staggered back a few steps, his hand going to the tender red mark spreading on the side of his jaw. Chaff had been nice enough not to break his nose and Maeko thought the mark went well with the bruise from falling down the steps outside JAHF, giving him a rebellious flair. Ash didn't look the least bit amused, however. A murderous rage rose through the shock in his eyes as he stared at Chaff, his hands balling into fists.

So much for not drawing attention.

Maeko stepped out of the way when Ash charged, she wasn't about to get in the line of fire. Chaff wouldn't do him any real harm, and right then she rather wanted to cuff him herself.

Chaff grinned, the look of a hungry predator about to make a kill. He stood his ground, then took a step back at the last second and grabbed Ash by the shoulders, spinning them both around and letting go so that Ash's momentum slammed him into the side of the omnibus. The bus rattled with the impact and Maeko winced. The horses started, half-rearing in their traces, and the driver cursed at them while he reined in the animals. Surrounding pedestrians backed away in alarm, though they didn't go far and more gathered, drawn by the irresistible lure of conflict.

Ash staggered a step and shook himself. His pale
eyes homed in on Chaff and he charged again. Chaff
lowered his stance as if he meant to brace for the attack,
but he sidestepped at the last possible second, his movement effortless and graceful as a dancer, and swung
around to clout Ash a sound blow to the back of the
head. Ash caught himself on someone's arm. When he
spun around this time, his face was crimson with rage
and humiliation. He charged again and she wondered
if he would ever learn, but this time he caught hold of
Chaff's arm on the brush off and spun himself around,
striking the taller boy a solid blow under his eye.

To be fair, it wasn't a bad move, but it left him in
close enough for any number of swift counterstrikes and
Chaff, despite his slender appearance, could take more
hits without flinching than it took to topple a brick wall.
Before Ash could retreat, Chaff punched him twice in
the ribs, yanked his arm free, and swept out with one
leg.

Maeko cringed. That wasn't going to end well.

A voice rose up above the increasing din enough to
catch her attention and she turned as Ash hit the ground
with a grunt.

"That's the one, right there!"

A Literati officer was pushing his way through the
gawking crowd. The man she'd nicked the wallet from
flanked him, pointing at her. A chill swept through her
when she recognized Mr. Jacard following along behind
them, the gray coachman hat shadowing his eyes. He
smirked when he caught her looking and tipped his hat
to her.

"My employer tips his fine hat to you." She shuddered
at Hatchet-face's voice in her head.

Jacard was showing up too often. Twice might be
coincidence, a third times suggested something more
deliberate. Right now, however, she couldn't waste time

investigating or she would wind up in Literati hands again.

Ash got to his feet and shook his head to clear it. Chaff watched him with the casual indifference of someone watching a fly buzz past. The omnibus driver was maneuvering his horses out through the press of people, snarling curses at all of them.

Maeko bolted between the two boys. "Time to go."

She threaded her way through the crowd. Squeals of surprise and indignant shouts behind her let her know someone, probably several someones, followed. She couldn't afford the luxury of looking back to find out who. She shoved onward until she burst free of the crowd and sprinted, ducking down the nearest side street.

This part of town was a cinch. This was where she learned her trade. After seven more turns down the streets and alleys, using an ashbin to scale a fence in one, she dared a glance over her shoulder. Ash followed, a trickle of red drying in one corner of his mouth. Benny panted along close behind him, his short legs pounding out a desperate pace. She saw no sign of Chaff, but also no sign of the toff, the officer, or Mr. Jacard.

She turned down another trash-lined alley and slammed through a door that hung crooked on its hinges. She stopped at the foot of some stairs inside the dingy, deserted building, the musty smell of mildew and stink of old waste thick in her nostrils. She grimaced, turning to the door when Ash and Benny stormed in. Ash shoved the door shut as far as it would go and leaned against it, breathing hard and choking on the rancid air. Benny slumped on the bottom step to catch his breath.

Ash looked up at her, anger still raging in his eyes even after the run. Then his gaze moved up to the top of the stairs and his scowl deepened. Turning, she looked

up at Chaff who stood there grinning down at her, a
faint darkening over one high cheekbone where Ash had
made contact.

"I see you took the slow route, eh Pigeon."

"I was trying not to lose the pups," she countered.

Ash made rude noise in his throat and Chaff glared
down at him.

"Your taste in mates has gotten sorry and sad."
Chaff sauntered down the steps and continued past her.

"Apparently so." She turned her back on the wounded look in Ash's gorgeous eyes and followed Chaff
through a doorway.

Bloody boys. Frustration welled. No amount of handsome excused their reckless behavior, even if Chaff was
just being protective.

Benny trotted past to walk with Chaff and she heard
the creak of the door as Ash pushed away from it to follow. They slipped out a side door into another alley and
went in search of transportation. When they reached an
omnibus stop, Chaff turned and scowled at Ash before
giving her a stern look.

"You sure you want to do this?"

Maeko nodded.

The conductor accepted their money and ushered
them aboard. Chaff offered Maeko a hand up,
something he'd never done before. She would normally
brush off such an offer anyway, maintaining the fierce
independence he claimed to admire so much, but this
time she took advantage of the chance to poke at Ash
for his earlier criticism. Chaff climbed up behind her.
Ash, scowling and refusing to meet her eyes, climbed in
third and slumped down in a spot at the far end of the
opposite seat. Benny squeezed into the last spot next to
him.

Chaff leaned close. "So who was the other bloke?"

"What other bloke?"

"The well-dressed toff behind the Lit and your mark who looked at you like a hound that just found the fox he's been tracking."

Her stomach turned. "I didn't see him."

"Don't lie to me, Pigeon. You know I can tell." While he talked, he stretched his arm and let it come to rest around her shoulders.

She looked down the omnibus catching the pained look on Ash's face. He turned away to stare off in the other direction, his reaction adding weight to the growing suspicion that he might be attracted to her, as crazy as that was. Guilt twisted in her chest. She stared at someone's feet on the floor across from them and let Chaff ramble on. They were almost to Tyburn when she noticed he had stopped talking.

"You've taken a fancy to that duffer, haven't you?" he asked in a low voice when she met his eyes.

Something in his manner made her uneasy, a guarded remoteness that strained their usual easy camaraderie. She looked away, resorting to the familiar comfort of silence. He leaned in again and she cringed to think how they must look from where Ash sat.

"C'mon. You can't hide it from me. You've never moped like this after dipping in a toff's pocket before."

His words grated on her. No, she hadn't, and that only made it more frustrating. She shrugged his arm off.

"You could do better," he commented, unwilling to let it go.

"Please stop." She gave him a cutting look. His expression darkened and a nagging voice in her head reminded her that she had asked for his help. Snapping at him might not be the best way to express her gratitude. Besides, her frustration wasn't his fault, not entirely at least. She swallowed her temper. "Sorry. It's been a long few days."

"That's all right." His words said one thing, his stilted tone and stiff posture said another.

She groped for something to win back his more congenial mood. "I ran into my mum."

The distance evaporated. He winced. "Ouch. On top of your encounter with the Lits. I guess you have had a bit of hard luck."

Should she tell him about her second escape?

No. He'd lecture her for being daft enough to get caught again and worse if she admitted to doing it on purpose so she could break Ash out.

"I'm chuffed you're all right. I didn't like leaving you at the Tower. You're not mixed up in whatever got those folks killed, are you?"

"No." *Coward*. But he would tell her to get out of it and he would be right. She couldn't convince him she wasn't in danger when she knew she was.

"Good."

His arm slipped back over her shoulders and she let it stay. It was nice, soothing, though she couldn't help wondering if this unusual physical affection was only a show to irritate Ash or if there were more to it.

Do I want there to be more?

She never used to worry about such things. It was Ash's fault, him and his pretty eyes making her think about silly things. This wasn't time to worry about who felt what toward her and how she felt in return. She had more important things to worry about.

"How'd your mum handle seeing you?"

That shut her momentary distraction down. "It was very...uncomfortable. I guess she figured me for dead. She seemed sad, mostly."

"I'm sorry. That couldn't have been easy."

She nodded, the constriction in her throat discouraging speech.

He tightened his hold, pulling her in against his chest.

It was only for a few seconds, but in those few

seconds, she wanted nothing more in the world than to curl up in his embrace and unburden all the stress of the last few days, of a lifetime. This was Chaff, though. He was her mentor, her partner in crime. They didn't have that kind of intimacy between them.

His arm relaxed.

The experience with her mother weighed on her, gaining potency as soon as she thought about it and his comforting made it more difficult to keep her jumbled emotions under control. Now she regretted bringing it up. Chaff allowed her to brood in silence and she dared to lean in to him, stealing comfort from the contact until they reached their stop.

Heavy clouds moved in, dropping early darkness in like a shroud upon the landscape and a drizzling rain came with it, drowning everything in dreary grayness. When the omnibus stopped about a quarter mile from the orphanage, Chaff stepped out into the aisle and let her off ahead of him, forcing Benny and Ash to follow. She considered kicking him for taking the opportunity to jamb another wedge between her and Ash, but that wasn't going to make him any more sensitive to their cause.

Besides, it was her fault for not explaining things to Ash, for not realizing that she might need to explain something she took for granted. If you lived on the streets, there were only so many ways to survive, most of them less pleasant than the one she had chosen. She'd learned to steal, run fast, and hide in the shadows to avoid ending up in a Literati workhouse or reformatory. Most of those weren't any better than the life of a street rat. In some cases, they were a sight worse. Ash didn't understand that, and in a way, she was glad he didn't have to.

She glanced back at Ash when he got off the bus behind Chaff, but he avoided her gaze. With a heavy exhale, she turned away and began to chew at her lip.

"Shall we walk?" Chaff clapped her on the back.

It was a gentle amiable pat, but her teeth bit into the inside of her lip, drawing blood from the healing sore where she had bitten it while making her escape with Hatchet-face. She started moving, picking up a swift pace for her short stature and licking at the blood on the inside of her lip, using the pain to take her mind off Ash. Perhaps, if this went well, he'd forget his anger.

They walked most of the way to a big four-story red brick building, the newest of the Literati orphanages. It looked much like a prison, complete with bars over all the windows.

Chaff stopped them and turned to face the group. His gaze rested on her. "What's the plan?"

An expected question that she'd already worked out the answer to, though she knew it would lead to more conflict. "You know how these places are laid out. You can lead. I'll follow. These two will stay here out of sight."

"Not bleeding likely," Ash objected. "I'm going with you."

Chaff started to speak and she gave him a stern look. Nothing he might say was going to help. In an uncommon show of self-restraint, he kept his commentary to himself.

She turned to Ash. He'd wiped the blood from his chin, but the lower lip swelled around a small split, another injury she'd led him to. "You don't have the skills to get in and out of there without being seen."

She hadn't intended the words to be offensive, just factual, but his expression closed up, shutting her out. Closing her eyes to a burst of frustration, she exhaled again.

"You don't know Samuel," he muttered, the words lacking the necessary conviction to sway her.

Not caring what the others thought of her deliberation, she took a few slow breaths to collect her thoughts, focusing on the task ahead of them rather than the emotions tied up in the current situation. When she felt calm and collected, she opened her eyes and looked at Ash, or through him really. It was easier to keep her composure that way.

"I know what he looks like," she said. "You stay out here with Benny. Keep out of sight and make sure neither of you is spotted. We'll nip in and back out quick as we can."

When he didn't argue, she spun on her heel and gave Chaff a nod, which he returned. He strolled up the walk beside the low iron fence that surrounded the grounds and scanned the street. Then, fast as a spooked cat, he hopped over and ducked into the bushes. After a long pause, she heard his soft whistle and strode forward. Two short whistles came from the bushes, Chaff letting her know the coast looked clear. Following his example, she sprang over the fence and crouched down, slipping into the bushes behind him.

He gave her a game grin, his irritability gone as soon as they were away from Ash. "If someone told me before I met you that my best pupil would be a twist, I'd have said they'd gone barmy."

"Girls can be criminals too. Get a move on." She poked him in the ribs and he jerked away, chuckling as he started slinking across the grounds.

They stayed low, working their way through scratchy, wet bushes and deep shadows, the soggy soil squishing beneath their feet. The tension and excitement of the caper kept her mind off other things. They stopped and crouched next to a tree a few yards from a door in the back of the building. Electric lights spilled their harsh glow out through some windows, but it was getting late enough that the residents would be settling in for the night, at least as much as kids ever settled.

"The Lit orphanages are all laid out the same. That door will take us in through a washroom," Chaff whispered. "From there we can sneak past the front desk. It should be quiet at this hour and it'll be easier if we can find out what room he's in on the roster."

She nodded, holding silence around her as a defensive barrier against the many distractions trying to hammer their way into her thoughts, like why Chaff was so extra protective around Ash and why Ash was so put out by Chaff's affection toward her and how she felt about all of that. He made a quick gesture toward the door and they scampered up to the building, crouching next to it. The damp sinking into her clothes started to make her shiver, but it provided one more distraction from the things she didn't need to be thinking about right now.

Digging into a pocket on the inside of his vest, Chaff pulled out a small pick set. Much nicer than the rusty little set she had. He considered the lock, then held the set out to her. She gave him a questioning look.

"This is your adventure, and besides, I'm willing to admit when I'm outclassed."

Normally, such a comment would have made her beam with pride, but in the current situation, it only made her feel nauseous. She grabbed the pick set and went to work on the door, cursing Ash in her head all the while for making her feel bad about her hard-earned ability to do such things. The lock clicked and Chaff squeezed her shoulder in silent praise before accepting the set back and tucking it away. He began to turn the knob.

She heard a soft sound from inside and shot a hand out, closing it over his. He froze, trusting her. Louder sounds of someone rummaging around beyond the door followed and he gave her an appreciative nod. She met his eyes. They weren't as shockingly pretty as Ash's perhaps, but they were lovely, with a charming glimmer of mischief that brightened her mood. Why hadn't she ever noticed that before?

He smiled then, a smile so warm and welcoming that she caught her breath in surprise and looked away, staring hard at her hand over his on the doorknob while her cheeks grew hot, thankful for the cover of darkness. Perhaps someone else did care for her, despite his declaration that one should never grow too fond of companions on the street. Although she hadn't intended it to happen, he'd become more than a mentor to her a long time ago. Was it so surprising that he might feel the same?

They waited there, crouched close together, until they heard the sound of feet departing and another door closing. Then they waited another few minutes in silent accord before she took her hand away and he began to turn the knob again.

He paused before opening the door. "Ganbatte." She grinned. "Ganbatte."

He pushed the door open.

The room beyond was dark and musty, a washroom that wasn't very well kept. It smelled of dirt. There were a few cupboards on the wall, none of which shut all the way despite how new the building was, and a pile of small, muddy shoes in one corner. She pointed to the shoes and he nodded. They took their shoes off, tucking them behind a broom with crisp bristles far cleaner than the floor. No sense leaving tracks around the building.

She listened for a moment, then opened the next door and they crept into the hallway beyond. A few doors stood closed along the left side and a room opened to the right with a single lamp sitting on a desk next to an open book. Chaff nodded in that direction. They started to move, then he grabbed her arm. A light bobbed toward the room from down another hall. They retreated into the shadows at the edge of the doorway to wait.

As the light neared, another figure stepped up beside the desk, materializing from the shadows in one corner. Maeko sucked in a breath when she recognized the detective. Chaff gave her a questioning look, but she didn't dare speak for fear of someone hearing. Then she noticed that two sets of footsteps approached from the hallway with the bobbing light. One sounded normal and even, the other halting, with every other step thudding hollow and heavy on the floor. Dread formed a writhing mass in the empty pit of her stomach.

Two figures entered the room, a tall, narrow faced woman with small dark eyes and a downcast young boy hobbling along beside her on a rigid false leg. The woman carried a candle, perhaps to avoid disturbing other residents with the bright electric lights. Em glowered, staring at the two as though their very existence was the source all of her troubles and Maeko felt a twinge of sympathy for the boy.

"That's him," she whispered.

Chaff's teeth ground together next to her, a sign that something peeved him and she had a good idea what. Thankfully, he couldn't put voice to his anger yet, though he would as soon as the opportunity arose.

Samuel was a slight boy, built lighter than his brother and father. His eyes, pale like Ash's, but tending more toward blue, stared listless at the wall to the right of their hiding place. His thin face hung slack, the world-weary look of a defeated creature.

She shifted forward, aching to help him and Chaff put a hand on her arm just as she had done to keep Ash from going to his rescue at the Blackwood's house. Shifting back, she brought her other hand to her teeth and began to chew at the nails. Releasing the one arm, Chaff reached up and took her wrist, pulling her hand away from her mouth, the painful tightness of his grip a testament to his irritation. With one coping mechanism denied her, she started chewing at her already wounded lip, tasting the coppery tang of fresh blood, though she barely noticed the sting.

"Here he is, Detective Wilkins, though I still think he would be better off remaining in our care. You don't seem the nurturing type." The woman held onto Samuel's arm as if hoping the detective would change her mind.

"No less so than you," Em countered. She stared at Samuel, impervious to the other woman's indignant huff. "Too many people involved in this case have gone missing, a few out of far more capable hands than yours. The warrant gives me the right to keep him in my custody until this investigation is resolved."

Em's expression softened then. She smiled and held out a hand to the boy.

With another huff, the woman pursed her lips and let go of Samuel. When he didn't move, she prodded him and he nearly toppled, unable to compensate fast enough with his bad leg.

The detective stepped forward, catching him and setting him right. She bent down to look him in the eye. "You all right?"

Sam gave a tremulous nod. Em chucked him under the chin and took hold of his hand before rising to turn a frosty look on the other woman.

I could almost not hate her right now. That was more than a little disturbing.

"Will that be all," the woman asked, wrinkling her pointed nose and turning away from the detective as if to avoid a foul stench.

"I certainly hope so." Em looked at Sam again. "Come on. Let's see if we can draw out your dad and your brother."

"Why?"

"Because they're in danger and we want to help

them." Em turned on her heel and walked from the room as fast as she could without toppling her small prisoner. She didn't bother with parting graces here anymore than she had at JAHF.

Giving one last put upon huff, the woman went to lock the door behind them.

Chaff tapped Maeko on the arm. When she looked at him, he gestured with a thumb over his shoulder back the way they had come. His tight jaw said there would be a scolding soon. She nodded and they made a silent retreat, slipping into their shoes and out the back door into the ongoing drizzle. Once they had crept a short distance away from the building into the cover of some bushes, his hand clamped tight on her arm, forcing her to stop.

She met his eyes, not surprised to find them alight with anger. "What?"

"You didn't tell me the boy was a raspberry!"

She stared at him for a second, watching a trickle of water run down the bridge of his nose while she worked his words through in her head.

Raspberry = raspberry ripple = cripple.

She hated it when he used less familiar rhyming slang, but then, she tossed bits of Japanese her mother had taught her his way on occasion, so it didn't seem reasonable to complain overmuch.

"Would it have mattered?" she asked the question knowing the answer because she would have felt the same in his shoes. Sam's handicap presented an unnecessary risk, one she should have been honest about up front. Logically, she understood his irritation, but that didn't mean it annoyed her any less.

"Yes. I would have told you to bugger off from the start." He pointed at the building. "We'd never have gotten him out of there without getting caught."

"We're going to get caught now if you don't keep your voice down." When she went to move on he kept her arm, holding her there with enough strength that trying to fight her way free would certainly draw attention. She blew out a breath and stopped pulling.

It stinks to be in the wrong. Sometimes, however, it was easier to own up to it, especially if she ever wanted to get out of these prickly bushes. "I'm sorry. I didn't think—"

"No. You didn't. You better clean your cogs and start doing so. That detective isn't playing a game and neither is whoever killed those people. Whatever bollocks you're into, you've gone in well over your head and you'd best get out before you get hurt. I don't care how much you fancy the bloke."

Her throat constricted and she looked away, peering toward where they had left Ash and Benny. He was right. She should get out while she still could, if that time hadn't already passed. Would he understand if she told him the whole story? Would he understand why she felt somewhat responsible for how things had unraveled? Probably not. He'd say, "Past mistakes is past, Pigeon. You can only do better going forward". He wouldn't see this as doing better. If she confessed that she also wanted to protect Macak, a cat of all things, he'd really think she'd lost her mind.

His hand loosened. After a few seconds, he took it away and mussed her cropped wet hair. "C'mon, Pigeon. The company's brilliant, but this rain's rubbish and the bushes are right prickly."

My thoughts exactly. She might have even smiled at that if she didn't have to face Ash soon. At least Chaff always got over being angry with her after he'd had his say.

Once they were back to the street, Ash stormed out of the shadows into the light of a gas-lamp, Benny trotting along behind looking cold and dejected. Ash's regard was despairing, made worse by the water dripping from flattened wet hair. A tempest of misery and anger raged in his pale eyes. She found herself starting to drag her feet as they closed the last bit of distance.

He pointed down the street. "I saw her coach leaving. She took Sam again, didn't she? She's always one step ahead of us."

Chaff stepped to one side and folded his arms across his chest, gazing at her with an expression that said this was her problem to deal with. Perhaps he was still annoyed with her about the fake leg after all.

She stared at Ash, standing alone before his tormented gaze. Chaff was right, this was too dangerous and Ash was too emotionally involved in the mess. He was going to get hurt. If there was ever an opportunity to drive him away, this was it, when he was already uncomfortable because of his rivalry with Chaff and upset with losing his brother to the detective again.

Even before she said the words, she felt the guilt and hurt inside. It was for his safety though. "If you hadn't started a row with Chaff, we might have beaten her here. You're not good on the streets. You're holding me back."

The hurt in his eyes was a knife twisting in her gut.

"I keep starting to really like you." Sorrow made his voice crack. "But just when I feel like we're becoming a great team, you say this. Since the moment I first saw you, bad things have happened to my family." He schooled his expression and tone to cold neutrality. "Maybe I am better off on my own. I don't need your help."

The ball of emotion knotted up inside her swelled to the verge of bursting. "Don't need me?" The words rushed out before she realized what she was saying. "I got you out of JAHF. I helped get your dad to Chelsea even though it meant confronting my mum. I tried to help you get your brother twice." She held two fingers up in front of his face for emphasis. "I even felt guilty about stealing from some wealthy toff for you."

Ash drew back, looking surprised, and then a hint smug at the admission.

What was she saying? She was supposed to be driving him away. She steeled herself against the pain and barreled onward. "I've gotten exactly nothing for any of it despite what you promised. We'll never be a great team. Not ever."

He stepped back, the hurt in his look attesting to her success. As she stared at him, the shield she'd put up between them crumbled, letting the disbelief and anguish in his eyes cut in.

I didn't really mean that. She started to shake her head.

All at once, his back stiffened and his shoulders squared up. The hurt expression gave way to a disgusted sneer. "You know, for a little while I almost forgot you're nothing but a money-grubbing street rat." Spinning, he stalked away from them.

Maeko watched Ash's retreating form. His parting words were a dagger twisting in her chest.

I should have told him why I wanted the money. I should have found another way to get him to leave. She moved to go after him and Chaff caught her arm. She yanked against him until he reached out and grabbed her other arm, pulling her back and caging her in his arms.

"Ash!"

The figure in the dark beyond the gas-lamp didn't turn or even hesitate as far as she could tell. He saw her for what she was. A worthless street rat. No one wanted a rat in their life.

"Ash!"

She fought against Chaff's hold, trying to turn around to kick her way free as she had done with Hatchet-face. Chaff, however, was too sound of mind to give her the opportunity.

He kept her firmly in place.

"Let him go, Mae."

She stopped struggling. It was the first time she could remember Chaff ever saying her name right. It sucked the will to fight out of her and she slumped against him, shivering with the chill of their damp shirts pressed between them. He supported her weight, his hold loosening to more of a gentle embrace now that she no longer fought to get away.

"I didn't mean to hurt him," she objected.

Chaff bent his head close to her ear, water dripping from his hair onto her shoulder, his breath warm against her skin. "Stubborn bird. You did too mean to hurt him. You've done it to me. Always driving others away to keep them safe. You can't be his nursemaid. If you chase him down now, it'll make things worse. Give him time to cool off."

Just because he was right didn't mean she had to like it. She stared in the direction Ash had gone, though he had vanished in the heavy dark drizzle. At least Chaff hadn't allowed her to twist around and kick him. Then she'd have both of them furious with her.

"You want me to go after him?" Benny piped up, eager to be of use.

Maeko shook her head and forced a smile for him. It was hard to be the new kid, especially when you were small enough to overlook. She knew. She'd been there.

Now that she had given off struggling, Chaff took his arms away, leaving one hand poised on her shoulder. She shivered again as the chill swept in where the heat of him had only just started to warm her back.

Everything really had gone wrong and it wasn't going to improve so long as the detective continued hunting down Ash's family for a murder they didn't commit. Unfortunately, Chaff was right about that mess too. She was mixed up in something much bigger than her, something she wasn't at all prepared to handle. She believed Ash's family was innocent, perhaps mostly because Ash did, but also because it didn't make sense for them to have killed those people. No one would take the word of a mere street rat as proof, but if she could find real, solid evidence, then maybe… Maybe…

Heldie?

The clatter of Heldie dropping her spoon when Em asked about Mr. Folesworth came unbidden to mind. Maybe there was more to the woman's unease than guilt over turning Maeko in. It wasn't Barman they needed to talk to, it was her. She had to know something. Her hands had trembled when she left the kitchen that night, nearly shaking the food off the plate.

Heldie had exhibited all the signs of a guilty conscience and Em, like many successful women trying to distance themselves from their origins, made the same mistake most blokes made, dismissing the woman as unimportant because of her gender. That gender invisibility was why Chaff often put Maeko in a dress and handed nicked items off to her when they worked the streets together. If someone noticed and called attention to the crime, the Lits would search all the boys in the area, but a girl following behind some random woman never got a second glance so long as she kept her head down so they couldn't see her Asian features. Perhaps, with her respect-worthy accomplishment of carving out a place in a man's occupation, Em had also acquired a man's shortsightedness.

Chaff was watching her. When she met his eyes, he looked away. "C'mon, I'll buy you two some grub."

"Given that I nicked the wallet, wouldn't it be me buying you two some grub?"

He returned a sly grin. "Last I checked, you were still working for me."

"Well, since you've already got the pinched dough, I guess we can call it even and skip the meal."

Chaff cocked his head to one side and narrowed his eyes at her, his grin fading. "What're you thinking?"

"I have an idea." She held up her hands to fend off the argument brewing behind his eyes. "I know I shouldn't stay involved in this, I know it's risky, but I can't walk away now. I can't...I can't let his family be destroyed." *Like mine. Like Macak's.*

Chaff shook his head at her, though the threat of an affectionate smile pulled at the corners of his mouth. "You are a sweet and stubborn bird. You know I can't stand back and let you get yourself hurt."

"Why not?"

The ever-present gleam of mischief in his eyes guttered out and he turned to stare off into the darkness. Rivulets of water ran from his damp darkened hair, tracking down the tightened muscles of his jaw, running over his cheeks like tears.

He does care.

It felt as if she caught a rare glimpse into his innermost soul and it left her reeling. His indomitable spirit was the one constant in her life. She started to reach out to him.

He turned then, the hint of vulnerability gone so fast she snapped her hand back in surprise. "At least let me buy us a ride to Cheapside. We've been kipping in the old lurk over there. No sense walking all that way and maybe I can talk some smarts into you before we get there."

No sense turning him down. It was the direction she needed to go. "If you want. You might not bother with the chin wagging though. I can guarantee it won't work."

He gave her shoulder a squeeze and smiled, some of the invincible good-humor returning to his eyes. "Have you ever known me to stop talking?"

With effort, she dredged up a small, weary laugh despite the hollow that had formed in her chest. Would Ash forgive her for her harsh words? Could she forgive him for his? She didn't suppose it mattered. They were from different worlds. If she could fix things, she would. Then, he could go back to his life and she could go back to the world Chaff had given her, the only world she'd ever known, though even that was changing now.

By the time they arrived back at Cheapside, the rain let up and Chaff talked her into sticking around for a bite before the last of the evening vendors closed up shop. A full stomach, he insisted, would help her think things through and, perhaps, bring her to her senses. She conceded on the condition that he promise not to follow her or have her followed once they parted ways. He agreed after another solemn silence that left her hanging in that awkward space between wanting to comfort him and wanting to retreat from whatever truth skulked behind that silence.

With a little of the coin she had nicked earlier, she purchased a sandwich from a street vendor while the two boys queued up at another cart to get meat puddings. She walked away from the cart, shook some of the remaining wet out of her hair, and raised her meal to her lips. A hand clamped on the back of her neck. The unexpected pressure propelled her forward and the sandwich flew from her hands, plopping into a puddle.

"Look at you." Em's tone dripped venom and Maeko almost looked up to see if the detective had turned into the snake-faced creature she imagined when Wells talked about her. "Already back on the streets."

Maeko's stomach clenched, her gut twisting in alarm as much as in remorse for the lost meal. She looked over at the other vendor cart and picked Chaff out of the queue of people still waiting there. He glanced her direction and his eyes widened a fraction. She managed a slight shake of her head and he made his gaze slide past to focus with apparent interest on something beyond them.

Em's hand tightened, her thin fingertips pressing into the flesh of Maeko's neck. "You and I need to talk."

Increasing the pressure, she forced Maeko to start walking down the street. A mournful glance at the sandwich soaking up grimy water in the puddle helped her turn fear and pain into anger. A boy in tattered rags darted out from somewhere and snatched up the meal, biting into the sludge-dampened bread with enthusiasm. At least it wouldn't go to waste.

"Perhaps if you stopped treating me like a criminal I'd be willing to talk."

Em's hand squeezed hard for a few seconds then loosened again. She spoke in a low voice, tight with controlled frustration. "You're a little too clever for your own good, rat, but you remind me a bit of myself when I was young, so I'll give you a chance. I know you helped that boy get out of JAHF and helped his father get away, so I'm guessing you also know where they are. You owe me for the harnesses you destroyed. Tell me where they are and I won't have a new set made out of your hide."

Maeko shrugged, wincing when Em tightened her grip again. She had very little time to find a way out of this. Several yards ahead of them, the familiar coach waited with the two soot-grayed horses sagging tired in their repaired harnesses. Sam sat in the seat by the driver, lured into compliance with lies and a bag of sweet cakes. It was a little tempting to give up and join him.

"You're after the wrong people. Ash's parents didn't kill anyone."

"You can prove that?"

To her surprise, Em sounded interested, perhaps enough so to listen to her theory. Then again, she hadn't proven anything yet. She didn't have an alternate suspect to offer aside from speculation about the Lits and Folesworth's partner in his nice coachman hat having a motive.

"My employer tips his fine hat to you."

Hatchet-face? He wasn't a good suspect given the timing, but if that was the job he'd been hired for, his employer could have hired a new killer after he was arrested. The scarred murderer might know something.

She could send Em to talk to Heldi, but without knowing where the detective's loyalties lay, that could make the situation worse. Maybe she should send her after the lead she didn't dare follow.

"There was a killer I had a run in with. He said he was hired to kill a wealthy family. I don't know where he is now, though."

"The bludger you helped escape from JAHF?" Em gave her a shrewd look, her steely eyes narrowing with skepticism. "Yes, I know about that. If you take me to Garrett, I'll let you go. No Lits this time. You have my word."

Maeko twisted enough to glower at her despite the extra pain it caused. "That lie won't work twice. I'm not daft. Besides, I'm telling the truth."

Em glared ahead then smirked wickedly. Her hand tightened again and Maeko winced, her head throbbing with the pressure. They were getting close to the waiting coach.

"I'm not usually one for roughing up young women, but I'm starting to think I might enjoy it in your case."

Maeko twisted, trying to relieve some of the pressure of the detective's grip. As she did so, she spotted Benny sneaking up behind and to the other side of the detective. He met Maeko's eyes and reached into the pocket of Em's long coat, his grab purposefully clumsy. Em twisted around, grabbing for his wrist with her free hand. Maeko twisted the other way, wrenching free of the detective's grip, and ran.

She didn't look back to see the consequences of the rescue attempt. You never looked back. Every street rat she ever met told her that. She could only hope Benny had the sense to get out of there. Chaff would do his best to make sure the boy escaped. He always tried to watch out for his own.

"Grab her!"

Reuben stepped out from alongside the coach, a lanky shadow shifting into her path in the growing dark. He was tall. She could work with that. She kept running. When his arms reached for her, she dove beneath them, curling into a somersault. She landed on her left shoulder blade. The resulting burst of pain was a small price to pay for freedom. She rolled to her feet, up and running again before Rueben had recovered from his failed effort. Sprinting past the coach, she glanced over in time to catch the dumbstruck expression on Amos's face as he looked up from the cigar he was about to light. He tossed aside the struck lucifer and gave chase, but she was in her element. She ducked down a side street, weaving a complex path through the neighborhood until the sounds of pursuit faded.

When she stopped, she slumped back against the chill brick wall of a building and took a few minutes to catch her breath. The gnawing ache in her stomach brought to mind the sandwich she'd dropped in the street. She could still smell the ham and bread on her fingers. Her mouth watered.

Bleeding detective.

The Lits must have told Em that they spotted her and Ash at Cheapside earlier. That made sense, enough so that she almost felt daft for not expecting her there. It was difficult enough keeping a watch out for officers without having to worry about that woman, too.

The few pedestrians along the poorly lit street didn't pay her any mind and a light drizzle started to fall again, adding to the insidious gloom that seeped into her. Light traffic included a trio of young chaps over their fill on liquor who could barely stagger a straight line while they taunted one another. They made enough noise for a group three times the size. Another time, she might have stalked them, seeking the prime moment to take advantage of their condition and empty their pockets, but Ash's disapproving scowl came to mind and she dismissed them. She had more important things to do.

She rubbed at the stinging marks in her neck from Em's fingers and almost sank down on the wet pavement to indulge in a refreshing cry. It wouldn't help anything, though it might ease the buildup of misery and frustration. Still, if she wasted time on that, the chances of Em finding Garrett and her mother increased. She didn't want to bring that kind of trouble down on Tomoe no matter how she felt about their relationship. Besides, what would that mean for all the pirates to whom her mother provided medical services?

Her head rested back against the wall, the drizzle mixing with a few warm tears that trickled down her cheeks.

Mum.

All those years, believing her mother didn't want or love her. Why else would Tomoe consider turning her over to an orphanage instead of finding some way to keep her? It didn't occur to her until they sat talking on the little porch that it might have been a devastating decision for her mother to make. Now that she better understood, she wasn't sure whether to try mending the broken relationship or let it stay dead. Right now, they had to interact for Garrett's sake. After this was over...

"Clean your cogs."

She smiled at Chaff's voice in her head. *Keeping me on task even when you're not here?*

The voice was right though, she needed to clear her head and focus on her immediate goal. Heaving a deep sigh, she shoved away from the wall and began to weave her way through back streets toward the pub where it all started. Her flight from the detective had taken her several blocks in the wrong direction, mostly because she didn't want Em getting any idea where she might be going. Hopefully, Heldie would be there. The more she thought about the woman's behavior the other night, the more certain she was that Heldie knew something. She could be the key to finding Lucian Folesworth and fixing this bollocks.

She started working through scenarios in her head the way she did whenever she and Chaff worked the streets together, so that she would have options in mind for many of the turns a situation could take. He claimed to admire her ability to puzzle things through ahead of time and that skill might be of considerable use when she confronted Heldie. After their last brief encounter, Maeko had a hunch that if she played upon Heldie's guilt over turning her into the Lits and her apparent friendship with Ash's father, the woman might at least feel obliged to listen.

A glance through the front windows found a bois-terous crowd in the pub. Another pirate band played, their exotic sound thrumming through the building. Two unfamiliar women bustled about serving tables. Heldie must be in the kitchen if she were there at all.

Maeko slunk around into the back alley. A new ashbin stood there, the mess she'd made now only a memory etched in her mind, the start of an unexpected journey. The door was locked. They'd wised up, but it wasn't about to stop her. She pulled Chaff's fancy lock picks out of a trouser pocket, grinning at the thought of his expression when he realized they were missing. Nothing made one feel more accomplished then picking a thief's pocket. He'd done it to her often enough.

She brushed away a few flakes of peeling paint and put one ear to the edge of the door, listening for the sounds of anyone nearby. Satisfied that she wouldn't be disturbed, she went to work on the lock. Moments later, it clicked open. She turned the knob, pushing the door in a few inches to peek into the dark hall beyond. Empty. She slipped through and started to slink down the hall.

She'd barely taken four steps when the door next to her opened. She spun to see Heldie standing in the doorway of a dark little room. A single flickering candle illuminated the cramped space. Dark shadows danced in the corners, given texture by more peeling paint. A small camp bed with a few ratty blankets heaped in the center of the dingy mattress stood pushed up against the back wall.

The woman stared at her with a look of profound dismay. Maeko stepped toward her, discouraging her from leaving the room, and Heldie took a quick step back.

"Ye again." Her voice had a panicky sharpness to it. "I thought that detective had ye."

"She let me go." It was best to get the small lies going right away. That made the bigger ones easier. "I need to talk to you."

Heldie leaned out to peer down the hall and Maeko got a good, nauseating whiff of her cloying perfume. The bright paint around her eyes looked smeared as if she'd been crying.

Before she got the idea of calling for someone, Maeko took another step forward. "You turned me in to the Lits, didn't you?"

Heldie frowned, her eyes and painted cheeks drooping with the expression, giving her the dumpy look of an old toad, only with heavy makeup and perhaps a shade less green. She took another step back and moved to one side, allowing Maeko enough room to enter.

The flickering candle sat on a petite, scuffed vanity. A spider web of cracks radiated out from a dimple in the center of the mirror, reproducing the light in each section until there appeared to be a whole array of candles on the vanities surface. The flame flickered when Heldie shut the door, sending shadows lurching across the walls. She stepped around Maeko and stopped, staring down at the little camp bed. When she turned around, she was wringing her hands. Maeko forced her gaze up from the mesmerizing motion to meet the woman's eyes. Heldie lowered her gaze to stare at her twining hands.

"I narked on ye all right. I ain't apologizin' neither. The streets ain't no place for a twist."

"Isn't that my business?" Maeko asked, surprised that the question came out calm and free of accusation.

Heldie exhaled and shuffled around Maeko to pull a half-burned candle out of one drawer of the vanity. She lit it off the first with shaking hands. It took two tries to get it set properly in a bent wall sconce, then she walked back to plop down on the bed and proceeded to twist a finger in her frazzled locks. The added light enhanced dark circles under her eyes and the lines of worry creased into her brow. She looked like a woman who had seen many rough days. Judging from her figure, she wasn't half as old as she looked. What kind of life could age a woman so fast? Perhaps she had firsthand experience with being a girl on the streets.

"It doesn't matter. I didn't come about that." The woman met her eyes, then looked away again. "I'm looking for someone, a gentleman by the name of Lucian Folesworth."

At the mere mention of his name, Heldie's finger stopped twirling for a few telling seconds and she schooled her expression, exaggerating disinterest.

"Why would I know anythin' 'bout that?"

"You can't lie to a liar," Maeko countered, hoping her conviction might shake truth out of the woman. "I know you've spoken with him." Another lie, but so long as Heldie believed her, it didn't matter.

Heldie twisted her hair so hard now that Maeko feared she might start pulling it out, but she pressed her lips together in a crimson line and said nothing.

"This is very important. Mr. Folesworth is in danger. Captain Garrett's been injured and his family is in danger too. If I don't find Mr. Folesworth all their lives could be destroyed."

Heldie's lower lip trembled and tears welled in her eyes. "Oh!" She slapped her hands down in her lap. "Barman's all upset about my turning you in and that detective keeps pokin' around. Now my brother and his family are in trouble. Is he going to be all right?"

Maeko stared, dumfounded. Most of Heldie's abhorrent speech patterns vanished. The woman was hiding more than she'd guessed. "Garrett's your brother?"

"Half-brother. He all but raised me when our mum died and my dad turned to the opium dens."

"His injury is being cared for," Maeko replied, finding her voice and fighting to hold in the rising excitement of success she could almost taste. "But someone needs to intervene on their behalf or this will destroy him and his family. Please Heldie, help me so I can help them."

Heldie swallowed, her expression rife with skepticism. "What can you do?"

"A lot of things. I can avoid the Lits. I know where Garrett is. I know who's after Mr. Folesworth." A slight exaggeration. "Mr. Folesworth is the only one who can put Garrett's family back together."

She tugged out a kerchief tucked in her bosom and wiped her eyes. "If it'll help them, I'll tell you what I can."

This time, Maeko couldn't hold back a victorious smile. "It most certainly will."

Heldie gestured for her to sit in a rickety chair tucked under the vanity. Maeko was almost too eager to sit still, but she didn't dare offend the woman now by refusing her offer. Sitting in the chair, which creaked even under her slight weight, she gave her full attention to the other woman and even tried for an encouraging smile, though it felt awkward. Whatever it took to guide the conversation where it needed to go.

Heldie cleared her throat. "It weren't but a few days before you showed up. A toff in some fine threads came in. A real swell. You ken the type, creases in all the right places, shiny shoes pokin' out, a tie, and kerchief." She used her hands to point at those remembered creases and shiny shoes on herself, finishing with a tiny tugging motion near her chest where the kerchief would be hanging out of a suit pocket. "He had a briefcase under one arm and a little crate with holes in both ends." Maeko nodded. That would have been Macak. The poor cat had to have gotten here somehow. "He was polite and of a better class than usually comes in here. A bit gloomy though, so I tried to be extra nice to him. Before he left, he asked if I'd do him a kindness."

Heldie eyed Maeko uneasily. Realizing that she had slid to the edge of the chair and was leaning far forward in her eagerness, Maeko forced herself to ease back into the seat again.

After several seconds spent picking at the hem of her cinched up skirt, Heldie continued. "He told me his brother'd be comin' by within a fortnight. Said I'd recognize him easy because they're twins and that I should tell him where to find him. He made me promise not to tell another soul. He tipped real nice too."

She paused and Maeko almost prompted her for his location when she started speaking again. "When that detective came askin' around, I knew this was something serious. I got a bit nervous, but I didn't' tell her anythin'."

Maeko nodded. "This is very serious. He needs to know what's going on, that other people are in danger because of this. You have to help me, Heldie. You have to tell me where to find him. It's the only way I can help him and keep Garrett's family from falling apart." *Or at least dump the bollocks in someone else's hands.*

The woman stared down at her lap, her mouth again set in a tight line.

"This is life or death, Heldie." She pulled out her best pleading look. When all else fails…

Heldie clenched her hands in her skirt. She was smarter than she let on and she apparently had her own secrets to keep, but she was softhearted and worried about her half-brother. Not the person Maeko would have chosen to confide in.

"All right. I'll tell you, but you have to promise you won't tell no one else."

Was there a special hell for liars? If so, it was already too late. She'd secured herself a room there a long time ago, unless there was a special hell for pickpockets too, in which case she'd have conflicting reservations. "I promise."

Still basking in the uneasy glow of this particular victory, Maeko slipped out the back door of the bar. She shut it behind her and turned around—

A man stood to one side, leaning against the wall between her and the open end of the alley, one foot crossed casually over the other. He struck a lucifer to light his cigarette, the flicker of flame illuminating his features. A flurry of images came together in her head from the Airship Tower, at JAHF, and in Cheapside earlier that day. Her heart started to race. Mr. Jacard. How had he found her?

"Maeko. It is Maeko, isn't it?" He tipped his hat with the hand holding the cigarette. "I'm Joel Jacard." He spoke in an easy, conversational tone as he pushed away from the wall with a foot and turned toward her, his movements unhurried. He shook out the match and flicked it aside. His free hand sank into his coat pocket. "I understand you have some information I need. I can pay a tidy sum for it. What do you say? Can we help each other?"

She longed to trust him, to tell him everything and let him deal with it, but, as best she could figure, he had the most to gain from Lucien Folesworth's disappearance. It didn't help that Hatchet-face's words popped into her head when he tipped his hat to her. Chaff said she had good instincts. This wasn't a good time to start doubting them.

"I don't want your tin." She took a step back and glanced to the side, taking quick measure of the distance between him and the opposite wall of the alley.

"And I was going to play nice," he said with unconvincing regret.

His hand moved to a different pocket and drew something out, something that glinted in the sallow light from a gas-lamp at the end of the alley. The way he held it made her mouth go dry and the click as he cocked back the hammer validated her fear. She continued backing up, wanting nothing more than to stay away from the ready weapon. He moseyed after her, looking down at the gun as he turned it in his hand, as if admiring the finish.

"You see, a dear friend of mine has gone missing and his family..." his gaze jumped up, fixing her with a piercing look, "...is dead. Detective Emeraude, she says you know who did it and where they are. Says you're hiding them." He smirked and ran his index finger over the trigger. "She told me to stay out of it, but she can't seem to keep a hold on you, can she? Neither can the Lits."

She backed into the wall and cast about for somewhere to go from there. The ashbin filled in the other side of the alley, cold steel narrowing her options. Her palms felt hot and sweaty compared to the cold damp of the rough wall against her back. Terror sent a flush of blood to her face.

"Perhaps you're that clever, but I think they simply haven't been persuasive enough." He continued to advance, flicking away the ash from his cigarette, the gun now pointed at the ground. "I've had enough of the cat and mouse game. You're going to tell me where they are?"

She shook her head.

He raised the gun, aiming at her right shoulder. She stepped to the left and he shifted his aim down to her right hand. She jerked it out of the line of fire and he moved it in so the barrel pointed at her abdomen. Her stomach turned and she hugged her arms around her middle as she moved away again, pressing into the corner. He kept the gun aimed just to her right, pinning her in the corner as effectively as if he had built a fence around her. With cruel nonchalance, he raised the gun and walked forward until the barrel touched the brick next to her ear. A whimper escaped her. She flinched away from it, her breath coming in frantic little pants.

When she had stared up the barrel of Em's gun, she hadn't felt this paralyzing fear. Em was a businesswoman, for all her jaded temper. Something about this man reminded her of Hatchet-face. The same unpredictable, not quite sane gleam lit his eyes. Only this man would use a gun instead of his hands to hurt her.

He took a long draw on the cigarette, then tossed it aside and blew the smoke in her face. Her throat tightened, her stomach churning as the stale smelling smoke stung her eyes and nose. Then, he rested the hand holding the gun on her shoulder and swiveled it so the barrel pointed into her ear. She sucked in a breath, wincing. He took her chin in his other hand and turned her to face him. His fingers were soft, a toff's hands. His eyes shone bright and feverish. A smile lifted the ends of his neatly trimmed moustache.

"You're not so fierce. If you trembled any harder you'd shake yourself apart."

I'm just a rat. I don't matter. A tear slid down her cheek. *Please, let me be invisible again.* She tried to pull her chin away and his grip tightened.

"I almost expected you to be oily, the way you slip away from everyone, but you're not, are you? You'd be a comely little bird if you let your hair grow and put on a proper dress. With your exotic looks you'd fetch a fine price at any brothel."

Never.

He brushed the barrel tip along the line of her cheekbone and licked his lips. She swallowed back a rush of burning bile. Throwing up on him might be reason enough for him to shoot her.

I'm not ready to hold up a stone. She clenched her hands tighter around her abdomen, trying to stop her shaking. It was useless.

"You don't talk much, though, do you?"

For the first time in her life, she wanted to talk. She wanted to ask why he was doing this, to keep him busy long enough to think up a way out, but her throat refused to make any sound more coherent then a tiny moan. She managed to stare back at him, trying to find the well of defiance that would keep her from sinking down into a shuddering, weeping ball the way she wanted to.

His smile broadened with manic delight. "I see. I wish I had more time. I'd love to play this game with you for a while, but I really must find the ones responsible for this tragedy."

His words gave her pause. Could she have been wrong? Was he trying to avenge his partner's family? She managed a small shake of her head. "They didn't do it." It came out a strained whisper.

"What do you care? Someone has to take the blame."

Someone has to... She stared at him. The woman and child lying on the floor of the flat rose up in her mind. She had been right. The thwarted partner taking matters into his own hands. "You killed them."

She thought he would deny it, wanted him to, really. She very much wanted him to give her some convincing proof that he was only a concerned friend and partner.

His eyes were wide and wild, at odds with his nonchalant tone. "Convinced of that, are you?"

"You were more interested in Macak than the dead woman and her child at the tower." She muttered it under her breath and gave a slow nod. "Mr. Folesworth's death would make you owner of Clockwork Enterprises and let you reopen weapon negotiation with the Lits."

"You're smart. Too bad you won't live to put those brains to use." He took a deep breath and let it out as if releasing a great burden. "I didn't want to hurt them. Feels good to tell someone that. I hired some bludger to do it, but he didn't show. I had to handle it myself."

Hatchet-face. "He was nicked by the Lits."

A flicker of surprise in his wild eyes and a bigger grin. "You're the bird that set him free? I owe you my gratitude. He's out there now, looking to finish the job for me. It's only a matter of time."

If there were any justice in the world, the two would end up cellmates. They deserved each other.

He traced the barrel tip along the side of her jaw then down her neck, coming to a stop at the hollow of her throat. He pressed it in hard. She jerked back into the wall to escape the pain of flesh pinched between bone and steel. When her mouth opened with a small cry, he hooked his thumb over her bottom teeth, yanking her head forward and jamming the barrel in harder still. She bit down, tasted blood. He didn't flinch, didn't let go. Another tear ran down her cheek and her stomach heaved against the force of her will as his blood trickled over her tongue.

He leaned close, cigarette-tainted breath filling her nose. "You need to start talking. Now."

The pub door swung open with a sharp screech and Heldie stepped out. Joel let go of Maeko's jaw and twisted to look over his shoulder. She shoved him with all the force of her terror. He slammed into the wall with a grunt and Heldie's red-rimmed eyes popped wide. She pushed him back toward Maeko.

A small form dropped from above. A flash of brass. Macak wrapped his legs around the toff's head, digging claws into his face, then sprang away. Taking advantage of his surprise, Maeko kicked out, hooking behind his knee with her foot, and swept it forward. He fell and she bolted, spitting to get the taste of his blood out of her mouth. Cold sweat broke out on her forehead and her stomach heaved again, threatening to interrupt her escape with a round of vomiting. She fought the sickness down, snatched up Macak and ran. A muffled bang sounded as she rounded the corner. The sound of Heldie slamming the door as she rushed back inside? She hoped so. You never looked back.

Her legs and lungs burned with the strain of more running, her reserves wearing down, but she forced herself on, sprinting as far and fast as she could with Macak clutched to her chest.

You were supposed to take care of him, Tomoe. Not that she minded his assistance, but how had he gotten back to the pub?

There were no sounds of pursuit, no gunshots. She didn't stop until her lungs screamed for air, then she stumbled into a building, leaning against it to catch her breath. She spit again. The salty tang of his blood stuck to her tongue.

The sky had turned leaden gray, the color of the soot that belched out of the many factories. It smelled of soot too, and of cold wet streets and waste. She shivered, not as much from cold as from the knowledge, confirmed by the encounter she'd just escaped, that she was plunging down deeper into the mess with every passing minute. At what depth did death wait?

I should have listened to Chaff.

Macak squirmed in her arms and she set him down. She rubbed at the spot where Jacard had pushed the gun in, feeling the tenderness of bruised flesh. Why did she have to be right about him? He'd hired Hatchet-face to do the deed, but who else was in on it? Were there Lits in on it? Or had he taken the action on his own? If she listened to pirate propaganda, no Lits could be trusted, but she knew better. No one could be trusted.

A meow drew her attention.

She crouched down and stroked the cat's head. "How'd you get away from Tomoe? Did you come back here looking for me? Troublemaker. You'd make a fine street rat."

Macak accepted the attention for a second, then trotted a few feet away, looked back at her and meowed again.

"You want me to follow you?"

He took another couple steps then paused again and looked at her.

"Well, you are pointed the right direction."

She wiped at her damp cheeks and began to walk, following the cat toward JAHF. Heldie's imperfect directions put Mr. Folesworth hiding in one of the warehouses southeast of JAHF, near where Hatchet-face had taken her. She didn't like going that way because she didn't know the back streets around that section of the waterfront well and mostly because she feared the scarred murderer might be haunting the back alleys, especially if he were making headway on his own search for Mr. Folesworth. This time of night, there wouldn't be many people around. Still, she had to go there to find Lucian Folesworth.

Naze?

The question came in her mother's voice. Why? Why did she even want to find Lucian? What would she do if she found him? Did she care that much about Ash? Could he care about her? They were from such different worlds. Could a street rat find a place in his world?

She could hear her own voice declaring, "I'm not a rat." *What am I then?*

It started to rain then, the kind of drenching downpour that soaked a person through before they hardly

realized it was coming down. The upside of that was
that anyone trying to follow her would have trouble
being discreet because the night streets cleared of all
but a few stubborn or desperate folk. The downside was
that she would have to work harder at hiding from Lit
patrols with so few people out...and the pervasive cold
began to creep in as clothes not yet completely dry from
the last rain gradually became saturated.

Macak shook himself every few steps for a time then
gave up, letting the downpour pummel him whenever
he couldn't find adequate overhang to shelter him.

Determined to get some good out of the situation,
Maeko stopped, tipped her head back and opened her
mouth. She let rain fall on her tongue and rinsed it
around, cleansing the last traces of Joel's blood away,
then spit it out and resumed walking.

Passing in front of JAHF without notice made her
feel clever until she remembered that they were understaffed. It was probably the least likely place to run into
a patrol. Beyond that, she found herself following Macak
along a path not much different from the one she had
gone down with Hatchet-face, and the chill of the wet
was enhanced by the icy prickle of remembered fear.

Why had she come out here alone? No one even
knew where she was, which didn't bode well if she got
into trouble.

But who could she have told?

If she'd given in to Chaff's questioning and told him
what she meant to do, he would have tried to talk her
out of it, perhaps going as far as using physical restraint.
He'd done that once before and she hadn't spoken to
him for days afterward. At the very least, he would have
had her followed despite his promise not to. All of which
suddenly seemed like great reasons to have told him.
He thought her crazy for not turning her back on the
whole mess, regardless of what role she played in it, an

assessment she was starting to agree with. As reckless as he could be sometimes, he knew when to back out of a situation, and she couldn't imagine anyone she would rather have at her side right then.

Ash, assuming he would even speak to her after their last exchange, might have insisted on coming along had she told him and he didn't have the right experience to thrive on the streets. Besides, his presence would have been a distraction. She would have worried about him and about what he thought of her. She didn't have to worry about him now. With his father injured and not fit to travel, he would have gone back to her mother's house in Chelsea and would probably stay there so long as he didn't know where to find his brother.

Her mother was never an option.

At least alone, she didn't have to worry about someone else getting hurt, except Macak, who at least had the sense to stay in the shadows as much as possible.

She spotted two Literati officers walking the streets and ducked into the shadows of a building to watch. Macak stood under her, taking advantage of the rain block she provided. The Lits went along in careful silence, peering down the many cross streets. They appeared to be looking for something or someone in particular rather than running a routine patrol.

Hatchet-face, perhaps?

She shuddered and moved out, following at a distance, her heartbeat speeding up with the effort of not making any sounds or movements that might draw attention.

They stopped at an intersection and she ducked back into deeper shadows to wait, chewing her abused lip. The one on the right made a silent gesture, indicating a direction and they continued their cautious search. Macak trotted to the same intersection and turned the opposite direction. She slipped along behind him with all the silence of the rat they named her.

She slowed then, looking around for the entrance, a door almost hidden behind a stack of old crates. The nearest gas-lamps at the corner did little to light her way in the rain. Several stacks of crates stood outside the buildings on both sides of the street, hulking forms in the darkness. The door she needed should be close by, but in the dark and with heavy drizzle obscuring her vision, she found it hard to see much of anything. Whoever the Lits were looking for, she doubted they would ever find them in this.

Macak's tail went up and he started trotting toward a stack of crates across the street. Maeko watched him. Then the cat jumped, twisting around to face her for a second before bolting up the stack of crates and in through a cracked window.

Someone grabbed her from behind and pulled her back. She stifled a scream when something cold and sharp pressed against her throat. Even with the drenching rain, the rotting sour smell of the muscular body constricting around her made her stomach clench and her head spin.

"I told you I'd find you," Hatchet-face crooned.

One arm snaked around her, pinning her arms to her sides and squeezing tight. He didn't leave her enough freedom to maneuver, and the knife pressed into her neck made her reluctant to try.

His breath rasped harsh in her ear and his muscles trembled either with excitement or with the chill of the same drenching rain that soaked her. The blade slipped on her wet skin. The sudden sting of a small cut elicited a gasp from her and she pressed into him to get away from the weapon. His arm tightened, taking in slack.

She could scream. The Lits might be close enough still to hear. They weren't going to give her another chance to escape, though. After the last slip, they would know better than to leave her unwatched in the cells.

Besides, if Hatchet-face intended to kill her, screaming might encourage him to hurry up and finish the job.

If I live through this, I swear I'll go straight to Whitechapel.

Her muscles continued to shake with cold, fear, and exhaustion. Her nerves buzzed with panic. The world around her tilted in her vision and it was taking more energy than she had left to come up with a calm coherent plan. Screaming might be the extent of her capabilities at this point. She had to try something.

"I met…" It was hard to speak with the blade against her throat. She managed to shift her neck a hair away. "I met Joel Jacard. I never took you for a Literati dog. You enjoy begging for his scraps?"

"I work for whoever pays," Hatchet-face said. "Not too late for you to join me. Say the word and I'll cut you in on the take. Otherwise, I'll just cut you." His tone said he would be content either way.

He adjusted the knife, cutting into her skin again. She flinched back harder against him, the revulsion of the contact bringing the burn of bile up in the back of her throat again. The officer's he'd killed getting out of JAHF passed through her mind.

"What if his partner was willing to pay you more?"

Hatchet-face was quiet. The knife eased away from her throat a fraction. Maeko screamed. His free hand clamped on her upper arm with bruising force and the blade pressed in, digging into one of the prior shallow cuts. Tears sprung to her eyes and streamed down her cheeks.

Hatchet-face laughed. "Who's going to help you here, rat?"

He didn't know the officers were nearby. The knowledge provided a glimmer of dubious hope. She almost screamed again, but the press of the blade, a cool promise of more than just pain, increased enough that she didn't dare do so much as swallow. Her shaking was bad enough now that it alone made the edge dig deeper.

A heavy thud made her flinch and Hatchet-face slumped, sliding to the ground. The blade cut a track across her neck and bit deep into her shoulder before it fell free of his hand. She spun around and grabbed her shoulder, holding the wound.

Standing over Hatchet-face and holding a heavy brass candelabra stained with blood was a man who, if one looked past his rain soaked ragged state, fit Em's description of Lucian Folesworth in every detail down to the odd little clockwork ring he wore on his right hand. He had deep shadows under his eyes, the dark turning them into black hollows. His hair stuck out, a touch unkempt, though the rain was slicking it down, and his fine togs were dirty and rumpled, as if he'd been sleeping in them.

Beside him stood Macak, looking quite pleased with himself.

The pain of the cut and a wave of overwhelming relief numbed her thoughts. Warm blood seeped between her fingers, mixing with the cold wet rain.

The man stared with wide eyes at the object in his hands as if it had assaulted Hatchet-face of its own malicious will. Wrenching his gaze away from the sinister candelabra, he looked at her, or at least at her covered shoulder. "You're hurt."

She looked at Hatchet-face, crumpled in a heap between them. A heavy flow of blood spread over the back of his head from a split in the flesh.

"Is he dead?" Her voice sounded strange, as if coming from across a great distance. The buildings still tilted around her.

The man drew in a sharp breath, alarmed by the notion, and looked down at the still figure. Just when she caught the slow rise and fall of Hatchet-face's chest, her rescuer sighed with relief.

"No. He's alive."

"Give me that." She held her bloodied hand out. "I'll kill him."

The man shook his head, drawing the candelabra in close to his chest. "Have you ever killed anyone?"

"No." She knew she couldn't kill anyone, even Hatchet-face, but the sharp stabbing pain in her shoulder fed her hatred for him.

"Then I'm not letting you start now."

She clamped her hand back over the wound. "Who do you think you are, my father?"

"I'd be surprised if you know who your father is. I feel it is my obligation to step into that role for a decision with such grave consequences."

The sound of two pairs of feet slapping on the wet street reached them.

"A few Lits passed by here a short time ago," she said, shifting her feet now with the urgent need to get out of sight. "That's probably them."

He looked at the hand covering the deep cut and the blood seeping down into her shirt, then glanced over his shoulder at a door standing ajar behind stack of crates. He tugged off his rings, jacket, and the tie hanging loose around his neck. "Take these and the cat through that door. Keep quiet. Don't get into anything. I'll take care of this."

"Are you Lucian Folesworth?"

He stared hard at her then, his hand shifting on the candelabra as if he considered using it as a weapon again.

"Wait for me. I have questions for you."

The approaching Lits were getting close. Macak darted in through the door. She took a few unsteady steps to follow then stopped, turning back to Lucian. "You might wipe the blood off his knife or they'll wonder whose it is."

He gave her a shrewd look and bent to the task.

She slipped through the door, shutting it softly behind her seconds before the officers charged down the street. Leaning back against the cold metal, she closed her eyes, grimacing with the brutal sting of the wound. Her heart still hammered in her chest, the wound throbbing in time, and a few quiet tears ran down her cheeks. She sank to the floor, still trembling while Macak pressed his damp body against her leg, and listened to the voices outside.

"What happened here?" a man's voice demanded.

Before Lucian could answer, another voice exclaimed, "It's bloody Dobson!"

Officer Wells. She recognized his voice. They must have taken him off the watch at JAHF after she and Ash escaped.

"How'd this happen?" the other officer asked with the heavy tone of assumed authority.

"I stayed late to do inventory in that warehouse there and I heard noise outside." Lucian sounded every bit as shaken as she felt. "I brought the candelabra with me. I'm not a big chap as you can see and nights alone here make me nervous," he explained. "This man attacked me. I reacted. I didn't intend to harm anyone."

"Nice reflexes," Wells commented. "We thought we heard a woman scream."

Lucian cleared his throat and chuckled, convincingly self-conscious. "Yes, I'm afraid that was me."

"You're lucky, Sir," the other office said. "We've been hunting this bludger for a while. He's extremely dangerous. Almost a shame you didn't kill him," he added in a lower voice.

Maeko nodded agreement.

"Heavy blighter," Wells muttered. He grunted and she could imagine the slim young officer trying to heft Hatchet-face's unconscious weight.

"Can I be of assistance?"

Lucian's voice was tentative, the voice of a man who wanted to be refused, but whose sense of propriety demanded that he make the offer. For all appearances, he seemed a good sort and she had to give him credit for his handling of Hatchet-face.

"This one's dangerous. We'll take it from here. Good evening to you, Sir."

She didn't stay to listen to them grunt and groan as they hauled Hatchet-face away. Instead, she rose unsteadily and moved out into the dark building. It appeared to be a storage building, with shelves of machine parts lining the walls and an overflow of crates and various items stacked in rows on the floor. It was nippy, at least for someone soaked to the bone, and smelled of grease and metal shavings. Beyond a tall row of crates, a flickering light beckoned.

With her hand still pressed over the worst part of the cut, she shuffled toward the light. A table stood tucked in just around the edge of the row of crates. Behind the table sat a solitary chair and several blankets were laid neatly out in a makeshift bed on the floor in the shadows farther back.

Does he actually make his bed every day or does he never sleep?

The door opened and she heard someone enter. The footsteps were light and refined, not heavy or scuffing like those of men out working late on a miserable night. Confident that Lucian returned alone, she continued her perusal of the makeshift living area with Macak's accompaniment. He sniffed around, looking as if he couldn't quite figure out what she found interesting about it all.

She set the rings and tie on the table and crouched down. Pain shot through the wound, making her wince when she held a hand out to Macak. He trotted over to her, his articulated metal leg clicking on the hard floor, and pressed his head into the offered hand, purring enthusiastically.

"Thanks for bringing help, mate."

The rain had cleaned his soft fur. Beneath all that dirt and grime, he had a striking black and white coat.

"Handsome boy," she murmured.

The cat's unrestrained adoration, rubbing his face into her palm repeatedly, brought a weak smile to her lips.

"It looks as if we have a lot to discuss, such as how you came to be traveling with my cat." Lucian stepped around them and set the candelabra down on the table.

"You shouldn't have let him run loose." She turned to peer up at him, wincing when the motion sent sharp pain through the cut.

The chastisement earned her a bemused smirk. "I lost him near a pub several nights ago. I've gone back every night to search for him."

She nodded to herself. A man who would go to such trouble for a cat couldn't be all bad. Of course, this cat was probably worth a lot more than most cats. "If only you could talk, Macak," she murmured. "What stories you must have."

"Unquestionably," Lucian said.

She drew away from the cat and tried to stand. Her balance failed and Lucian reached a hand out, catching her arm to keep her upright. She placed a hand on the table and nodded. He let go of her and took a few seconds to put his rings back on. When he came to the tie, he stared at it for several seconds and left it there. He did pull the jacket back on, fussily straightening the wrinkled front. After running a hand through his wet hair, as if that might improve something, he finally met her eyes again.

"Before I delve into the mystery of the young lady who has entered my lair," he said, sweeping his arm with a dramatic flourish to indicate their surroundings, "perhaps we should see to that wound."

He dug around in a corner and drew out a clean white shirt. When he gestured her closer she shook her head, already dreading the pain. He gave a stern look, stepping back into that unsolicited fatherly role and pointed at the floor in front of him. Reluctant, she stepped up to him and took her hand away from the wound. With a rather unconvincing scowl, he dipped the clean shirt in a cup on the table and dabbed at the wound through the split in her shirt. It burned.

She twisted away. "What is that?"

"Brandy."

"It burns."

"I'm afraid it's that or the absinthe. I wasn't planning to tend knife wounds tonight. Now stand still."

Clenching her teeth, she offered the shoulder again and gave a curt nod. He resumed his work, cleaning the area around the cut so he could see how bad it was. She took hold of the table with both hands and gripped tight, digging the little bit of fingernail she still had into the wood to keep from pulling away from his ministrations.

"What were you planning to do, drink yourself into oblivion," she asked, taking note of the several bottles upon the table.

"Not that it's any of your business, but the thought had crossed my mind." She wavered on her feet and he placed a stabilizing hand on her shoulder then pointed with his narrow nose to the bruise forming in the hollow of her throat below the shallow cuts there. "What happened there?"

"Some friendly bloke tried to push a gun barrel through my neck."

He raised his brows, pausing in his cleaning. "Does that have anything to do with why you're here?"

She nodded.

He began to dab at the wound again. "Perhaps we should back up a little and start with how you know who I am?"

Pleased to have some distraction, she gave him a thorough account of how she had come upon Macak and lost him again. She told him about escaping JAHF with Hatchet-face, which earned her sharp scowl of disapproval. However, he did compliment her on her apparent resourcefulness, which earned him some grudging respect. When she got to the part about arriving at his flat in Airship Tower, her throat clenched and a staggering dread swept through her.

Did he even know about his family?

Maeko stared at Macak who sat on the chair industriously grooming his chest. His tongue slipped down onto the metal of his false leg and he drew back. With his tongue still sticking out, he gave the metal appendage a disgusted look before resuming his bath on the other leg.

Lucian finished his doctoring, tying a bandage made of strips of the fine shirt, which he had disassembled with a small knife, pressing down tight around her shoulder to keep pressure on the deepest part of the cut. She relished the pain. It was easier to bear than the hollow misery swelling in her chest.

"There. That should do it for now." He considered his handiwork and nodded to himself. "You were just getting to my..."

He trailed off and she looked up to find him staring at her. Only then did she notice that tears streamed down her cheeks. She stared back at him. How was she supposed to tell him his wife and child were dead? This shouldn't be her responsibility.

"Did I hurt you?"

When she shook her head, his brow furrowed. Then, all at once, the color drained from his face, making the circles under his eyes stand out even darker. Macak scurried out of the way when he sank onto the chair.

"My wife? My daughter?"

She could see in his eyes that he already suspected the truth. Still, she shook her head, trying to deny it for him, the tightness in her throat painful enough now to rival the knife wound.

Is it harder to lose everything when you start with so much?

"Please. You must tell me."

Her legs felt weak. She moved back to sit on a crate and stared hard at the one burning candle. With a sick feeling in her gut, she told him about the dead woman and little girl she had seen lying in the room. He made her describe them in detail, needing to verify every feature of the two bodies.

"I never thought he would hurt them." His voice cracked.

He put his elbows on the table and dropped his head into his hands, his fingers clenching in his hair. She watched uncomfortably as his shoulders started to shake and small sounds of misery emerged from behind his hands.

Listening to his sobs made her tears dry up. Something, perhaps some flicker of her mother's empathy that had snuck into her when she wasn't being diligent, made her get up and place a hand on his shoulder. One of his hands clutched at hers, holding it tight while he cried. The contact felt awkward and somehow wonderful at the same time, as if someone actually needed her. She stood there, letting him take what comfort he could from the contact for as long as he wanted it.

When he finally let go and wiped at his eyes, she crouched down next to the table and looked up at him.

"You know your partner did this, don't you?"

He nodded, his face a sunken, pale mask of despair.

He laid one hand on the table and she took it in hers, a gesture that earned her his full attention.

"There is more I need to tell you then, and a lot of lives hang on what we do next." She assumed at this point that she would be a part of whatever happened next. Over her head or not, she was inescapably wrapped up in this now.

This Detective Emeraude, she said Thaddeus hired her?" Lucian, his eyes rimmed in red and his sharp nose an unflattering shade of pink, had collected himself enough to listen to the rest of her story, stopping her several times to clarify details.

"Yes. If Thaddeus is your brother, that is," Maeko replied, stroking the warm comforting ball of cat curled up and purring on her lap. He joined her when she sat down on the crate and his reassuring presence helped her recount a more accurate run of events to Lucian than she had given anyone else. It was only fair to give him all of the facts, since he already lost so much, and his next actions would help decide the outcome of the convoluted mess.

"A woman detective," he muttered to himself. "How out of character. Thaddeus never had much respect for professional women. I suppose he didn't get my telegram if he hired someone to find me." His eyes lit upon her and he shrugged. "It seems I owe you some explanation. I came here to hide from Joel. As you probably know, he is my business partner in Clockwork Enterprises."

Her stomach clenched and a lump formed in her throat. It was easy to forget who he was in this setting, but this man could sell his smile for more money than she would see in her lifetime. His inventions included numerous remarkable gadgets designed to do every-thing from mixing ingredients in a kitchen to feeding massive forges in the some of the big foundries. He was the man behind the Clockwork Enterprises brand she saw everywhere.

More importantly, helping this man could be the key to finally having enough money to free her mother.

On the less positive side, his company had backed the Literati, helping them face off against and crush the last rising Luddite movement. From there, with the support of many such wealthy benefactors, the Lits had gained enough political and social momentum to win control of the city government, absorbing the City of London Police into their own team of law enforcement officers and pushing out the jurisdiction of the Metro-politan Police Service. Supporting Lits didn't make him a friend, but perhaps this turn of events might make him an ally.

Macak licked her hand with his rough tongue, re-minding her to keep petting him. She obliged. "I don't understand how someone like you ends up hiding in a warehouse. Why did Mr. Jacard turn on you? Was it the weapons deal?"

He gave her an appraising look. "You know more than I would expect for someone in your position."

She shrugged. Let him think her clever and worldly. He would be less inclined to try to deceive her that way.

"Sometimes all status earns you is more powerful enemies." He leaned back in his chair and stared at the candle. "A few months ago, a man came to my office and offered to buy my company. When I refused, he became enraged. He threatened to have me put down for my insolence and assured me that he had the means to make it happen. I had him removed from the facil-ity, but I was shaken by his conviction, so I told Joel about the incident. Joel expressed concern, worrying over what would become of my family and the company if something were to happen to me. He convinced me to have a will written up leaving him the company in the event of my untimely death, with a regular support stipend provided to my wife and daughter."

Tears came to Lucian's eyes and he closed them. For a few minutes, he rubbed at his temples and she could see his jaw working as he struggled not to break down. She stroked Macak and waited. When he had his emotions in check, he continued.

"I didn't realize what a fool I was until I saw the man who offered to buy the company staggering drunk outside of a pub as my coach passed by one night. He wore common clothes, not the fine attire he'd worn to our meeting, and appeared quite shocked to see me. When I pressed him, he admitted that he had been paid handsomely by Joel to threaten me as part of some elaborate joke.

"I didn't want to believe it. Joel and I have been friends as long as I can remember. I couldn't let it go, though. With a careful bit of eavesdropping and investigation, I discovered not a joke, but an elaborate plot by him to arrange an *accident* in the factory. He wanted it done quickly so he could resurrect the Literati weapons contract I vetoed and, to balance that with a show of the company's compassionate side, he would unveil and take credit for another invention I'd been working on."

"The clockwork leg?"

He smiled at the cat. "Yes, the clockwork prosthesis. I was devastated and, frankly, terrified. I didn't know what to do or who to trust, so I took my weapons sketches, the blueprints for the leg, and Macak, and snuck away one night, intending to hide out until I found out who I could trust and prove what Joel was planning. I never thought…" His voice cracked and he swallowed. "Joel always fancied my wife. They got on famously and he coddled little Elizabeth as if she were his own daughter. I never thought he would hurt them, especially if Anna knew nothing of my whereabouts. I would have brought them with me if I had even suspected."

While Lucian battled another wave of emotion, she focused on Macak, pondering a heart shaped patch of black fur on the back of one white leg. She closed her eyes, just for a moment, and fell asleep.

Macak made a squeak of protest when Lucian ejected him from her lap and prodded Maeko to her feet. She barely woke as he guided her to the blankets at the back of the room.

"You won't be able to move your neck soon if I let you sleep there," he said.

She muttered a few weak protests and he used steady pressure on her good shoulder to drive her down to the bedroll. She fell asleep again almost before he finished throwing a blanket over her.

When he woke her later, pain nagged at her and deep weariness tried to hold her down in the welcome embrace of much needed sleep. Lucian propped her up in the chair and handed her a cup. She took it, groggily raising it to her lips, and choked when licorice flavored fire burned down the back of her throat. She coughed. Spears of pain shot through her wound. It felt hot and swollen under the bandage.

"Sorry about that." He snatched the cup and set it down. "I thought it might help you wake up."

"Trying to kill a person does tend to make them more alert," she rasped, her throat still on fire.

"Merely a swallow of absinthe. I'm certain you won't die from it." He held a white shirt out to her, no longer wearing one beneath his frock coat. "Here. You can't go running around the city covered in blood. This will be much too big, but it is clean." He frowned at the garment. "Well, cleaner and more intact than yours."

"It's nicer than most of the togs I've worn," she answered, but didn't move to accept it. "I'm not leaving. I need your help."

"On the contrary, my dear girl, I believe it is I who needs your help." He set the shirt on a corner of the table and placed one hand on a cloth satchel beside it. "This contains detailed copies of the blueprints for the clockwork prosthesis and of my new will. I've been working on them since I arrived here. I was going to entrust these to a woman who helped me before, but, since you knew where to find me, I see my trust in her was misplaced."

"Don't be upset with Heldie, Mr. Folesworth. I don't think she told anyone else. She's just a bit simple."

He chuckled at that and she glared at him, daring him to call her simple. His amused expression faded, and a sad smile took its place. "I apologize. You may be poor, but you are positively not simple. I think the word to describe you best would be unexpected, though remarkable is also in the running." He regarded her with such a sorrowful look then that she had to look away, her tear-blurred gaze sliding down to the satchel. "I must apologize for my appalling manners. I never even asked your name."

"Maeko," she murmured.

"Just Maeko."

Shame burned in her cheeks as she nodded.

"Japanese?"

She looked up at him, surprised.

"I've always been fascinated by other cultures. I suspected, from your features, that you had a good helping of Asian blood in you." He coughed and nodded to himself. "I need someone to take these copies to this Detective Emeraude and bring her here or at least tell her where to find me. Can I ask you to be that someone?"

What he asked wouldn't be easy. Searching for the detective without ending up in Literati hands would be difficult and she would have to think fast to get the woman to listen to her after their last encounter. Still, if Em came and spoke with Lucian, he could tell her about Joel and clear Ash's family. That was why she had come searching for him, wasn't it?

A prickle of trepidation climbed up the back of her neck when she nodded. "Yes, sir. I'll do it."

His face relaxed, relief soothing some of the depth from the lines that etched his brow. "I have the originals hidden away with my weapon sketches, but these still mustn't fall into the wrong hands."

She nodded. Her empty stomach churned. "You should know your good friend Joel is looking for you and for the pirates accused of murdering your family. I'm afraid he's on the right trail. He did this—" she pointed to the bruise from the gun barrel "—and he hired that bludger you hit with the candelabra to find you."

Lucian bowed his head as if the weight of his thoughts was becoming too much to carry. "My mistakes have had an unfortunate impact on your life. I'll do what I can to see that you're compensated when this is over."

"I could use some tin." At his look, she said, "Not for me. It's for my mum."

He gazed at her for a minute then nodded. "I'll see what I can do, but right now I can only give you money for transportation…and the shirt off my back." He added the last with a wry smirk.

When he handed her the shirt this time, she took it and went around a line of crates to change, biting her lip against the pain in her shoulder. The shirt hung loose on her. She had to roll up the sleeves, but he was slender enough that the top button at least hit high enough to be decent. She walked back around and Lucian stared at her for a bit before shaking his head.

"Such a pretty young lady shouldn't be running about in men's clothes."

Widow Jameson had said almost the same thing, though it was the memory of Ash saying she was too pretty to pass as a boy that made her duck her head to hide the burn of embarrassment behind her hair. Then she recalled with a stronger flush that she no longer had enough hair to hide behind. Ash. He probably hated her now, if he ever liked her in the first place.

"You don't have to sweet-talk me, Mr. Folesworth," she replied, a cynical edge in her tone. "I'm helping you because it'll help the people I care about."

He tilted his head to the side and regarded her, her bitterness rolling over him like a light mist. "I wasn't cajoling. In all honesty, if you grew out your hair and put on a dress I think you'd find that most young men would agree with me."

She shuddered. "Joel said something similar."

His expression darkened. "That's a discussion for another day, perhaps. Here." He handed her a coin pouch. "There should be more than enough in there to get you around the city a few times while not enough to draw attention. I do hate to put this burden on you. However, since you know what this detective looks like and I daren't be seen until I have protection, I don't see that I have many other options."

She gave him a discerning look. "Why didn't you go to the Lits for help?"

He exhaled, his shoulders sinking, and leaned on the table. "For all that I supported their rise to power, I'm afraid I don't know who among them I can trust. Joel has many allies in Literati organizations and my refusal of the weapons contract hasn't made me popular with them. I fear that, without sufficient proof of his guilt, they may be as much of a threat to me as he is. For now, I put my life in the hands of a lovely young lady masquerading as a common street rat."

She took the pouch and tucked it in a pocket, then lifted the satchel from the table and hung the strap over her good shoulder. "It's no masquerade, Mr. Folesworth."

Macak jumped on the table and walked to the nearest edge. He meowed up at her. She smiled and scratched his head. It was hard to leave him again, like tearing off a piece of herself, but she needed to know he was safe. "Don't worry. I haven't forgotten you mate, but you're safer here right now. I'll be back. Promise."

She hurried away, holding back foolish sorrow. After she helped Lucian out of his fix, maybe he'd be willing to let her visit Macak, though she found that hard to imagine.

A street rat dropping by the home of one of the wealthiest men in London? Not likely. Best to move on and forget any of this ever happened.

After opening the door a tiny crack to see if it was clear, she slipped out and hastened away from the building to lessen chances of someone seeing where she had come from. Morning light gave a pale glow to the thick, smelly yellow fog draped over this part of the city like a moldy blanket, rolling in off the water of the Thames a few streets over.

Until she reached more populous streets, she startled at every sound. As soon as she could, she boarded an omnibus, clutching the satchel close, all too aware of how appealing a mark it would be for others of her trade. Jostling in the cramped seats made her wounds hurt and she felt the warm spread of fresh blood seeping from the cut under its makeshift bandage. The smaller cuts on her neck earned her more than one awkward glance, but the collar of the shirt hung too loose and her hair was too short to cover them, so she pretended not to notice. She could hardly get off fast enough at her stop.

As she walked up the street to her mother's house, the exhale of a fancy steamcoach coming around a corner caught her attention. Her nerves crackled and she ducked down alongside a wall at the next house down. A coach that nice was probably passing through, but her pulse still raced with fear, keeping her from leaving the spot.

The door of her mother's house opened just as the steamcoach chugged to a stop out front. Maeko peeked around the corner. Lottie stared at the coach for a second, closing the front door behind her. The door of the coach opened. Lottie set her jaw and walked toward it. Maeko's breath caught in her throat when Joel stepped out, cold sweat rising on the back of her neck. She clutched the strap of Lucian's satchel tight. Did he find out somehow that Garrett was there?

Lottie stopped in his path. "Can I help ye?"

Joel didn't answer immediately. He eyed the house from under the brim of the gray coachman hat in scowling silence and Maeko trembled with the certainty that he would somehow spot her. He finally turned his frown on Lottie.

"A cabman told me he dropped an unusual trio here the other night. A drunken man and two youths—"

Lottie cut him off with a sharp wave of her hand. "Yer barkin' old news, Guv'nor. A private detective was by last evenin' askin' after the same folks. I'll tell ye just what I told 'er. They did come 'ere and the older bloke 'ad a gammy leg. They looked like they was in some kinda trouble. I told 'em they had the wrong 'ouse and sent 'em on their way. Now I've got errands to run if ye don't mind."

Lottie started to step around him and his hand shot out, grabbing her arm in a pinching grip. He yanked her close, putting his face in hers. "I do mind. I have to find them. If they're not here, then where did they go?"

Maeko chewed her lip and twisted the satchel strap in her sweaty grip. Would he dare do anything to Lottie there, in the open, where anyone could see? She'd seen the crazy in his eyes, but there had been a certain calculating shrewdness there as well.

Lottie lifted her chin, staring into those eyes. "I didn't ask 'em and I don't much care long as they stay away from 'ere. I run an 'onest business, so, unless ye gots some togs as need launderin', I suggest ye be on yer way."

Joel glared at her. She winced as the flesh of her arm bulged around his tightening fingers, but continued to hold his gaze. Then he let go, the perfect shapes of his fingers rising red on her pale skin. Lottie sneered at him before stalking away. Maeko held her breath as he stood glowering at the house. When he didn't move, she tucked herself alongside the low wall and focused on breathing soft and shallow. After what seemed an eternity, the steamcoach chugged off down the road. She took a deep breath.

Too close.

She sat for a time until the shaking eased then hurried to the door and slipped into the dim house, tucking her chin to try to hide the visible cuts. A patched blanket hung from the ceiling, sectioning off the back of the main room where she assumed Garrett still rested. Her mother sat in a corner, her fine boned hands working at stitching a hole in another blanket. The door clicked shut. Her head snapped up, her eyes wide, then she breathed a small sigh, the anxious lines in her face fading.

"Sumimasen." Maeko forced an apologetic tone, though it rankled a bit. Right now, she needed to set aside awkwardness with Tomoe. Besides, barging in on someone harboring a wanted man was a daft thing to do. "I should have knocked."

"Yes." Tomoe cast her eyes down. "The cat—"

"I know. He found me. He's safe."

Tomoe looked up in surprise then frowned. "Are you well? You look pale."

Someone stepped around the curtain.

Ash.

Maeko closed her eyes, hiding the giddy rush of relief at knowing he was safe, especially now that she knew both Joel and Em had come so close to finding them. She opened her eyes again, inhaled the rich aroma of something cooking, and reached to pull the satchel off her shoulder. Searing pain ran through the cut in her other shoulder. The room spun. She reached for a table to steady herself and missed.

Tomoe half rose, but Ash was there first, catching her arm. He focused on the wounded shoulder and his eyes widened.

"You're bleeding." The distress in his voice brought a flutter to her stomach.

Did he actually care?

Turning her head, she saw that blood had soaked through the cloth bandage and a line of bright red seeped through the shoulder of the shirt. The room spun again. Ash still held her elbow and she leaned into his hand to keep her balance. He took her chin in his free hand and lifted, turning her head to get a better look. His brow furrowed. His hand moved down then, one finger tracing beneath a cut on her neck. She jerked away, not because it hurt this time, but because it felt shockingly pleasant.

He flushed and pulled his hand back. "What happened?"

"I was attacked in an alley," she replied. "It's nothing."

"Nothing wouldn't still be bleeding."

"Bring her here," Tomoe pointed firmly at one of the chairs next to the little table.

She stood her ground. *No. I won't be beholden to her.*

Ash took hold of her wrist and tugged, gentle but insistent. His cautionary look when she didn't budge said her there was a lot more force in reserve that he would use if necessary. "Don't be stubborn. Let your mum take a look at that. Or do I have to carry you over?"

She relented, knowing she was too weak to put up a fight. He led her to the table and pushed her down into a chair, careful not to touch the injured shoulder in the process, then reached for the satchel. She scowled at him, but let him take it when he scowled as fiercely back, his green eyes flashing a warning. He set the satchel on a pile of folded clothes on a stool in the corner.

"She's your patient now, Ms. Ishida."

Tomoe's gaze homed in on the growing bloodstain with professional scrutiny. She sat in another chair beside Maeko and unbuttoned the top few buttons, pulling the shirt askew to expose the shoulder. Maeko grabbed the front and held it together over her chest for modesty's sake. Tomoe helped adjust the shirt so it wouldn't fall open then turned to the crude bandage.

The torn cloth stuck to part of the wound and Maeko gasped, tears springing to her eyes. Tomoe scowled at the bandage and pursed her lips, the taught expression making a scar that ran at an angle under her nose stand out stark against her skin. She got up and left, returning a few minutes later with a bowl of water. She took a wetted rag from the bowl and laid it, dripping wet, over the bandage.

Maeko shivered as cold water dribbled down her skin under the shirt. She closed her eyes, gritting her teeth against the relentless sting as the water soaked through. A warm hand took hold of hers under the table and squeezed it. She opened her eyes. Ash had moved a chair up to sit on her other side. He smiled encouragement and she closed her eyes again, her chest aching at the fact that he chose to offer her such support even after the mean things they'd said to each other.

Tomoe worked the cloth free a little at a time and made a small hissing sound, not pleased with what she found beneath it. Ash's hand clenched on hers, easing up when Maeko gave him a sharp look. He managed an apologetic smile, though the color had faded from his face. Not fond of the sight of blood, she supposed, though she chose not to look at the wound herself, as much for the pain the movement would cause as for the sudden worm of squeamishness in her stomach.

"This should be properly closed."

Maeko's empty stomach clenched tight and she broke out in a cold sweat. Closed. Stitched. A painful prospect.

"Are you sure? Can't you just wrap it tighter?"

Tomoe didn't answer. She considered the wound for a minute in tightlipped silence then went to rummage around in a concealed cupboard set deep in one wall. She returned with a cup of something and held it out to Maeko.

"Drink this."

Maeko shied away, remembering the burn of the absinthe Lucian had given her. "What is it?"

"It has laudanum drops in it. It will reduce the pain and help you to relax."

Maeko choked down a swallow of the bitter fluid with her mother looking on sternly and felt the faint burn of alcohol in her throat. She started to hand it back. Tomoe stepped away, nodding encouragement. Maeko's stomach churned. Chaff once told her that it was easier to swallow strong liquor if you exhaled first. She blew out, holding her breath so she wouldn't smell it, then poured it down her throat and promptly choked, coughing. So much for that technique.

Tomoe laughed into her hand, glancing over it

almost shyly at Maeko who giggled self-consciously in return. Tomoe smiled, a beautiful expression, even with her scars, and took the cup away then began gathering and laying out the materials she would need to suture the wound. Maeko watched with a growing dread. A person never minded needles much until they were pointed their direction.

Her mother sat down again and her eyes tracked to the smaller cuts across Maeko's throat and the bruise below them. "How did this happen?"

Too many questions would stem from the truth. Maeko retreated to the old sanctuary of silence.

Tomoe wasn't going to let her stay there. "Maeko?" A firmer tone now. A demand with no foundation.

"It doesn't matter," Maeko snapped. "It can't be undone."

Tomoe clenched her jaw, the muscles twitching with suppressed irritation. She began to clean the wound. Maeko's limbs were beginning to feel heavy with the effect of the laudanum, but she still had plenty of power to twist away from the pain. Ash squeezed her hand again and she did her best to stay still, gritting her teeth while Tomoe finished cleaning. When she pressed the needle tip into the angry flesh at the edge of the wound, Maeko jerked away.

Tomoe looked past her, nodding to Ash who released her hand. He slid his chair closer and moved to the edge of it so that he now straddled the back corner of her chair. Sitting between him and her mother with the table in front and the chair back behind, there was no longer room for her to move away. Ash took the wrist of her injured arm in one hand, placing it on the table and pinning it there. He was stronger than she gave him credit for and she couldn't help resenting the restraint. Then he put his other hand against her cheek on the injured side, turning her face away from the wound and the contrasting gentleness of that touch made the flash of resentment fade. When her mother resumed working and she tried to pull away, his grip on her wrist held her firmly in place. The growing sedation of the drug made it even harder to fight him. A whimper rose in her throat and tears burned in her eyes.

"Sorry, Maeko," he murmured.

Grinding her teeth, she turned further away from the pain, tucking her face against his neck. The contact might have proven embarrassing under normal circumstances. In that moment, the smell of him and the warmth of him helped ease the fear. The laudanum lulled her, lessening the sharp sting of the pain.

"Ash." Her lips brushed the skin of his neck when she mumbled his name.

He inhaled. There was a long pause, then, "Yes."

"I didn't mean what I said when…" she trailed off, trying to recall what she had said. Something about him being a prat.

"I know you didn't."

She winced at a sharper pain in the wound and pressed into him, closing her eyes. His thumb brushed her cheek, leaving a line of tingling warmth in its wake.

Tomoe stitched and bandaged the wound with steady practiced hands. What felt like an eternity of tension and pain finally ended. Without those things, it became impossible to fight the floating drowsiness of the laudanum. Maeko remained curled against the warm body next to her. The heaviness in her muscles kept her there and the trembling that plagued her while her mother worked subsided. Peacefulness stole over her. She was aware of Ash moving her hand off the table and setting it in her lap. He left his hand resting on top of hers and she smiled drowsily, pleased to let it stay.

ingers brushed Maeko's cheek. She opened her eyes to find Tomoe gazing down on her. She lay under a blanket on the small couch, though she didn't recall how she'd gotten there. Lucian's bloodstained shirt had disappeared and she now wore a light blue blouse, probably something of her mother's. It fit better than Lucian's shirt, though the feminine pleats and ruffles, while understated, thwarted her efforts at not drawing attention to her gender. That got more difficult with every passing month anyhow. Age had an annoying way of emphasizing the wrong bits.

Someone had set plates and food out on the little table. Lottie sat in one chair. Ash sat in another, staring at his plate as if it held the answers to all the secrets of the world in its chipped surface. She remembered him holding her while her mother tended the wound and until she fell asleep. It wasn't the extraordinary pain of the experience that stuck in her mind and brought a vivid flush to her cheeks, but rather the care in his touch and the comfort she'd taken from it.

So much for trying to pretend she didn't like him.

Tomoe shifted her position, screening Maeko's embarrassment from the view of the two at the table. "You must eat, Maeko-chan, to regain your strength."

Maeko-chan? The affectionate address crashed up

against years of rejection and hurt, chipping away at it. Her throat tightened with memories of a loving if unusual home, a life that ended with screaming and blood. She glanced at her hands, remembering them covered in red.

I couldn't help. Couldn't stop the bleeding or take away the pain. Perhaps, if I could have done something, things would have been different.

She squeezed her eyes shut. Tomoe placed a hand on her arm. It made the misery sharper, but she faced the pain and found something new within it. A whisper of what could be. She opened her eyes and let Tomoe help her up, guiding her to the table with a steadying hand cupped under her elbow. When she was seated, Tomoe took her hand away, leaving a spot of warmth behind.

A shroud of awkward silence hung over the group.

Maeko glanced around at them, puzzled. Perhaps Ash's father wasn't doing well. "How's Captain Garrett?"

"He ate a good meal just a bit ago." Lottie dished pork pie onto her plate as she spoke, as if the question had broken some dining stalemate. "I think he's feeling a bit better."

The serving of the pie released its savory aroma, not an unpleasant thing, but right then Maeko felt weak more than hungry. Laudanum on an empty stomach killed her appetite as sure as a bullet killed a fox.

Several seconds passed in silence. No one other than Lottie took anything to eat. Ash and her mother were watching Maeko.

"What's with you two?"

Ash heaved a sigh and almost met her eyes. "I didn't keep up my end of the deal with your mum, did I? I ditched you and you got hurt."

Tomoe's lips pressed into a thin line, a subtle confirmation.

"Oh rubbish!" Maeko snapped. They both sat back in their chairs and she turned on her mother. "You should know better than to blame Ash for that. I'm not any easier to get along with now than I was when I lived with you. Besides, I'm not a child anymore. It's my job to take care of myself, not his."

A smile tugged at her mother's lips and Maeko was shocked to see pale rose rise in her fair cheeks. Without a word, Tomoe proceeded to serve Maeko and then Ash before serving herself. Ash looked confused. When he glanced askance at Maeko, she started to shrug, but another flash of pain cut the motion short. He cringed in sympathy and the hang of his shoulders said he still felt guilt for her injury, unwilling to accept that he deserved no blame.

"Do you need more laudanum?" Tomoe asked.

Maeko hesitated, blinking back tears the pain brought to her eyes, then shook her head. "No. It makes me tired and I've wasted too much time already."

Tomoe pursed her lips and focused on eating, stabbing at her pie with disturbing ferocity.

Ash swallowed a bite. "What are you planning now?"

She chewed at the bite she'd taken, afraid to swallow while her stomach still threatened to send it back up. How much did she dare say in current company? It was odd enough having her mum here. She'd been on her own too long to abide someone else trying to discourage her from doing what she wanted and, in this case, needed to do, even if only out of concern for her safety. Besides, the more information she gave Tomoe, the more concerned Tomoe would be, and the more likely they would end up in a row about it. She didn't want that.

She finally swallowed the bite, figuring it would gain her no ground to spit it up on the plate. When it didn't come rushing back up, she said, "I need to find someone."

Ash licked at his split lip and stared at her. Rather than press for more information, he set down the hearty bite he'd been lifting to his mouth. "Can I help?"

She looked at him, at his bruised face and swollen lip, injuries he'd suffered following her around. Then she met his eyes and admired the willingness she saw there. Regardless of what she had to do or where she had to go, the look said he wanted to help. She held back a smile. No point offering too much encouragement, though going in search of Em with him at her side had considerable appeal, especially now that she had her wounded shoulder to consider.

Something of her thoughts must have come through in her expression, because Ash grinned in triumph. "It's settled then. We'll get going after you've eaten something."

Settled?

What if something else happened to him because she let him come? She opened her mouth to object, then noticed that Tomoe had stopped attacking her food like it still needed killing.

"It would be nice to have some help," Maeko said, watching her mother.

Tomoe smiled at her plate.

Maeko got up and walked over to the satchel still sitting in the corner, feeling the eyes of the others follow her until she slipped behind the curtain. She knelt next to the camp bed and started to set the satchel beside it. Garrett's eyes opened, clear and bright. He would heal well.

She dug into the satchel and pulled out the blueprints, holding them up for him to see. "Are these what you wanted?"

Bright enthusiasm lit his eyes. Like a man in thrall, he reached up with one hand and began to run a finger over the first drawing. His finger paused occasionally, his eyes moving across the page as he read over notes on the document.

"This is amazing," he whispered, his voice thick with awe. Then his gaze shifted to look at her over the drawings and his brow furrowed. "How did you get these?"

She smiled for his sake. "It's a long story. I'll tell you all about it when I find out how it ends." Actually, she might not see him again after that, but it sounded nice. "These are only copies. I was hoping to leave them with you along with this satchel for safe keeping until this is resolved."

His smile faded and she sat back on her heels, lowering the drawings down to rest on top of the satchel.

He lifted himself on one elbow with a low groan and looked her in the eyes. "You need to stop this. I know you're trying to help, but this isn't a game. You're in over your head and you're going to get hurt."

As if to reinforce his words, a sharp pain shot through her wounded shoulder. She forced herself not to react. Like Chaff, he was being too protective. She was doing this to help his family. He at least ought to have the decency to thank her.

"You should talk. You've been shot once," she hissed, keeping her voice low so the others wouldn't hear. "At least your family needs you. Nobody needs me."

Her throat tightened. She pushed aside the satchel and the blueprints and stood before he could respond, darting back around the curtain.

How long had she survived on the streets, never thinking back on what she had left behind? How long had she been content living among thieves with no one controlling her life? Wasn't that better?

The longing for a home and a family stabbed through her chest, a serrated blade sawing through hard-earned indifference. She balled her hands into fists and willed it away.

You've always had Chaff.

But that wasn't the same. As important as he was to her, he wasn't blood family, and now the almost brotherly role he'd played in the past had become confused with something less…familial.

Ash and Tomoe were watching her, both wearing looks of concern. Maeko schooled her expression and pushed away those thoughts. She met their eyes and said, "Let's go."

Tomoe scowled, her gaze going to Ash, who sank as if he meant to sit back down. Maeko gave him a stern look and turned toward the door. She would leave him there, and if he hadn't known that before, he knew it now. He straightened again.

Tomoe said, "Maeko-chan, your injury needs to heal."

"I know, but I have to go."

Tomoe nodded, as though she'd expected the answer. "Then if you must go…be careful."

Maeko stepped toward the door and put her hand on the knob. There, she paused and turned a little so she could see her mother in the periphery of her vision. Her throat clenched. "Thank you for your care, Okaasan."

She heard Tomoe start to cry as Ash followed her out the door. He placed a hand on her arm, stopping her before they reached the street.

She spun on him, letting frustration overpower the ache in her chest. "What now?"

He let go and lowered his gaze. "I wanted to thank you."

Irritation guttered like a windblown flame and went out. "For what?"

He looked up, his pale eyes drawing her in. "For trying to help. For…" His eyes locked with hers and his mouth hung open as if the words had become stuck upon his lips on the way out.

Butterflies fluttered in her stomach before his riveting gaze. She shifted her feet. "I really didn't mean the things I said outside the orphanage. I was just narked."

Ash looked away again. "That bloke, the one that helped us, is he…important to you?"

"Chaff?" When he nodded, she shrugged. "Of course he is. He taught me how to survive and he's helped me out of…" She trailed off, noticing the slight souring of his expression. All she could do was stare in slack-jawed wonder. Then she giggled and he gave her an irritable glower. "You can't be jealous."

"Of course not," he snapped.

Liar. It was hard not to smile. "We should get moving." She started to walk away.

"No. Wait." He hurried after her and caught her arm again.

When she turned, he was very close this time. She knew she should back away, but something held her there.

"I was angry and afraid for my family before, but none of that's your fault. Your mum and I talked a long time. I know why you want the money." Alarm bells went off in her head, but he continued before she could speak. "I didn't tell her. That's between the two of you. But I misjudged you, Mae. You're not just a rat. You're so much more than that. You truly care about the people in your life."

His hand came up, hesitating between them. Then he touched her cheek, brushing his thumb over the skin there. Her heart beat triple time and she almost held her tongue, afraid to break the spell. It felt incredible to be the object of such attention, but he was wrong.

"I'm a street rat, Ash."

He drew a breath and met her eyes. "Maybe you are, but you're also beautiful, inside and out."

He leaned in and she almost did the same. He would kiss her if she let him. It was a shocking revelation, and part of her wanted to let him so bad it hurt inside. They stood facing each other, the silence lengthening while she tried to think of something to say. His gaze drifted to her lips. She almost relented, almost shifted closer... when Chaff's smile came unbidden to mind.

What? Why do you have to confuse things?

She glanced away, cheeks warming. Running for her life and dodging capture were things she could do. Things she understood. This was new and scary territory.

"We should get going," she said.

Ash released a soft, disappointed exhale, his hand dropping away, and nodded.

When they had been walking for a few minutes, he asked, "What is okaasan?"

"It's Japanese for mum."

He nodded approval and his gaze drifted to her shoulder. "Will you tell me how you got hurt now?"

Their relationship had changed some, but not that much. Besides, Hatchet-face was dealt with. There was no point in upsetting him with that story now. "No."

He looked taken aback by her answer, but he adjusted. "Can I at least know where we're going?"

Maeko kept walking, not wanting to talk about it too close to Tomoe's house. She shifted her arm carefully to see how mobile it was. The shoulder stung with most movement and she couldn't lift it without considerable pain and pulling on the sutures. She almost wished she had given in and asked for more laudanum before leaving, but she had to be alert.

When they were well out of earshot of the house, she answered him. "We need to find Detective Emeraude."

"What!" Ash stumbled, tripping over his own foot when he turned to look at her. His mouth hung open. She kept walking and he righted himself, matching his pace to hers again. "Why would we want to do that?"

"I found the man she's looking for." Ash's brows popped up, giving him the look of a startled puppy. Fighting back a smile, she said, "He can convince her that your family is innocent. We need to find Em and take her to where he's hiding so he can explain things to her."

He responded with a slow admiring smile and she stared forward, chewing at her lip.

"I can't believe you've done all this to help my family. You really are incredible, you know."

She caught herself before shrugging this time and kicked a pebble in her path instead. It rebounded off the window of a sagging brown house. A dog barked inside.

Noisy buggers.

Would he feel the same if he knew all the things she'd done to survive on the streets? Stealing, fighting, begging, and even digging through the clothes of a dead vagrant once in a moment of desperation. She didn't think she could tell him now.

She scuffed her heels along the pavement and regretted cutting her hair again when a warm flush rose in her cheeks.

"Was it just the money for your mum or did something else make you decide to help me?"

"I just felt like helping. Don't make a storm in a teacup out of it." She tried to underplay the situation, hoping he would lose interest in that line of questioning.

Ash responded with a haughty grin and it took considerable willpower to resist the urge to kick him.

"You know, you almost look like a real girl in that blouse."

Maeko swung out with her good arm and punched him in the shoulder. He ducked away, lessening the impact of the blow, though not quite escaping it the way Chaff usually did. His pale eyes sparkled with delight. A lady across the street, walking with her gloved hand resting on the arm of an older gentleman, wrinkled her nose at them before a passing carriage blocked the view.

"You're not much of a young gentleman," Maeko grumbled.

"Oh?" He raised his eyebrows and looked around as if searching for something. "Should I be? Have you seen some young ladies around?"

This time she struck out faster, catching him a solid blow to the upper arm. He winced, rubbing his arm and laughing. She had to struggle hard to hold back a grin. Her mother's voice popped into her head.

'Never smile at a boy who teases you, it will only encourage them.'

It was a little late to worry about that. "Why did I let you come along?"

"Because you find me irresistibly charming," he replied with a wink and a handsome smile.

She shook her head. What could she say? It wasn't like he was wrong. Let him read what he would into her silence.

Using the tin Lucian had given her, she paid omnibus fare to a number of markets around the city. At each, she went to the usual haunts and sought any of Chaff's boys out working the afternoon crowds. Not surprisingly, every one of them refused to approach the detective on her behalf. She gave them all a thorough description of Em and her companions and told the boys to come find her around Cheapside in the late afternoon if they had any information as to the detective's whereabouts.

Given that she had run into Em there recently, Cheapside seemed as good a place as any to spend time hunting for the detective or someone who might have seen her. It would probably mean running into Chaff with Ash in tow, but she had to trust the boys to behave themselves for the sake of more pressing concerns. What worried her more was the chance of running into Joel again, though she didn't think him mad enough to pull a gun on her in the open. If she wanted to find Em, she had to risk it.

By the fourth stop, Ash was getting used to the measuring looks the street boys gave him and had started to return the scrutiny, picking up his own haughty flair. He warmed to the process as soon as he earned a few acknowledging nods instead of the usual disinterested dismissal and Maeko had to fight hard not to giggle as she watched his progression.

When they finally arrived at Cheapside, she led Ash to a quiet corner and told him where to find Lucian Folesworth. She had him repeat the location back to her several times to be sure he would remember.

His expression darkened with each insisted upon repetition. "Why are you making me memorize this?"

"Don't worry. I'm not planning to abandon you." She gave him a teasing grin, recalling their first escapade escaping JAHF when she had considered just that.

"You better not." He smiled.

She gave him a very serious look then, hoping he would take the gravity of her manner as enough reason to commit the location to memory. "If we get separated somehow, I want you to keep looking for the detective and take her there. No matter what happens, she needs to talk to him if your family is going to get out of this mess."

His smile vanished and he nodded, willing to take her seriously in that light. "I'll remember."

"Brilliant. It's getting on toward evening. If we're going to find her today, we should split up. We can talk to the local vendors and cover more ground that way."

He nodded, his expression sober now. She wanted to hug him for not going into this with the spirit of wild adventure that Chaff tended to take into all his endeavors. Then again, now that she thought about it, she could use some of that lively spirit to keep her going.

"You take that side." She pointed across the street.
"I'll take this side and we can meet up at the far end. And
Ash," she called when he started to turn away. Whatever
she meant to say slipped away before his attentive gaze.
Blast those pretty eyes. "Just... Ganbatte."

He looked confused.

"It means good luck, sort of."

"Ah." He grinned. "Good luck."

She watched him stride away.

Ganbatte. Such a habitual phrase, that private
something she and Chaff said to each other before they
engaged in their less than upstanding livelihood each
day. Ash didn't know that. He hadn't shared that past
with her. They were so very different.

Suddenly yearning for the comfort of the lean street
rat, she exhaled heavily and started down the street
alone. She hadn't reached the door of the first business
on her side when a shout from across the street drew
her attention. She spun to see Ash shoved up against
the cold brick wall of one building, his arm twisted
up behind his back by none other than foul tempered
Officer Tagmet. Pedestrians along the pavements either
hastened away or stopped to stare.

The Literati officer glanced over his shoulder and his
eyes met hers across the street through a break in traffic,
narrowing with hatred. His gaze darted away then,
skipping a short distance down the street from her.

"Grab her, Wells!"

She didn't bother checking to see if Wells heard
the order or if he were even there. She turned and ran,
cursing under her breath in a fashion most contrary to
the ladies' blouse she wore.

If only she had refused to let Ash come. Now he was
in Literati hands and she couldn't even hold it against
him. She'd been so intent on searching for Em that she
hadn't noticed the officers either. With a sharp snarl

of irritation, she darted down the nearest side street and ducked in alongside a building behind a group of dapper young toffs in suits. One of them glanced over his shoulder at her, giving her odd attire a quizzical look, but a roar of laughter from his companions drew his attention back to them.

She held her breath when Wells came around the corner and ran past, stopping a few feet from where she stood. He stared down the street at all of the people who weren't her and punched the air in frustration, cursing under his breath.

She pressed back against the wall, watching him until it occurred to her that he might be of help. *I must be madder than a March hare.* "Officer Wells," she called.

He turned and tensed, his hand sinking to the club at his belt. He took a step toward her and hesitated, his eyes darting around as if searching for a trap.

"I need your help." She infused her tone with a hint of desperation. It didn't require much acting at this point.

The wary expression remained, but he took a few more steps, his hand still hovering close to the club. He looked her up and down once then nodded. "It was you both times, wasn't it? You slipped out between the bars."

"Yes."

His expression hardened. "You killed two good officers."

The young man glanced at her again and stepped closer to his companions.

She moved a few yards away from them. Wells followed at a careful distance.

"I didn't kill anyone," she said.

"But you did let Dobson out, didn't you?"

She cringed. He was right. She might not have done the deeds, but she made them possible. "I never meant for anyone to get hurt, but at least you've got him back now."

"How do you know that?"

"You heard a woman scream last night, right?"

His lips pressed into a tight line and he shook his head. "That bloke covered for you?"

"He didn't know any better," she said, relieved that he still didn't realize who that bloke was. "I need to find Detective Emeraude. Please. It's important."

"I don't know where she is now, though she's certain to come by JAHF in the next few days. She's been checking in regularly to see if we have any new information on her case. She's still looking for you and that boy too." He gestured back the way they had come with a jerk of his head and her throat clenched. "Come with me now and you can talk to her when she comes in next."

Em wasn't the only one checking in. She remembered Joel coming in the night she and Ash escaped. Was he still making stops by JAHF? What would happen if he found Ash there? "It can't wait that long. I need to find her myself. Now."

Wells drew back from her and his small eyes narrowed. "Are you asking me to let you go? An accomplice to murder and you want me to stand back and let you walk away?"

That didn't sound promising. "Yes." She nodded, pleading with her eyes. "Pretend you couldn't find me."

His nose crinkled up as if he'd taken a bite of spoiled meat. He stared hard back out toward Cheapside. "After everything you've done... Tagmet would be livid, and I can't say he'd be out of line."

"Please." As much as she hated to do it, she clasped her hands together and held them up before her in a begging posture. "I have information Em needs to find Lucian Folesworth."

"You're deeper in this mess than I thought." He looked hard at her now, perhaps trying to decide if he could believe her. "Tell me what you know and I'll find her."

"No. I can only tell Em. Mr. Folesworth's life could be in danger if I tell anyone else." He wasn't going to go on her word alone. He struck her as a good man, and it was becoming clear she couldn't pull this off alone. She had to take a chance. She had to do the unthinkable and trust a Lit officer. "There are Literati involved. I don't know who I can trust. Do you, Officer Wells? Do you know who I can trust?"

He clenched his jaw, torment rising in his eyes. He glanced down, his voice low and overflowing with distress when he spoke. "I wish I could say you're wrong, but I know there's something bigger going on. I can't prove it yet, but I've seen enough to convince me there's a deeper conspiracy here. Though how you figured it out is beyond me, unless..." He met her eyes then, searching. "You've talked to Folesworth, haven't you?"

She nodded, holding her breath.

He clenched his jaw and kicked at the pavement with the heel of one boot. "I must be bleeding mad. Get out of here, but if I find out you lied to me, I'll shoot you on sight next time."

For once, she believed he might. "Thank you. About Ash?"

"Tagmet won't let him go so don't even ask. You're pushing your luck already."

She hated to leave Ash behind, but she could see in the officer's eyes that he wasn't going to give any more. "You'll take him to JAHF?"

Wells gave a curt nod. "We'll hold him there until Miss Emeraude shows."

"Make sure nothing happens to him."

"He'll be locked up. What could happen?"

"Just make sure."

He blew out hard and nodded again then stepped to one side to give her a clear exit. "Chivvy on then, before I come to my senses."

She heard indecision in his voice and bolted past, putting as much distance as possible between them as fast as she could.

"I'm sorry, Ash," she apologized under her breath as she left Cheapside behind.

She could only hope he would understand. If not, well, it would put an end to whatever relationship had started between them and save her from making a hard choice later. It wouldn't work, not without him giving up his world to live in hers. He wasn't a street rat and, if she could do anything about it, he never would be.

Her shoulder protested every jarring step, so she boarded the first omnibus she saw, using it to get her further away from the area while she pondered her options. Someone climbed up behind her, squeezing into the last bit of space on the seat and she winced when they bumped her injured shoulder. Leaning closer to the person on the other side to keep her injury out of harm's way, she stared out into the busy street and chewed at the inside of her lip.

It would be too risky to return to Cheapside right away. That meant she needed to continue her search elsewhere, and the more she thought about the many options, the bigger the city seemed to get. She had to assume that Em was still hunting for Ash and his family and for Mr. Folesworth. Where would she go to look for them? The markets? The pubs? The slums over in Southwark? Whitechapel? The city docks?

She ground her teeth. It was hopeless. There were too many options.

"You care to explain how you got out of that predicament, Pigeon?"

She turned and a wave of relief burst through her. "Chaff!"

He chuckled. "Don't think anybody's ever looked that chuffed to see me."

"You have no idea." She almost hugged him, but pain in her shoulder held her back. Things always felt like they would work out with him around. She needed that feeling now more than ever.

"Nice work dumping the lout. That was slick."

"Ash isn't a lout," she snapped.

"If you insist." He responded with a dubious look, mischief sparkling bright in his eyes, and she silently reprimanded herself for letting him get at her. "I have to know how you got that officer to let you go. He had you cornered. Someone else might think you'd turned nark the way he just stepped aside, but I find that hard to believe."

"I begged."

Another dubious look, but he didn't press. "Nice blouse, by the way. A bloke might almost think you were trying to pass as a girl." His gaze dropped to her neck then and his face pinched with displeasure. "Though most the birds I know don't go around getting into knife fights."

"I'd bet most girls *you* know actually do," she countered. She decided to redirect the conversation before she gave in to the wild compulsion to kiss or kick him. "Where's Benny?"

"He got nicked when he helped you get away from that detective the other day. But don't fret," he added in response to her sharp inhale, "he wasn't street material. He kept whinging over how the orphanage at least offered regular meals and passable beds. I think he wanted to go back."

"I hope he's all right."

He glanced away, but not before she caught the flicker of regret in his eyes. "I heard the strangest rumor from some of the boys that you were trying to track down that woman detective. I told myself that couldn't possibly be true." He gave her a sideways glance. "My dodgy little Pigeon would never go searching for that kind of trouble."

She sat up, hope sparking her nerves to life like a lightning strike. "Have you seen her?"

He stared at her now as if she had gone barmy and shook his head, assuming an expression of dramatic disappointment. "I thought I raised you better than that."

She put a hand on his arm. "This is important, Chaff. When did you see her? Where? You have to tell me."

He gave her hand a wry look. "I dunno, Pigeon. You've been askin' for a lot lately and not offerin' much back. Information's expensive."

Her jaw dropped. She closed it and drew her hand back. "What? Why would...? This is about Ash, isn't it? You don't like him."

"Of course I don't, but it isn't about him." He cocked his head and raised one eyebrow. "Well, not entirely. I have a reputation, and helping you like this when you ain't contributing to the family jeopardizes that reputation. You see the problem."

She fought the sinking feeling in her chest. It was true. The streets were dangerous, more so if word got out that you were going soft, but was that all that mattered to him? She could tell he wasn't being completely honest by the hurt in his blue eyes. If he cared, why didn't he say so? For that matter, why didn't she tell him she cared? Was it because she'd met Ash?

"Tell you what. You tell me what you know and I'll give you seventy-five percent of my street take for the next month. You know I'm good enough to make that profitable, and the other boys will think you're right brilliant." He still looked resistant. It wasn't all about money and reputation then. She held back a smile. "And I won't mention Ash."

"Ever?"

They could renegotiate later. "Around you."

He laughed. "All right. It's a deal." His grin was wicked. "You know I'm a fool for you, Pigeon. I'd've settled for fifty."

"Well you'll get forty now." She punched him in the shoulder.

He laughed and a man standing to get off scowled at them both.

"Scamp," she grumbled. "So where's Em?"

"It wasn't no more than an hour or so ago. She was asking around about you, that boy whose name we won't mention, and some other folks. She even asked me, shattering my long held belief that I'm invisible to the rest of the world. Deeply disappointing, that." He smirked when she shifted in the seat, impatient. "I told her I knew you and had seen you over at Covent Garden this morning. The duffer gave me sixpence for my trouble." His eyes lit with the sparkle of a merry thief at that.

She stared at him, absorbing the importance of his words.

The omnibus driver pulled the horses to a stop, trying to keep them in hand while a steam powered ash collector hissed and clanked down a cross street, heading in for the night.

She stood. "Then I'm going the wrong way."

Slipping past him, she pushed her way to the exit and hopped off.

"You've gone daft!" He jumped off after her and caught her arm no more than two strides from the departing omnibus.

Pain sparked in her shoulder. She spun around and opened her mouth to yell at him. There wasn't time to argue. Then she clamped her mouth shut again. She had to find Em and she had to get back to Lucian in case

Ash told someone other than Em where he was. There was only one way she could do both with any efficiency.

She smiled and Chaff let go, taking a wary step back. "Don't look at me like that."

"I need your help." He took another step back and she held a hand up to stay him. "Please. I know I've asked a lot already, but I need to find Em and tell her where the bloke she's looking for is. I also need to get back to him immediately. Since you already know where she is—"

"No!"

She stepped up to him and took one of his hands in both of hers, squeezing it gently. The glaring resistance in his eyes started to fade. "Please. I can't do this alone."

"No."

"Chaff," she spoke his name, intending it as a plea, though it came out more breathy and flirtatious than beseeching.

He swallowed. His eyes tracked down to the cuts on her neck and he squeezed her hands. "This'll finish this bollocks, right? It'll get you out of danger?"

When in her life had she ever been out of danger? She nodded. "It'll finish it."

"What do I need to do?"

She grinned, triumphant, and told him where to send Em. She had him repeat the location several times just as she had done with Ash.

"Got it?"

He nodded.

She grinned and popped up on her toes, intending to plant a grateful kiss on his cheek. At the last second, he turned and their lips met. His hand cupped the back of her head, holding her, though not so firm that she couldn't pull away if she tried.

Ash appeared in her mind and a twinge of guilt accompanied the image. She cared about them both, but she hadn't expected this. This changed so many things.

Rather than pull away, she closed her eyes, giving in to curiosity and a burst of longing. Her lips softened against his and warmth swept through her, tingling beneath her skin. Their breath mingled. His kiss was gentle yet demanding and her heart raced in response to him the way it did after a narrow escape from the Lits. She wasn't so sure she shouldn't be running now.

Before the war between physical pleasure and mental uncertainty could resolve, he released her and she took a few cautious steps back, lightheaded. The flush in her cheeks burned hot.

She turned to the familiar realm of teasing to get her composure back. "I thought you weren't supposed to get attached to your mates on the street."

Chaff licked his lips. "My rules. I get to break them." He winked and started to walk away, calling over his shoulder.

"Ganbatte, Pigeon. I won't let you down."

"I know." Her voice sounded small and breathless.

CHAPTER SIXTEEN

Maeko watched Chaff walk away, his strides long and easy as if he hadn't a care in the world, as if he hadn't just turned her life upside-down. Questions raced through her mind. What did this mean for their working relationship? Did she want this? She touched her fingers to her lips. What about Ash?

The delicious pleasure that had warmed her was slowly fading, leaving confusion and the evening's chill in its wake. She shivered, glancing up at the darkening steel gray sky.

Chaff would come through for her, she was confident in that, but what about everything else? If she could get Em to Lucian, that would end this fiasco, but what then? Would they all go back to life as usual?

She couldn't though, could she? Not after finding Macak, not after meeting Ash, not after talking to her mother, and certainly not after Chaff's kiss. Life would never be the same again.

A droll laugh slipped out. *Who would ever think I'd long for the simplicity of picking pockets and running from Lits?*

Nevertheless, for a little longer, life was very simple. Right now, it was a matter of getting back to Mr. Folesworth and Macak before someone else did. She might be fretting over nothing. Ash might not tell anyone where Lucian was. Joel might not find out JAHF had Ash in custody before Em met with Lucian. Still, she had to be sure, and it would take Chaff longer to catch up with Em than it would take her to get back to the warehouse. She hoped Em had the sense not to shoot Chaff on sight for giving her a false trail earlier.

Maeko started to chew at her lip and stopped when it brought the brief kiss back to the forefront of her thoughts. She turned around and watched another horse drawn omnibus roll to a stop. This one was also going the wrong way. She shifted from foot to foot, impatient to be moving again.

Lucian might be angry when he found out she hadn't taken the blueprints and the will to the detective. And nice as he seemed, she wasn't sure how much she could trust him. Or Em for that matter. Maeko needed some leverage to ensure they cleared Ash and his family of fault in the murders. It also gave her the opportunity to make sure Garrett got a chance to talk to the man about the clockwork leg. A little irritation from the founder of the most powerful company in London was worth the insurance those documents gave her, wasn't it? What could he do to her, throw her into a Lit workhouse until she ran away?

Someone bumped her injured shoulder while rushing to catch the departing omnibus. She staggered, barely keeping her balance, and clenched her teeth against the burst of pain as stitches pulled at wounded flesh. The careless bloke leapt up next to the conductor in the door of the omnibus, out of reach of any retaliation. She blinked back tears and glared after him.

Now the ache in her shoulder was a burning pain. She could feel the slow seep of fluid under the bandage. There wasn't much she could do about it other than hope the jostling hadn't torn any stitches loose. Fussing with the bandage to check on it would only make a mess she couldn't fix on her own.

With pain, exhaustion, and gnawing hunger her only company, she shifted from foot to foot and waited for the proper omnibus. The evening sky grew darker with creeping dusk and a thickening of grumpy clouds. Her mother's light blouse did little to combat a growing chill in the air, made worse by the contrasting heat in her shoulder. By the time the omnibus she wanted pulled up, she was shivering, something that further exaggerated the pain of her wound and the weakness of hunger. The ache spread down from the cut into her upper arm now, reaching below her collarbone in front and her shoulder blade in back, distracting at best.

She trudged on board and sat near the back on the lower deck, resting her head against the side. The cool surface provided a refreshing contrast to the stuffy, smelly heat of the overcrowded bus. She closed her eyes, wincing each time a bump sent another spear of pain through the injured shoulder. Despite the pain, she started to doze, jerking awake when the bloke next to her bumped her arm as he stood to get off. Sucking back a cry of pain, she clenched her teeth and glanced out the window then followed him. They had passed the stop where she should have gotten off, but it wasn't too far now to the warehouse so she started walking.

Lacking the warmth of bodies crammed on the omnibus, her shivering returned with renewed vigor, leeching away at her failing energy. She trudged along, distracted by discomfort and the sooty, pungent yellow fog rolling in off the river, obscuring the streets.

It wasn't until she heard the lapping of water against the docks that she realized she had missed the turn. She stopped and stared into the thick fog, trying to get her bearings, frustrated anger bubbling up as a scream in her throat. She forced it down.

You're fine. Stay calm. Stay quiet. There'll be no

Hatchet-face this time, just a little more walking.

Her feet ached in the poor fitting shoes.

Turning around, she began retracing her steps, hugging herself against the chill.

Something brushed her leg and she twitched away in surprise. Macak turned and rubbed along her leg again, purring. He looked up, meowing, perhaps wondering why she hadn't started petting him yet. She reached down to scratch his head.

"What are you doing outside again? Can you take me to Mr. Folesworth."

The cat purred, accepting a few more scratches, then started off, glancing back once to make sure she followed.

When they turned down the proper street after what felt like an eternity later, she darted to one side to crouch by a stack of crates. A Literati steamcoach like the one they'd taken her to JAHF in was parked down the street from the warehouse entrance. It stood empty, which meant whoever had come in it was nearby. They could be in the warehouse already, assuming they were even there for that. If not, she might still have time to warn Lucian before anyone else got there.

"Does he have company?" she whispered, scratching gentle fingers down Macak's spine. His back rose into her hand and his purr grew louder. *At least someone's enjoying themselves.*

Macak turned around and gazed up at her, arching his back in search of more attention. He pressed against her, seeming reluctant to move on. She started scratching again and peered through the fog. She could make out the door to the building. It stood slightly ajar, the faint glow of candlelight visible through the crack, a promise of welcome.

But what kind of welcome?

She rubbed her forehead. It was damp, perhaps with

moisture from the fog or the residuals of the cold sweat
that had come over her earlier. She wiped her hand on
her trousers, then picked up Macak with her good arm
and held him close, comforted by his warmth against
her. The cat purred louder still and nuzzled her cheek.

"You shouldn't be out here," she muttered, slinking
across to the door. No, out here he could be hurt or lost,
or picked up by foolish street rats with an overblown
sense of their own worth.

She stopped outside the door. This was daft. She
should wait for Em. Macak gazed up at her, his yellow
eyes full of trust and adoration, so much to live up to.
She nudged the door open with her foot and crept in.
With Macak still in hand, she used her injured arm to
pull the door closed behind them, wincing when it
clicked shut and the wound gave a sharp protest. Cold
dread crept up her spine and she opened the door again,
leaving it cracked so she could make a quick escape if
necessary, but not enough for Macak to get out.

Flickering candlelight beckoned from beyond a high
row of stacked crates toward the center of the warehouse
rather than the corner where Lucian's desk and bed
were. Creeping toward the lit area, she spotted someone's legs sticking out just beyond the end of the crates.
Someone was lying down in a rather unlikely spot. Her
skin prickled. She set Macak down, shooing him back
toward the nook where the desk was with her hands.
He gave her an insulted look, trotted a few feet that
direction—whir, click, whir, click—then sat and began
to groom his normal front paw.

Crouched down so low her fingers touched the
floor, she crept toward the light to the end of the crates
and peeked around. Lucian sat in a chair at the center of
a large open area, his hands bound behind the seat and
his feet tied to the chair legs, a massive red lump above
his left temple. He looked shriveled, small, and helpless

in his bonds. A familiar figure in a gray coachman hat stood staring down at him, holding a large pistol with a bulbous middle trained on the bound man.

She leaned a little further out to see who belonged to the legs on the floor and sucked in a sharp breath. Ash lay there, his hands bound behind his back, the rope pressing deep into his wrists. He was staring murder at Joel, but the black gag tied around his mouth forced him to keep his homicidal thoughts to himself. The hair behind his ear was sticky with blood and he had a fresh bruise on the visible side of his face.

Had Joel beaten him to find out where Lucian was or had he found out some other way and brought Ash along to keep him from telling anyone else?

If she inched out around the crate, she could reach his hands.

"Where are the blueprints?" Joel's voice was calm, fearless as it had been when he confronted her in the alley.

She shuddered, her heart hammering against her ribs. Holding her breath, she snuck along the crates far enough to get a hold of the rope binding Ash's wrists.

"In safe keeping," Lucian replied, giving no indication that he had seen her, if he even had yet.

Ash tensed when her fingers touched his wrists, but he didn't turn or make a sound to give her away. She went to work on the knot.

"I was hoping for a more useful answer. Shall we try again?" The ominous click of the pistol cocking made her mouth go dry. "Where are the blueprints?"

"Why are you doing this?" Lucian demanded.

The knot began to loosen.

"Why?" Anger crept into Joel's voice. "Because I've played second to you my entire life. I've watched people lavish praise on you for your brilliant inventions while I stood in the shadows and kept the business running.

I watched you build a life with a woman you knew I loved. I've—"

"A woman you killed." Lucian's voice cracked on the last word.

The sound of movement behind her caught her attention, but there was nowhere to go without alerting Joel to her presence. She shifted closer to the crates and started to turn. A cry burst from her throat when someone grabbed a handful of her cropped hair and yanked her up. She clutched at the hand, struggling to get her feet under her as the unseen attacker hauled her away from Ash.

Joel spun around, the pistol swinging around with him.

"Watch where you point that thing," her captor shouted.

Maeko struggled against the man holding her. He let go of her hair and shoved her off her feet. She landed hard on her knees in front of Joel, who aimed the fat pistol between her eyes. He sported a small cut under one eye with blood drying in a trail down his cheek, evidence that his efforts had at least met some resistance, and there were scratches from Macak's attack on his forehead.

He tilted his head to one side, his eyebrows rising. "You again?"

"She's just a street kid who's been bringing food to me. Let her go." Lucian's voice sounded strained.

"Wouldn't that be a fine arrangement?" Joel twisted to look over his shoulder at Lucian, still pointing the gun at her head. "Too bad I know she's more than that. Much more. Her dirty little fingers are deep in this mess. Maybe she even knows where the blueprints are."

He looked down at her again and she glared at him, though staring down the black, unsympathetic barrel of the gun had her trembling worse than the cold had done. The wild look in his eyes made her feel sick.

He tucked the barrel of the gun under her chin, using it to guide her to her feet, frowning at the cuts on her neck and the bruise he'd given her. "Pretty little thing, if a bit scratched up. If I were arranging such a dalliance I might have gone for something a little less used looking." He met her eyes, his deep blues sparkling with mad gaiety. "I dare say, she's a bit shy on manners too. Do you know she abandoned some hapless trollop to take her bullet for her?"

Her throat tightened. "Heldie?"

"A friend of yours?" He grinned. "Did you think I'd let her walk away after she'd seen us there? I told you I was in a hurry. I didn't have time to waste on awkward questions."

She stared at him. Wells' voice sounded in her head, accusing her of killing the two officers. Now here was another life lost because of her.

"The girl knows nothing. Let her go, Joel. This is between us."

"It is between us." Joel seized her injured arm in a viselike grip, the sudden surge of pain making her head spin. "It's between all of us now. Oh, and the cat," he added, swinging the gun around to point it at Macak who had sauntered out to sit beside Lucian's chair. He pushed a button on the grip and gears spun, rotating the bulbous center a half turn.

Macak laid back his ears and hissed. It was the wrong response. Joel's eyes narrowed, his expression taking on brutal intensity. Maeko could see the pressure of his finger on the trigger increasing.

"Rude little beast," he growled. "Perhaps I should shut you up."

"No!"

Her scream made Macak bolt seconds before the gun fired, the blast making her ears ring. A dart ricocheted off the floor and sunk into one of the many crates.

Macak scurried off between some crates and vanished into the darkness.

Joel snarled. He grabbed her injured shoulder and shoved her away, sending her careening into the crates near Ash. The pain was blinding, the momentum too powerful to stop. She ducked her head, twisting her shoulder toward the crates to take the impact, the wrong shoulder she realized as she hurtled into them. Wood cracked and splintered around her, crates on the back of the pile crashing to the floor.

She landed curled up in a pile of ragged wood, breathtaking pain raging in her shoulder where stitches had torn free, the faint metallic taste of blood in her mouth. For several seconds, she couldn't move, couldn't recall where she was, how she had gotten there, and why it hurt so much. Then she caught movement in the corner of her eye, Macak darting out to check on her, and heard the click as Joel shoved another dart into the gun.

"Stop this," Lucian commanded.

Joel sneered at him and kicked the chair over. Lucian's head struck the floor with an awful crack. Macak bolted away again, into the crates on the far side of the room. Joel pursued, shoving crates around in search of the cat.

A thick sliver of wood several inches long stuck out of Maeko's forearm, blood welling around the obstacle. She swallowed hard against a rush of bile. Blood trickled down her chin from a small cut on her upper lip. She licked at it absently. So much of her body seemed lost in a haze of pain.

You have to move.

She turned her head and saw Ash next to her. His hands were moving, almost worked free of the bonds she'd loosened. The Lit officer who had grabbed her earlier stood a few feet away, watching Joel's frantic search, his presence confirming that at least some of the Lits were in on the plot. He started to turn toward them,

his pistol in one hand, hanging loose from his fingers.
Maeko grabbed a piece of wood and shied it at him to
keep his attention away from Ash. It hit him square in
the nose. The man's eyes snapped to her, his face flushing with instant rage.

Good plan. Now what?

The officer charged her, deflecting her feeble kick
with a swipe of his hand and grabbing her around the
throat. Bright agony blurred her thoughts when he lifted her off the floor by her neck.

"You little—"

A chunk of wood struck him in the back of the head
and he staggered, dropping Maeko and the gun. She
landed hard on her knees again, another pain among
many now. The officer spun and charged Ash. The two
went down in a flurry of flying fists. Joel twisted around
at the commotion.

There, inches away, lay the officer's gun. Maeko
grabbed it, the weapon cold and heavy in her hands,
and started to turn it on Joel, cocking the hammer. The
officer got a hand free and pulled his club, raising it
over Ash's head. She turned the gun on him and pulled
the trigger. The man stiffened, the club falling from his
hand, and he curled over, falling on top of Ash with
a wretched groan. She cocked the hammer again and
swiveled toward Joel. A sharp pain burst in her side. She
fired.

The bullet hit Joel in the shoulder and he staggered
back, catching himself on some crates.

"Bloody darts!" He moved the gun to his other
hand, struggling to aim, and pressed the button on the
side. Gears turned, the barrel rotated—

Macak leapt from the top of a crate, wrapping himself around Joel's hand in a flurry of teeth and claws.
The gun skittered away and the cat leapt off, sprinting
into the cover of the crates again.

Joel sank to his knees, clutching his wounded shoulder as the main door slammed open. Em sprinted into the room, snatching the gun from the floor before shoving Joel to the ground. Reuben and Amos followed her in, their guns also out and ready. After a brief glance around, Amos holstered his and knelt by Ash and the officer. Reuben took over the task of securing Joel while Em moved on to Lucian.

Maeko's arms felt heavy. The smell of sulfur from gunshots stung her nose. She dropped the gun—it was spent anyway—and glanced down at her side. The bright orange end of a dart stuck out of her shirt. She yanked it out with fumbling fingers, gasping at the sharp pain. A trickle of blood ran down her side from the puncture.

Em started untying Lucian, who appeared unharmed from the fall other than a small bleeding gash over one eye.

"Maeko!"

Was that Chaff? She couldn't imagine him saying her name right twice in one week. When he knelt down in front of her, however, she couldn't deny it was him. She made an effort to smile. Her lips didn't move. His gaze tracked to her cut lip, then her freshly bleeding shoulder, then the fat sliver protruding from her arm, and finally to the spot of blood soaking through the blouse on her side.

His eyes widened. "Are you shot?"

She couldn't find her voice so she looked at the discarded dart.

Chaff picked it up.

"It's deadly poi—"

There was a thud and grunt when Rueben silenced Joel with a kick to his wounded leg. "Nobody asked you."

Lucian, now untied and on his feet, gave Joel a murderous glare. He picked up the gray coachman hat lying

on the floor, dusted it off and put it on, then took the
dart from Chaff and turned it in his fingers. "It's not
poison. I designed that gun. It's a prototype for the zoo.
These darts hold a sedative, and not a terribly strong
one. It'll wear off in a few hours."

Em glanced at Joel. "Why a sedative?"

Joel was indisposed, however, his face pinched with
pain from the kick to his wounded leg.

Lucian continued to turn the dart in his fingers.
"To sedate Macak perhaps, though this dose might have
killed such a small animal. Or maybe to sedate me and
move me if I didn't cooperate." He scowled with hate-
filled eyes at his writhing partner. "We'll have to ask
him later, I imagine."

Let Hatchet-face question him. She was too tired
for her mouth to form the words, though. Maybe later,
when she had rested, she could suggest it.

Amos still knelt beside the wounded officer. Ash
had gotten to his feet. He hung back, swaying a bit and
glowering at Chaff's back.

Unaware of the daggers being glared into him,
Chaff took Maeko's hand and turned it to look at her
arm. "Sorry about this, Pigeon."

A prickle of trepidation raced up her spine seconds
before he yanked the sliver out of her arm. Pain shot
from the wound, and she would have hit him if her limbs
weren't rendered useless by the sedative. He cringed in
sympathy and kept hold of her hand while Em wrapped
a rough bandage around the arm.

"Reuben, take Mr. Folesworth, Asher, and the rat
in my coach to get their injuries seen to. We'll get these
two," Em scowled at Joel and the officer each in turn,
"into the steamcoach and get them locked up."

Lucian looked at Maeko and his lips pressed into
a tight line in his troubled face. "Detective Emeraude,
there are some important documents in the crate next

to the door if you would grab them for me. I need to get Macak."

Em nodded again, holstering her gun, and turned to do his bidding. Maeko wanted to offer her admiration at how easily he got the willful detective to obey, but she could barely keep her eyes open.

"I'll help get Maeko to the coach," Ash offered

He and Chaff exchanged a long, silent look, then Chaff nodded and they lifted her between them amidst several pathetic whimpers of pain that she was appalled to discover were coming from her. They walked her out to the detective's coach, Reuben striding ahead to open the door.

A familiar figure leapt down from beside the driver, sticking an awkward landing on his fake leg, and threw his arms around Ash who left Maeko in Chaff's care to return the embrace.

"Sam!"

The younger boy buried his face in his brother's shoulder, muffling his response, but she got the feeling it was meant to be between the two brothers anyway.

Chaff supported her up into the coach and she sank into the seat.

"You!" Em's voice rang out. "The healthy rat! Come help throw this offal into the Lit coach."

Chaff grinned. "I guess she means me."

"Don't let her take you to JAHF," Maeko managed to mumble through her rather uncooperative lips.

"She promised not to earlier."

She fought her sinking eyelids. "Remember..." She had to pause for a breath. "You can't squeeze between the bars."

He chuckled and brushed his fingers over her cheek. "I'm going to help the peevish bird load her baggage, then I'll come find you. You'll be fine, Pigeon. I'll see you very soon." He ducked out of the coach.

Sam went back to the driver's seat, grinning delightedly while silent tears ran down his cheeks.

Maeko managed to sit up, making room for Ash to climb in beside her. He hesitated on the step, meeting her eyes.

"You did it. You saved my family. You are the most amazing person I've ever met. I hope you'll give me the chance to show you how much this means to me." He started to look away, then made himself meet her eyes. "How much *you* mean to me."

Her throat tightened. Only moments before, Chaff had stood on that same step. She couldn't choose, not yet. She managed to struggle out the words through the fog of sedative. "I care about you, too, Ash. But…"

She trailed off when he held up a hand.

"I'm not asking you to choose right now." He paused. "But I'd like a chance to convince you when you're up to it, if that's not too much to ask."

She hoped her smile looked more encouraging than drunken, though it felt more like the latter. "I think we could arrange that."

He looked at her for a moment, then climbed in and sat beside her. "Then let's get you fixed up and go from there."

She smiled, hoping her gratitude showed.

Lucian with Macak and Rueben climbed in next, sitting on the opposite seat. Reuben reached for the door, but Em caught it from outside.

She leaned in to pass some rolled papers to Lucian, then gave Reuben a stern look. "See you take care of them. The little rat especially. With her skills, she'd make a fine assistant."

Maeko closed her eyes and leaned back. She rather fancied the idea of being a detective's assistant, but she couldn't focus on such things right then. The throb of her wounds, the ache of hunger and drowsiness from the sedative were more than enough to hold her attention.

"I think you should leave the young lady out of your affairs," Lucian stated.

"She's no young lady," Em countered.

Maeko heard the door thud shut.

"She could be," Lucian murmured.

Maeko sank to one side. An arm slipped around her and pulled her close. Her head came to rest against Ash.

"You plan to help Maeko then, Mr. Folesworth? Seems like she's done an awful lot for you." Ash's voice sounded muffled with her head against his chest.

"I do owe her a great debt," Lucian agreed. "It will be repaid. I can assure you of that."

Something cool and moist touched Maeko's nose and she forced open her eyes. Macak stood on Ash's legs, staring into her face. He meowed once, a soft, inquisitive sound, and licked her nose again.

She smiled weakly. "Brilliant job, mate."

Macak curled into a ball on Ash's lap and began to purr. She shifted one hand, finding enough strength to flop it onto the cat's side before her eyelids sank down again. Ash kissed her head and Lucian said something, perhaps more in response to Ash's question. They were things she should be paying attention to, things that might have an effect on her life, but the sedative was in control now, its lure irresistible after so many exhausting and stressful days fighting off sleep.

There's only so much a rat can do.

A faint sense of satisfaction warmed her. Maybe she was only a street rat, but she was a street rat who had just helped save Ash's family and the life of one of the most important men in London. If nothing else, she'd earned a bit of rest.

Later, she could deal with boys, debts, and all the other things. Chaff. Ash. Her mum. For the first time, she knew she wasn't alone and it felt good.

She settled into Ash's patient embrace and drifted off into a blissful sleep.

THE END

ACKNOWLEDGEMENTS

To Michael, thank you for bearing with my bad moods when writing isn't going well and supporting me in my pursuit of my dream (possibly for your own sanity as much as mine).

To my mom Linda, for encouraging me, believing in me, and reading chapters one at a time as I wrote them. I know it can be frustrating waiting for the next installment and always get a little pleasure out of you pestering me for more.

To Rick and Ann for being two of the best friends, editors, and fans a person could hope for. I am very lucky to have you both.

To my good friend and fellow author Eldritch Black. Thank you for sharing long rides to the coffee shop full of cathartic rants and commiseration every Thursday and for being an amazing writing companion.

To Aradia, for knowing I would succeed from the first time we met and being an inspiration in your dedication to your own art.

To my other mother Nancy, for being an early reader and offering encouragement for my work.

To my agent Emily and my original editor Stephen, thank you both for believing in this story and helping me accomplish my dream.

To all the other amazing friends and loved ones I missed above who supported me along the way, your belief in me keeps me plugging away no matter how frustrated I get. Thank you.

Lastly, thanks to my sixth-grade teacher, Mr. Johnson, for being so pleased and excited when I told you I was going to be an author and to my eighth-grade algebra teacher, Mr. Siebenlist, for almost letting me flunk because you were so delighted that I was writing books in class rather than notes.

AUTHOR BIO

Nikki started writing her first novel at the age of 12, which she still has tucked in a briefcase in her home office, waiting for the right moment. Despite a successful short story publication with Cricket Magazine in 2007, she continued to treat her writing addiction as a hobby until a drop in the economy presented her with an abundance of free time that she used to focus on making it her career.

Nikki lives in the magnificent Pacific Northwest. She feeds her imagination by sitting on the ocean in her kayak gazing out across the never-ending water or hanging from a rope in a cave, embraced by darkness and the sound of dripping water. She finds peace through practicing iaido or shooting her longbow.

•

Thank you for taking time to read this novel. Please leave a review if you enjoyed it.

•

For more about me and my work visit me at
http://nikkimccormack.com.

•

OTHER NOVELS BY NIKKI MCCORMACK

The Girl and the Clockwork Conspiracy
The adventure continues.

Forbidden Things, Book One: Dissidents
Forbidden Things, Book Two: Exile
Forbidden Things, Book Three: Apostate
An epic fantasy.

The Keeper
Book one of the Endless Chronicles.

CPSIA information can be obtained
at www.ICGtesting.com
Printed in the USA
FFHW011907301019
55888001-61759FF